OH!
THOSE
PARSIS

BERJIS DESAI

ZERO DEGREE PUBLISHING

Oh! Those Parsis ©2019 Berjis Desai
First Edition: June 2019
By ZERO DEGREE PUBLISHING

ISBN: 978-93-87707-88-7
ZDP Title : 19

ZERO DEGREE PUBLISHING
No.55(7), R Block, 6th Avenue,
Anna Nagar,
Chennai - 600 040

Website: www.zerodegreepublishing.com
E Mail id: zerodegreepublishing@gmail.com
Phone : +91 98400 65000

Illustrations by Farzana Cooper
Cover Design : Mrudul Pathak & Debojyoti Kundu
Typeset by Vidhya Velayudham
Printed at Manipal Technologies, India

To

my mother, Mani, who taught me to read
and
my father, Minoo, who taught me to write.

FOREWORD

Every great age has its epic and its bard. Homer, Valmiki, Firdausi and Kalidas, to name but a few. The rapidly dwindling, but nevertheless feisty and remarkable, Parsis have got no less, in the form of Berjis Desai, a renowned lawyer.

Berjis's eye upon the community is providential since he curates and archives for posterity our unique customs, likes and dislikes, strengths and frailties, language (unparalleled adaptations of Gujarati), virtues and vices and above all idiosyncrasies. This book is a kind of time capsule or Rosetta stone for future generations.

He writes as an Oscar Wilde would, with biting sarcasm wrapped in mellifluous and disarming language. His writing evokes the technique of pointillism known to art. A multitude of detail which, nevertheless and quite magically, allows the reader to step back and view the landscape as a whole. Elgar's Enigma Variations come to mind. Each detail is accurate and as he says there is "not an iota of fiction" in the book. Yet truth is often stranger than fiction and every piece carries a parable underlying its light heartedness.

He follows another great Parsi lawyer historian P.B. Vachha who has written the locus classicus on the Bombay High Court. Both adopt the dictum of Ferishta the historian of the Nizamshahi Court which was "Write without fear or flattery".

Berjis strikes one as unassuming and almost introverted. Yet with pen in hand he is transformed into an artist who paints with a bold brush and a flowing pen that is at once both colourful and seductive. Erwin Griswold, Dean of the Harvard Law School famously said "The true language of a lawyer is poetry". He may as well have said anecdotal prose in the case of Berjis Desai.

Berjis is an easy and engaging read and effortlessly draws the reader into a different world. His turn of phrase is nothing short of brilliant and with it he spins a web in which you exult and are lost in time. The result is a wonderful quilt of history, both anecdotal as well as scholarly, eccentricity (a quality which abounds in our community) and yes, a tinge of nostalgia for ages gone by and foreboding for what perhaps looms ahead of us in the future.

Berjis captures the essence of the quintessential Parsi in some delightful cameos which are woven into a rich tapestry. This is all the sugar that we promised India and a generous helping of spice, as well! It will bring back a flood of memories for every Parsi, from Polson butter (with coupons on the side of the pack, which I used to collect!) to Udvada *boi*. The book contains several gems such as "Parsi swearing is sweet", and the community's dabbling in the occult, ghosts, superstition, spiritualism and astrology; the taboo topic of sex and the sincerity of relationships between master and maid! But there is serious introspection and writing as well, such as the fate of intermarried Parsi women. To these he brings an astute legal perspective. Each piece displays a deep understanding of our traits and indeed Zoroastrianism itself. There is a warmth and affection for his subjects. He caricatures without ridiculing; he maligns, without malice!

The book covers literally the A to Z of the Parsi way of life. It is the details that embellish and excite the reader's mind: the Parsi preference for pearls over gold and our fascination for guineas. Yet there is always some axiomatic truth underpinning his narrative. Take the poignancy of Parsi "old money" heirs locked in their sprawling antique filled homes and their aristocratic lifestyles with dwindling bank balances, trapped in a sort of time warp.

When you manage to put the book down, you will wonder at the unique ability of Parsis to laugh at themselves and their multifariousness and perhaps despair at how the community is fast losing its sense of humour and tolerance.

Berjis likes to describe himself as a failed community activist. I demur. By any standard Berjis is not a failed activist, lawyer or writer. He has excelled in these fields and we are the beneficiaries of the treasure he has now produced.

DARIUS J. KHAMBATA

(Darius Khambata, Senior Counsel, is former Advocate General for the State of Maharashtra and has served as Additional Solicitor General of India).

INTRODUCTION

PARSIS are from a different planet. They confuse other Earthlings. Imagine a human being who is at once genial, high strung, funny, rude, crude, kind, brilliant and barmy. Most of the time Parsis are lovable; sometimes they are annoying. They are in a hopeless demographic decline – barely 85000 in the world. This decline makes people sad. Rather soon, Parsis will be sorely missed. They are an anthropological rarity worthy of being preserved. However, they themselves are merrily oblivious to their imminent extinction and continue to make others glad and mad.

Deciphering the Parsi psyche has been my favourite pastime since I was a teenager. I wrote nasty letters to the editor of Kaiser-e-Hind (Emperor of India), a then weekly Parsi Gujarati newspaper of liberal hue, barraging the trustees of the perennially despised Bombay Parsi Panchayet by calling them blue blooded bumblers who were obstructing progress and reform. Most of them were acquaintances of my father, who edited the Bombay Samachar, Asia's oldest existing newspaper, including a column on Parsi affairs called Parsi Tari Aarsi (PTA) (Parsi Mirror). Although he appeared to be embarrassed by his son's impolite adjectives, inwardly, he was happy with my growing iconoclastic tendencies. He, of course, never published any of my letters or articles in his newspaper. I was not yet out of my teens when he succumbed to colon cancer. Jehan Daruwalla, his successor, radicalised PTA and encouraged me to contribute. A couple of years later, I joined the Bombay Samachar as a sub-editor while I was attending law school in the morning. Daruwalla and I had fun and games with the PTA. Later, I too edited PTA (2002-2013).

In early 2014, Jehangir Patel, editor of the Parsiana, the community's most respected newsmagazine, invited me to write a column rather insipidly titled, Bawa Musings. This column appeared, with a solitary break, in 80 issues of the Parsiana from April, 2014 to August, 2017. This book is a collection of most of those columns. Barring some slight corrections, the columns appear in this book, as they were printed in the Parsiana.

Apart from Parsis themselves, non-Parsis too are curious to know more about the Parsi way of life. These columns have attempted to cover most aspects of Parsi culture. It has covered topics as diverse as maids, mothers and murders; *legho*, liquor and *lagan nu custard*; sex, superstitions and swear words; fish, fertility and funerals; goondas, *ghelsappas* and *gadheras*; noses, *nataks* and nostalgia; insanity, occult and xenophobia.

These columns have been classified alphabetically and subjectwise, from A (Alcohol) to Z (Zoroaster). Consulting the Index will help the reader to select a topic of his choice. For instance, if one is interested in Parsi doctors and Parsi drama, look under D; for Parsi murderers and the Parsi penchant for maids, look under M, for sex, superstitions and swearwords, look under S; and so on. A glossary explains Gujarati phrases (apart from those translated in the column already) and other typically Parsi expressions and abuses for the benefit of the non-Parsi reader.

Many a non Parsi reader may believe that several of the eccentricities and idiosyncrasies mentioned in these columns are simply the author's imagination. I assert that there is not an iota of fiction in this book. In any event, if the reader enjoys the irreverent joie de vivre of the Parsis, my purpose of showcasing this tiny, harmless and eccentric community would have been achieved.

BERJIS DESAI

Mumbai
25 December, 2018

CONTENTS

The A to Z of the Parsi Way of Life

Parsi swearing is sweet

Rather than being abusive the expletives are more idiomatic and often used to express affection

During the membership interview at the Ripon Club some 30 years ago, we were asked if we were joining for the mutton *dhansak* on Wednesdays. We smiled sheepishly and said we were vegetarian. A general look of disgust was evident. Do you enjoy a tipple? was the next question. Not really, we said. What kind of a Parsi are you? an old gentleman blurted, vegetarian and teetotaler, do you at least abuse? Not wanting to be blackballed, we gently nodded.

Not having had the fortune of residing in one of our baugs, our childhood knowledge of swear words was poor, despite studying at the Bharda New High School. At eight, we had innocently asked our grandmother the meaning of the M-word (incestuous relations with one's mother). In the mayhem that followed, we were made to gargle with salt water and recite the *Yatha Ahu Vairyo* seven times to sanitize our tongue. However, we made rapid progress a year later, during our *navar* sojourn at Navsari. We remember an elderly *mobed* reciting a limerick, with a pronounced lisp, peppered with *badaam daraakh* (Parsi colloquial for swear words). What impressed us was the original abuse unleashed by another *mobed* at the *navar* candidates alleging incestuous relations with their maternal grandmothers and how the learned priest would like to make *aléti paléti* out of some severed body parts. This time we had the wisdom not to recount our learning to our visiting grandmother. Priestly endorsement gives confidence to the community to swear.

Parsis seldom indulge in abusive swearing. Our swearing is more idiomatic. In this department, none can better the Dadar Parsis to whom swearing is nothing but lubricating a conversation. In the Watergate scandal, the American nation was shocked at the extensive abuse by US President Richard Nixon and his men. Those were the early seventies and the F-word was still unprintable. The transcripts of the Nixon tapes were, therefore, replete with "(expletive deleted)." If ever the transcripts of the recorded conversations of Dadar Parsis at the railing are published, they will also be full of (expletive deleted). A typical conversation goes something like this: "Good morning (expletive deleted). Has the (expletive deleted) newspaper arrived? Why does the (expletive deleted) ganga (cleaning woman) come so late these days? Has (expletive deleted) nallo (child) left for school?" Swear words are mere fillers in a sentence and rarely intended to be abusive. On the contrary, the greatest affection is expressed by the most colorful abuse. Devoid of bitterness, rancor or anger, Parsi swearing sounds sweet. Very often, it is used to express love and affection: "Madar... I missed you!"

Its political incorrectness is so delicious. Our fellow communities love it, as an integral part of our idiosyncratic culture. When it comes to swearing, there is hardly a class divide. Baug Parsis, bungalow Parsis, masoor paav Parsis and NCPA (National Centre for the Performing Arts) Parsis; they all enjoy it. Some ladies too. When a lady crusader for reforming *Doongerwadi* received an anonymous call at midnight threatening her with dire consequences, she let off the most appropriate response in a language so colorful that the goon at the other end instantly disconnected.

When Parsis swear, it seldom sounds vulgar or filthy. So much bonhomie and camaraderie flows from the manner of abusing that it does not offend the sensibilities of even the prig and the prude. Parsis do not regard swearing as sinful or objectionable. We knew of a well known Parsi solicitor, deeply religious, who would enter his cabin every morning, fervently pray before the photo frames of the Prophet, Mushkil Aasan, Dastur Kookadaru and other saints; and in the same breath instruct his old peon to summon the M… waiting for him in the reception.

Parsis can lay legitimate claim to have invented at least two original swear words — *ghelsappo* (mad) and *ghelchodio* (mad fornicator). Even the mild mannered, who spurn the M-word and the B-word (incestuous relations with one's sister), think it kosher to use these swear words along with the ever popular *chutio*. Parsi Bol, that fascinating collection of Parsi sayings and idioms, may well invite someone enterprising to publish a book called 'Parsi Gaar,' a collection of select Parsi swear words.

We recall settlement talks in an acrimonious Parsi family dispute, with several prominent senior Parsi solicitors present, in the chambers of a very grim faced Parsi advocate who appeared humorless. Before the gathered gentlemen could get down to serious business, the grim one asked his peon to fetch the Concise Oxford Dictionary. He flipped to the section containing vernacular slang and drew the attention of his fellow Parsi brethren to the B-word therein. He then whipped out a letter addressed to the editors of the Dictionary, which he requested all of us to sign. The letter sought to express the deep anguish of the Bombay Parsis at the exclusion of the M-word from the Dictionary, and their great surprise at the decision of the learned editors to prefer the lesser swear word over the greater and the most popular Parsi swear word. The only non-Parsi present had a totally confused look of unbelonging as all the Parsi solicitors happily signed this letter of protest.

Our late friend Navroji Gamadia, who was as aristocratic as they come, was very fond of reciting a couplet extolling the happy-go-lucky nature of our community, and which appropriately sums up this fortnight's column. *Husta rumta daharo jaiy; ruré téni bén* (may the day pass happily; the one who cries, sees his sister...) (expletive deleted).

Wetting your nose tip

Parsis have enjoyed a healthy relationship with alcohol

If a Parsi vegetarian is a rarity, and a Parsi teetotaler is an oddity, then a Parsi vegetarian teetotaler is a disgrace. The community has had an unbroken love affair with alcohol and yet only a handful have a drinking problem. Alcohol de-addiction centres have a lot to learn from the Parsi approach to drinking.

Parents don't lie to children about their daily tipple being a medicine. Nor do they drink in stainless steel glas*ses* (those who do, ought to be prosecuted). Many a child first tasted alcohol from his grandfather's fingertip. We tasted narangi (orange flavored country liquor - those days illegally distilled), at the age of seven, in rather strange circumstances. Aloo Aunty, a spinster (now long deceased), working in Cama Hospital, befriended us at the Victoria Terminus bus stop, discovered that we resided in her neighborhood and took us home for some delicious snack or other including, if you please, sautéed ox tongue (now it thoroughly repul*ses* our vegetarian disposition). Aloo Aunty's boyfriend would savor narangi at tea time and was bemused that we relished the taste of his concoction. One evening, the customary sip became a gulp and Aloo Aunty was soon banished from our young life by our stentorian grandmother who was horrified that her idyllic grandson had been sundowning bevda (slang for illicit hooch).

Parsis hated prohibition and, therefore, disliked Morarji Desai (a former prime minister and chief minister of undivided Bombay State) who imposed prohibition and was a fanatic temperance activist. There is this not so apocryphal story of Desai attending a Parsi wedding at Albless Baug and then having the police raid the guests enjoying a secret tipple. "*Saaré saparmé daharé police moklaavi! Maré muo*! (Had us raided by the cops on an auspicious day. Death to him)'," cursed the enraged Parsi ladies. Apparently, the curse did not work as Desai lived to be 99, extolling the virtues of consuming his own urine (a Parsi who ran the dining car attached to the prime minister's special train once narrated to us, with great disgust, how Desai's pre dawn drink was collected in a sparkling, sterilized tumbler and thoroughly relished by the ageing prohibitionist).

Seizure of illicit liquor in 1972 in Bombay by C. D. Bhesadia, assistant commissioner

Parsis in Gujarat, suffocated by prohibition, named their illegal tipple Morarji Cola, and often dashed to nearby Daman, a central government controlled territory outside Gujarat. The famous Oliaji Hotel in Daman was a welcome watering hole for parched Parsis who after gorging on a huge breakfast of eggs, mutton mince and *boi* (mullet) would start guzzling toddy, juice from the palm tree collected in earthen pots tied overnight; innocent and fresh in early morning, but mischievously alcoholic before noon. Anyone drinking toddy in a glass was a novice, looked down upon by the hardened Parsis sitting on their haunches with a rolled banana leaf in their mouth through which another would pour toddy straight from the earthen pot. If your guzzling power was deficient, you would risk asphyxiation. Parsis adored the Parsi married prime minister Indira Gandhi who sent Desai into political oblivion and even jailed him during the Emergency in 1975. This must have warmed the cockles of the hearts of our Daruwallas, Pithawallas and Toddywallas who had been forced by Desai to diversify into more dull busines*ses*.

Parsis handle their drinks extremely well and generally do not make fools of themselves in public. They may get a trifle *boi*sterous at wedding feasts after three or four Parsi pegs, larger than the famed Patiala peg, but seldom become obnoxious. The community's capacity to nurse, manage and hold drink is famed. We knew of an ex-sailor and his lifelong affair with *mahua* (a local brew made from *mahua* flowers, very potent). His son was warned by a legendary Parsi physician that his father would not last a fortnight as his cirrhotic liver had turned into a mini distillery. The sailor outlived the doctor and survived for 30 years thereafter on a staple diet of his elixir which he would begin to consume before noon.

Lest you wonder how a virtual teetotaler like your writer knows about liquor, we must hasten to narrate the story of the legendary Homi Seervai, the eminent jurist who had never tasted alcohol in his long life of 89, educating the Bombay High Court with the greatest erudition on the properties of different kinds of alcoholic beverages in an excise case. There are unmarried divorce lawyers as well.

No article on Parsi drinking habits can be complete without referring to two cute Parsi expressions for boozing: "*Kai chhato paani chhé ké?*' (are they serving liquor?)" and "*Chalo jaraa nakh bhijjavva jaiyé* (Let's have a drink, or literally, Let's wet our nose tips)." Given their love for the sundowner, it is a bit surprising that in the 1930s quite a few Parsis became theosophists following the teachings of Mme Helena Blavatsky, Annie Besant and Charles Leadbeater and formed a Parsi Vegetarian and Temperance Society, which had a miniscule membership. However, this did not prevent Parsi entrepreneurs from becoming alcohol producers, the notables being Lord Karan Bilimoria of Cobra Beer and the Contractor family in Sikkim who produced the most delightful after-dinner liqueurs of exotic origin. Even the Islamic Republic of Iran permits Zoroastrians to brew and consume aniseed liquor. Readers are cautioned though not to confuse Tehran with Riyadh. Spicy *dhansak* and succulent kababs washed down with aniseed liquor flavored with lime, after an invigorating trip to the *Demavand Koh*! This is truly keeping your spirits high (with our apologies to the *Ilm-e-Khsnoomists* for the totally unintended pun).

Why Parsi women are superior to men

Let us begin with a disclaimer. This article contains several unscientific generalizations and the evidence is only anecdotal. However, those blessed with powers of observation and a dispassionate mind will concur. Those who violently disagree will only prove the point. So our thesis is that Parsi women are considerably superior to Parsi men in all departments of life, barring the armed forces, judiciary and thoroughbred racing. The jury is still out on the Bombay Parsi Punchayet. Sometimes it is difficult to believe that they are from the same community as the men. Being superior does not always mean being nicer. Lord Curzon, a Governor General in British India is believed to have said: "I am Lord Nathaniel Curzon; a very superior person." Perhaps he was superior but not particularly nice. Parsi men are certainly nicer, maybe out of compulsion.

If we were to assure all unmarried Parsi women in Bombay that even if they were to marry non Parsis, their children will be regarded as Parsi Zoroastrians and their husbands permitted to reside in the baugs and they themselves need not worry about their rights, the number of interfaith marriages will quadruple. The reason is that Parsi girls find Parsi boys to be unambitious and without fire in the belly. The only fire in the belly is for dhansak. The cream of the boys have been licked clean by non-Parsi felines (and the why of it is that non-Parsi women appear to be nicer, sweeter, softer and politer) and the remnants are not very attractive husband material. The glamor of airline stewards, pilots, singers, bodybuilders and motorbike enthusiasts has now dissipated. Corporate high fliers and supersmart techies are in demand. Even the high earning Parsi men appear to be namby-pamby, Mummy obsessed, awkward, and incapable of making the Parsi girls swoon.

The ladies are academically brighter, hardworking, more committed and have a superior work ethic. Boys are engrossed in bikes, beers and bodies. Women are concerned about their careers; the men, about their carriers. Parsi ladies make good entrepreneurs and Parsi boys make good employees. Women score higher than men in having an ethical perspective and a more finely honed value system. Naturally, the wasters and wafflers do not appeal to their more accomplished female counterparts. How can the same genes and the same conditioning result in such disparity among genders is a question to be debated by sociologists. Parental role models may be an answer. There is often emulation of the same sex parent, resulting in perpetuation of stereotypes.

Alpha females, like Alpha males, drip aggression. Domineering and dictatorial, the Parsi ladies are formidable. The young Parsi lad witnesses how Pappa trembles in trepidation before Mummy's relentless onslaught. The child, out of empathy for his inferior parent, either never marries or finds non-Parsi women more malleable and attractive. The Parsi girl emulates the mother, and thereby remains a spinster who commands many in a stentorian voice or prefers to marry a non-Parsi high achiever. This gender disparity is resulting in more interfaith marriages.

Parsi women are quick and lethally committed to public causes, whether it is animal cruelty or saving Worli Sea Face or keeping the Oval Maidan free from political party meets or fighting noise pollution. Local mafia dons are terrified of unpurchaseable Parsi lady agitators. Parsi husbands would rather spend their afternoons at the races or sundown the evening with two Parsi pegs rather than worry about the fate of some classical music society or stench of Bombay ducks at the Sassoon Dock. The fairer sex oozes public spirit; the men are mildly amused but are inwardly happy with the lady being away from home.

Parsi men certainly have a better sense of humor and greater *joie de vivre*. They also make better judges, lawyers, soldiers and horse trainers. Fellow communities do not trifle with Parsi matrons while they are very fond of Parsi men. Few like the straight talking, blunt and uncompromisingly honest females. Perhaps, the only failure of Parsi women is not bringing up better sons.

Dinshaw Daji and Veera Sorabji in *Mua Luchaao*(Bloody Louts)
Photo: Laughter in the House, 20th Century Parsi Theatre by Meher Marfatia

Garo, sudro, legho né daglo

Parsis retain their affection for traditional attire

The Karani brothers, who published many editions of the *Khordeh Avesta*, also published a *dhobi ni chopri* (washerman's book), mostly for the use of Parsi households. Those were the days when laundries were few and mostly unaffordable. The dhobi would pay a weekly or fortnightly visit to most Parsi homes. Like a Japanese tea ceremony, it was an interesting ritual. On the appointed day, the dhobi would walk straight into the bedroom and arrange the washed clothes neatly on the bed. He would then open a small cabinet, cutely called *mèla kapraa nu pinjru* (dirty clothes cabinet) and empty its contents on the floor. Therea fter, the lady of the house would walk in, armed with Karani's *dhobi ni chopri*, and take an inventory of the washed as well as dirty clothes, after which the dhobi would carry away the latter. This prompted many a skit in Adi Marzban revues: *"Jao dhobi, kapara nikalo, bai aata hai* (Go, dhobi; remove clothes, Madam will soon be with you)!"* Altercations with the dhobi were frequent (missing clothes, smelly clothes, soiled clothes, someone else's clothes, over-starched clothes - the shirt sleeves would poke your armpits - and the dhobi's two month vacation) in terrible Hindi. The *dhobi ni chopri* would list amongst other things - *sudro* (sudreh), *mathabanoo* (lady's headscarf worn while praying), and of course, the ubiquitous *légho* (white pyjamas).

Parsis are ob*ses*sed with the last mentioned item of apparel. There was a famous comedy called *Dadi Lengho* wherein the hero changed this garment about nine times in a day. It is not to be confused with the lengha which non-Parsi men and women wear. The Parsi *légho* ends much above the ankle; is never fitted with elastic but is tied with a cloth *naroo* (a drawstring of much fascination and double entendre: "*Marhoom na léngha nu naroo dhiloo hatoo* (the deceased was a womanizer)." Our uncle, a thespian with Adi Marzban's troupe, introduced his fellow thespian, one Jiju (long deceased), to the Freemason order. During the initiation ceremony, the hapless man's *légha nu naroo* would not unravel while putting on the Masonry regalia, despite concerted efforts of our uncle and fellow masons, causing much consternation to the grandmaster conducting the ceremony.

Natak scene showing traditionally attired Parsis.

Photo reprinted with permission from Laughter in the House

At the end of a tiring day, when you reach home and change into shorts or a so-called sleeping suit, you are not an authentic Parsi. Once in his sanctum, a true Parsi dons only his *sudro né légho* (of course, with the kusti tied). The feeling of utter liberation which the body feels after discarding the shirt and trousers and undergarments and wearing the muslin *sudro* with the *légho* made out of longcloth (we knew of a Parsi dandy who wore a silk *légho*), is akin to what oppressed peoples feel upon attaining Independence from foreign rule. In the celebrated comedies staged by Parsi doctors, the famous radiologist Dr Jimmy Sidhwa, as Parsi Pavarotti, sang a hilarious piece on "*mèlo légho* (dirty pyjama)."

Only a micro minority now wears a dagli at Parsi weddings, navjotes, *paidasts* and *uthamnas*. Even fewer don traditional headgear like the conical *pheto* or the circular *pugree* - most families had a tradition of wearing one or the other headgear, but not both types. Of course the trustees of the Parsi Punchayet continue to wear traditional headgear at public *jashans* to signify that they are the honorable leaders of our community adhering to the great traditions and virtues of honesty, humility, simplicity, selflessness and service. The sheer image brings tears to our eyes. Even the Chinese silk *garo* (richly embroidered sari with certain motifs), both the authentic and the artificial, seems to be losing its allure. Almost every Parsi household was once proud to possess at least one traditional *garo*, as a family heirloom. Most Parsi women are no longer fond of the sari and often appear ill at ease at navjotes, weddings and the Tower of Silence when it is customary to don it. A few decades ago, the coming of age of a Parsi girl was marked with a little ceremony of putting on her first ever sari.

However, the Parsi love affair with the frock continues unabated. Non-Parsis are often puzzled about why elderly Parsi women wear the frock in public as it is considered the prerogative of only young girls. In Parsi colonies and the corridors of the B. D. Petit Parsee General Hospital, frock clad ladies move about in gay abandon. Fifty years ago, eyebrows were raised if a Parsi woman wore the *salwar kameez* (popularly known as "Punjabi dress") or draped the sari straight across the left shoulder instead of the usual drop over the right shoulder (appropriately termed "*chatta haath no chhèro*" as against the "*oondha haath no chhèro*.") The "*chatto*" coupled with a bindi stuck on the forehead would instantly classify a woman as more Hindu than Parsi - almost like extra-religious worship. In the pre-Independence era, some Parsi women who were Gandhians or theosophists often dressed thus. Of course, affluent women shunned both the sari and the frock and preferred Western dress. In a strange sort of way, even today socioeconomic class is often evident from the attire of a Parsi lady.

In days gone by most men of substance seldom stepped out without wearing a velvet Parsi cap or even a *pheto* or *pugree*. The Anglicized ones put on a sola hat. We remember a senior French teacher at the Bharda New High School who would always wear a white *daglo* with a slightly upturned white hard hat. Generations of schoolboys christened him as Napoleon (from the front) and *bumbawalo* (fire brigade man) from the back. Now only the *Ilm-e-Khshnoomists* and assorted traditionalists stride in the sunlight with a red (as Pundolites prefer) or even a dark blue velvet cap, preventing their *khoreh* (divine aura) from dissipating under *juddin* (non-believers) gaze. However, we must confess that we find it disgusting when Parsis enter an *agiary* or *Doongerwadi* with a handkerchief tied around the head. Very unParsi indeed. If you don't have a cap, borrow one from the *agiary* counter; you can always shampoo away the dandruff later.

Parsis are no longer proud of their traditional attire though one of our avid horse racing friends recently entered the Royal Enclosure at Ascot wearing a *dagli* and *pheto* (to avoid looking silly in the mandatory black or grey top hat with a waistcoat and tie), relying on a rule which permits overseas visitors to wear their "formal national dress." Are Parsis fancying themselves as a "nation" now?

When did you come to Bombay?

The class divide between the early and later Parsi migrants to Bombay has diminished

Parsis started migrating to Bombay from towns in Gujarat like Navsari, Surat and Bharuch in the early part of the 18th century when the East India Company had already gained control over Bombay. Many were disadvantaged or fortune hunters. Migration was in their DNA, their forefathers having migrated from Iran to the West coast of India, centuries ago. The Great Indian Peninsular Railway had not yet started and Bombay was a foreign country to these adventurers. Most became traders and stood out amongst the rest of the populace, as they talked, looked and thought different.

Fortunes were slowly made and also lost by those who sailed to China and neighboring lands selling silk, spices and opium. They braved adverse conditions, even though life was often, in the words of the philosopher, Thomas Hobbes, "solitary, poor, nasty, brutish and short." Tough as nails, amoral if not immoral, they had the first mover advantage of the risk taker. After the Great Indian Mutiny of 1857 was quashed and Her Majesty's Government took over from the decadent 'Company Sarkar,' greater number of Parsis left their cocoon of comfort in Gujarat, lured by the temptress called Bombay. They distrusted strangers and preferred their co-religionists, who were summoned to Bombay, to work for the now fast growing business*es* of ship building, construction and export. We shall call them the early migrants. Between the two World Wars, almost every family had someone in Bombay. We shall term them the later migrants.

When India became independent in 1947, there was a divide between the early and later migrants. Barring exceptions, of course, the early migrants were richer, spoke better English, had residences in the posher parts of the city and were connected to well known business families. The later ones became professionals like doctors, lawyers, engineers and architects or took up employment with Parsi establishments like Tatas or the Central Bank of India or the Wadias or the Godrejs. The former educated their children in schools like Cathedral and John Connon and Campion, the latter in Bharda New High and St Xavier's. The early ones kept dogs, engaged '*ayahs*' and '*mistry*' and '*Boy*' (maidservant, cook and valet), ate at a dining table using fork and knife and marrow spoon, were members of the Willingdon Club and the Cricket Club of India (CCI), enjoyed Beethoven and Mozart; the other class conversed in Gujarati at home, were scared of dogs, engaged '*Gangas*' and '*Ramas*' (household domestics of a lesser kind), sat on a mat on the ground to eat with their fingers and sucked the bone marrow with a whistling sound, enjoyed Radio Ceylon for Binaca Geetmala and later Vividh Bharati for Hindi songs, and were not 'clubbable.'

Community institutions like the Bombay Parsi Punchayet, the large charitable trusts endowed colonies (housing the migrants), *atash behrams* and *agiaries* and Parsi associations were all controlled by the elite. At best, the hoi polloi were engaged as secretaries and accountants. A lot of deference was shown by the underclass to the landed gentry. We knew of a certain Mr B, who ran a large business and was a busy man. He knew the patriarch of a famous family who stayed in a resplendent bungalow at Malabar Hill but had never done a decent day's work in his long life, bungled his finances and was adjudged insolvent. The latter would now and then summon Mr. B to have a cup of tea at the bungalow and indulge in utterly banal talk; Mr. B would leave his thriving business and drive down to meet his '*Seth*,' though he had nothing to gain from it. The brash nouveau rich had not yet emerged.

The early migrants were pioneers who dared great odds to build a city and an impeccable reputation for their community. They founded the traditions of trust and huge charity, as their hearts bled for their brethren whom they had left behind. They were generous to a fault, as they contributed to every field of human endeavor in the city. No one taught them corporate social responsibility, as compassion came naturally. The reputation, Parsis enjoy today as a community in India, is largely attributable to these early migrants. Like always, the future generations were largely disappointing but their greatness is not compromised thereby.

The early elite

In the last 50 years, things began to change. The elite, too Anglicised, forgot their roots and became indifferent to community matters. Some are mildly amused, others are disinterested or even disgusted. Wealth, power and influence surely but steadily shifted to the so-called underprivileged who retained a strong sense of communal identity. The *sethias* were replaced by the street fighters. Class distinctions were reduced though not obliterated. The *masoor paavs* (now don't ask for a translation!) trounced the National Centre for the Performing Arts (NCPA) Parsis. The mindset of the community changed inexorably.

What is Polson, Mummy?

Parsi food brands of yesteryears evoke nostalgia

It floated merrily in a glass dish filled with water; golden yellow and salty. Refrigerators were not yet a feature in middle class homes and sliced bread was still a shy débutante on the breakfast table. When one went to the provision store, one asked for Polson, not butter. Don't say ink, say Quink, advertised a fellow brand with global links. Polson required no advertising. It was wholesome, contained fat, tasted yummy, and it was Parsi. Honest and unadulterated. People wanted good butter and did not know about bad cholesterol. The Polson family was low profile and dignified. We will never break this monopoly, thought the lesser brands of butter.

Then there was Parsi Dairy Farm (PDF) milk. A battalion of blue shirt clad *bhaiyas* (delivery men who hailed from Uttar Pradesh) carrying round metal containers of rich creamy milk (skimmed, then, meant watery) would spread out all over Bombay, and the customers' aluminum *tapélis* (utensils), placed under the container's tap, frothed with pure milk. One had to use one's connections to obtain Parsi Dairy coupons to be given in exchange for the milk. The somewhat rude manager would condescendingly look at the Johnny-come-lately

aspiring to be on the elite list of those receiving that creamy elixir. In winter, the *bhaiyas* would bring *doodh na puff* (sweetened creamy whipped milk froth, left exposed overnight to cool in the morning dew). Countless Gujarati, Marwari and Bohri homes were also loyal customers. The brand was underwritten by community virtues. Decades later, the family litigated and fragmented.

Our grandmother's cousin, a smiling, portly lady, would visit every first Tuesday of the month and invariably bring for her a Dippy's can containing the most divine pumpkin *murabba* (sweet preserve), bought from Swabal Stores outside the Cusrow Baug gate. Manning the counter for decades was a genial but expressionless man named Rustomji. The can would be opened using a mean looking, World War II vintage contraption. Dippy's made canned dhansak, vindaloo, *papri* and other Parsi dishes as also jams, ketchup and fruit crushes. This was a partnership between Jiji Dastur and Noshir Pochkhanawala, son of the Central Bank's founder, Sir Sorabji. Noshir was as English as they come and had a long happy marriage with Pini, daughter of Sir Nusserwanji Engineer. They used to host the most memorable sit-down dinners for guests who did not know each other which meant painfully labored conversations on inane topics, while gorging on some divine desserts. For a decade or so, Dippy's was quite popular until it wound up reportedly due to fears that some bawajis may perish due to botulism (tin poisoning) while eating the pumpkin *murabba*, having regard to the suspect quality of Indian tin, unlike the good old British metal.

Pickles made with jaggery, mango and home ground spices; *gharabh nu achaar* (pickled fish roe); vinegar; mango chutney and *murabba*s; *methia nu achaar* (spicy, oil based, mango pickle); *bafénoo* (whole ripe mangoes pickled in spicy gravy, skin et al) and other such exotic stuff was produced, and even exported, by the Kolahs of Navsari. The founder of the clan, Edulji, was apparently an incurable romantic, according to the Navsari watchers in our family. The business was later split into concerns owned by Kersaasp, Jehangir and Rustom; the last selling a legendary homemade ice cream from shops near the *atash behram* (still existing) and Tarota bazaar. Until market forces compelled the introduction of exotic flavors, the ice cream was always pink and had a distinct aura about it. A visit to Navsari would be deemed incomplete without the "pink." As children, we used to put half the money given to us as *ashodaad* (offerings before the holy fire) and use the remainder to buy "pink" or drink lemon (not lemonade) in thick glass bottles fitted with a marble which had to be pushed inside for the liquid to pour out. We were told that these bottles could be used as deadly missiles during a fracas. One of the Kolah branches sold sandalwood and frankincense too. *Kolah nu achaar* was a great brand and also witnessed some fratricidal wrangling between brothers over the trade name. We had occasion to visit a warehouse storing the delicious stuff in huge black vats. Extraordinarily fat lizards on the walls eyed us lazily. There were also vats of ultra strong vinegar whose smell opened up our sinuses.

OK Wafers was another Parsi brand started by the genial Keki Kotwal who used the best potatoes and oil and was quality conscious even five decades ago. A part-time bonesetter and slip disc curer taught by the famous Manchershaw Madhiwalla, Kotwal served the populace, free of cost, kicking butts and backs into shape. Although a good and honest Samaritan, Kotwal was short-tempered and there is a story about how he roughed up a then famous gynecologist in the lobby of The B. D. Petit Parsee General Hospital.

These were Parsi brands which had an appeal beyond the community. Generations fondly relished these homespun brands of a community which was perceived as robust, honest and good natured. Polson now floats only as a pleasant memory; no *tapéli* goes under a

PDF milk container; an office block has come up where once Dippy's made pumpkin *murabba*; the OK Wafer company was sold long back and that pink ice cream has lost its aura.

The Parsi Dairy Farm bhaiyas

What is the roz and mah today?

The Parsi calendar still retains its significance

A few days before the *muktads* (all souls days), Parsi establishments like the Union Press [printers of *lagan ni chithis* (wedding invitations)], Karani Brothers (prayer book publishers), Kersaasp Kolah *[gor keri nu achaar* (makers of jaggery and mango pickle)] and K. Wadia (diamond jewellers) would print and distribute the Parsi calendar, always in red, print bold enough for the visually impaired to read, rolled cylindrically (one had to straighten it by putting it under the mattress for one night), to be hung on the wall proudly below Zarthost Saheb's frame. Some calendars were plain vanilla, while others provided details of the *salgirehs* (birthdays) of popular *agiaries* and *atash behrams*; the eight *chogadiyas* of day and night (12 hours of day and 12 of night sub divided into eight sub periods of propitious timing; classified as excellent, auspicious, favorable, neutral, beneficial, malevolent, inauspicious and inimical). Those were the days, my friend, when children learnt by rote the 30 days and 12 months of the Parsi calendar. Today, most children ask, "What is a Parsi calendar?"

The *roz nu varas* (birthday according to the Parsi calendar) would precede the Gregorian birthday according to a simple formula: divide your age by four; if you are 16, the Parsi birthday will precede your birthday by four days, and if you are 100 by 25 days. If you prayed everyday, you would know the roz and mah easily; if you prayed sometimes, then you could always sneak a sly peek at the *agiary* calendar. Even if you could no longer rattle off all the names, at least you were expected to know the roz and mah of your birthday and those of others in the immediate family. The Parsi birthday, which once upon a time was the only birthday celebrated, has now become a low key dress rehearsal for the "English" birthday, as it has been dubbed. On the Parsi one, you ate *sev* (vermicelli fried brown and garnished with thinly sliced almonds and raisins) and *dahi* (plain yoghurt); offer sandalwood and light a *divo* at the *agiary*; and maybe have dinner at a restaurant.

Apart from birthdays, practising Zoroastrians still remember certain days of the Parsi calendar with reverence. Meher mah and Meher roz is the day you visit the boon-bestowing popular *Aslaji Agiary* at Grant Road; if you are not an early bird, you will have to await your turn to worship the holy fire after jostling with stout *humdins*, some of whom stand transfixed praying for their extended family, while those behind them try hard not to commit the sin of uttering colorful expletives in the *agiary*.

The other *parav* (when the same Ameshaspand presides over both the roz and mah on a day) is Avan mah né Avan roz. The infallible wish fulfiller, *Avan Ardavisur banu* is famous for granting legitimate boons (if you really desire something, the universe will conspire to give it to you), and her *yasht*, the longest in the *Khordeh Avesta*, if recited with dedication and a clean heart, can be miraculous. Even if you recite it only once, on her *parav*, but without missing a single year, she is mighty pleased. We know friends who pencil these *parav*s in their diary, electronic or otherwise, and will just not miss a single year, even if there is a death in the family on that day and whether they are in Paris or Poona.

Most Parsi calendars highlight two other important days - Zamyad roz and Avan mah; Govad roz and Dae mah - on which devout *humdins* perform *baaj* prayers on the death anniversary of Dastur Jamshed Kookadaru and a *behdin* called Homaji, respectively. If, like the Catholics, we granted sainthood (on second thoughts, thank God, we don't), without the slightest doubt the pious Dastur would be the first to be beatified. Panthaky of the Kappawala *Agiary* for 43 years, his miracles of healing, both physically and spiritually, including alchemically turning a brick into gold to finance the exact deficiency of funds needed for construction of the Anjuman *Atash behram*, are legendary. His is a living presence,

reverentially worshipped even today. The *behdin*, Homaji, in the days of the Raj was falsely framed in a murder charge of having kicked a pregnant woman and hanged publicly. He was exonerated after his death and, as foretold by him at the gallows, his accuser did not survive Homaji's uthamna. He is a symbol of the spiritual power of a crucified innocent.

A brilliant solicitor and partner in a law firm of antiquity, now no longer alive, would daily consult the Parsi calendar to know the birthday of every *agiary* in Bombay and Thana, which he would first visit and worship, reaching office only at tea time.

On Adar mah, Dae-pa-Adar roz, Parsis would paint an *afarganyu* on the kitchen tiles near the cooking gas stove and celebrate the fires. On Bahman mah, Bahman roz, they would eat *khichdi né koru* (yellow rice and pumpkin purée) and children would visit homes like a desi version of Halloween, selling homemade jellies (that was 50 years ago in Navsari). On Fravardin *parav*, Parsis visit the Towers of Silence and remember the deceased. On the Kadmi New Year, Iranis would place cucumbers and other foodstuff favoured by their dear departed near the *dakhmas* until some sourpuss in the Bombay Parsi Punchayet banned it (we are told the Iranis are thinking of finding substitutes for the cucumbers to place at the *dakhmas*). Come Dae mah, the Parsi staff of big and small Parsi establishments, be they banks or public sector companies, have *jashans* performed. The *muktads* start on Ashtad roz né Spendarmad mah leading to the five Gatha days when there is no roz and no mah (if you pass to the great beyond during Gatha days, on which day will your *masiso* (first month after death) and *chhamsi* (sixth month after death) fall is a riddle you can ask Ervad (Dr) Ramiyar Karanjia, the only sensible learned priest, or continue to survive on the ventilator until Hormazd roz and Fravardin mah, that is the Parsi New Year.

Apart from the Shahenshahi calendar, there also are the Fasli and the Kadmi calendars. Only The Mumbai Samachar publishes daily entries from these calendars, in its daily *panchang* column.

A typical Parsi household would proudly display the Prophet's portrait and the Parsi calendar in the living room; these days it remains hidden in the wardrobe, to be stealthily consulted. Unopened cylindrical calendars are being used by children as mock swords. Some of the Parsi establishments which published them have themselves disappeared. *Parsiana* reminds its readers about the soon to be forgotten calendar by printing it in one of its issues. A culture or civilization whose calendar is rarely consulted is being badly ravaged by time.

Of lahuvaas, handaas, fituris and kaklaats

Caricatures of deviationist behaviour cut across the classes

The genteel, docile proper bawaji is now a rare commodity. There is an increase in the number of *lahuvaa*s, *haandaa*s, *fituri*s, *kaklaat*s and *pallonji*s. These are highly technical terms which are difficult at times to distinguish even for a seasoned community watcher like your writer. To illustrate these definitions is flirting with libel, so forgive us the slightly roundabout way of explaining these caricatures who are found both among the *Masoor paav* Parsis and the NCPA Parsis. And please do not try to categorize your in-laws and increase the number of contested divorces before the Parsi Matrimonial Court.

The easier ones first. A *kaklaat* is a garrulo us, incessant talker of nonsense which is jarring on the nerves. The listener feels physically exhausted after a *kaklaat* departs. *Kaklaat*s steal your energy. A well versed *kaklaat* will not let you interrupt his diatribe and he never listens to you. He is usually loud and raucous but there is also the soft speaking, whining variety narrating her sob story. They must not be confused with *manjan*s (tooth powder) who are mechanical repeaters of the same point ["Meher *to ékdum* Colgate *nu nallu* packet *chhè* (Meher is truly a small packet of Colgate tooth powder)."] An authentic *kaklaat* will create a shindig, a disturbance. In pristine Gujarati, *kaklaat* means plaintive crying, like a bird distressed at the loss of her young ones from the nest. In Parsi dialect, however, a true *kaklaat* will make the most peace loving person want to smash a flower pot on his offending head.

A *pallonji* is more than a show-off. A plain vanilla puffer goes by the little known but endearing term of *foortaji*. A *pallonji* is a compulsive attention seeker who spins yarns, exaggerates, pretends to be what he is not. If he is at Allbless Baug, he wants to be the bridegroom and if he is at *Doongerwadi*, he wants to be the corpse. At community functions, he will be found sitting in the front row, turning around all the time to ensure he is being noticed. His morbid fear is that he will be ignored. A serial 'vote of thanks' giver, he is quick to garland or wrap a shawl around the chief guest. Irrespective of his ability, he volunteers to take the lead in any initiative or movement or crusade. A publicity hound, he wants his mugshot published everywhere. In our days as a journalist, one such *pallonji*, who was once upon a time a minor minister, would insist every other day that his picture accompanies every silly press release, he issued as chairman of some State board. Irritated with his constant requests, we published his photo next to the obituary column which greatly offended him and he protested to the editor. Next time, we sandwiched his visage between two news reports of criminal fraud. He never again called the newspaper. We had also encountered a female *pallonji* whose every picture appeared identical, with the same exaggerated tilted head, a pasted mile long smile, and a garland in her podgy hands. If a *pallonji* is wealthy, he loves to flaunt his wealth. *Pallonji*s are not usually evil but mostly odious.

*Kaklaat*s, *manjan*s and *pallonji*s are benign but *fituri*s can cause a lot of stress. They are the touch-me-nots. Itching for a fight, their lungs yearn for a shouting match. Quick to take offence, they love brawls and fisticuffs. They endeavor to provoke and are most disappointed when they meet some *thanda pani nu matloo* (a calm person) who refu*ses* to bite their bait and lock horns. *Fituri*s are in full form at Bombay Parsi Punchayet elections and in Court corridors during hotly contested community litigation. They feel

reprinted with permission from Parsi Bol 2

cheated out of a slanging match if their opponent refu*ses* to engage in some old-fashioned *maramari* (fights) and *garagari* (exchange of cuss words). *Fituri*s are cantankerous, crotchety, hyperactive Parsis. Freud would have classified their high agitation as a substitute for sex.

The nuance between a *haandaa* and a *lahuvaa* is rather subtle. The latter engages in loutish behavior like interrupting a Adi Marzban masterpiece called *Asha Nirasha* (hope and despair) on Parsi New Year's Day by shouting, "Ardeshir, *saré saparmé dahaaré humé rarva nathi aaya* (we have not paid entrance fees to cry on an auspicious day)." The *haandaa* in the audience, while wholeheartedly agreeing with the *lahuvaa*'s views, may not necessarily approve of such loutish behavior in public. *Haandaa*s love the gross and the crass and enjoy the discomfiture of the prigs. Once at a Yehudi Menuhin concert in Bombay, when the great violinist was playing Violin Sonata No 5 in F Major, with his talented sister, Hephzibah, before a largely Parsi audience, the latter's microphone (those were not the days of sophisticated acoustics) emitted a sound like someone breaking wind. One *lahuvaa*, to the great consternation of the very proper Parsis, loudly remarked that Hephzibah must have eaten too much dhansak. The *haandaa*s at the concert, terribly bored with the slow movement, must have been secretly thrilled with the *lahuvaa*'s interjection.

If you ever come across a *haanda* at heart, who is also a loud *lahuvaa*, and has the mannerisms of a *pallonji*, can sound like a *kaklaat* and create a *fitur*, do let us know, so that we can recommend him to fill any vacancy that may arise in the august community institution.

Saaro saparmo divas has evolved

Navjotes and weddings are celebrated differently now

Dosu, feeling youthful at 72, decided to end his bachelorhood by marrying Pervin, 30 years his junior. On the wedding day he looked rather emaciated in an ill-fitting dagli and duckback trousers, as compared to his voluptuous bride. Those days, the entire *moholla* (locality) would join in the merriment lasting over six days. The wedding procession was led by Dosu's sisters-in-law carrying the traditional *ses* (German silver tray). A politically incorrect heckler enquired if there was a *batrisi* (dentures) in the *ses*, much to the amusement of the crowd and discomfiture of the hapless Dosu who had to manage a toothy grin.

Until the 1950s, most Parsis found their marriage partners amongst cousins. Genetic inbreeding, was then as a concept, as unknown as broccoli bake. Paternal cousins were preferred, which made matters worse. Our paternal grandmother's was perhaps the last child marriage in Navsari, then ruled by the Gaikwads of Baroda. The bride was six months old; the groom, her paternal cousin, of course, was 10. She was, rather unwisely, given a wine cake to suck, upon which she nearly choked. In the 1950s, an interfaith marriage was as common as a volcanic eruption. Aristocrats marrying *mudum*s (foreign wives) were secretly envied but the girl who dared to marry a *juddin* (non-Parsi) had no option but to elope. Our father signed as a witness to one such marriage and had to face the wrath of the orthodox for being a collaborator. 'Register marriage,' as civil marriages were then dubbed, were deemed silent and shady. The all-Parsi one was widely anticipated as a source of much joy, gossip and entertainment.

The ladies of the host household would visit the homes of most invitees to extend a personal invite at least a month in advance on an auspicious day (not Fravardin *roz né* Fravardin *mah*). It was called "*téru karva aayach* (have come to give the invite)." In the towns of Gujarat, an elderly *mobed* would visit different *mohollas* and recite the invite sonorously. When the printed *chitthi* (invite) first appeared, many lamented the advent of the impersonal invitation. The initial *chitthis*, for decades, were printed in red ink on white paper. The quality of paper, printing, envelope and the ubiquitous postage prepaid reply card indicated one's socioeconomic strata. The wording was uniformly boring. The *lagan ni chitthi* though spawned many bawdy versions, which cannot be fully reproduced in the respected family publication which you are reading; but just to give you a flavor, translate the following into Gujarati: "Our son, Lovji, with a missing vital part, will marry Coomi, again with some missing anatomy, on an *amaas* and *garhan* (no moon and eclipse) day at a godforsaken hill where incestuous happenings occur, when dinner will be served containing an exotic combination involving female buffaloes and *bhabraaveli bhaaji* (sprinkled with spinach), sparrows and *chaarvéla eeda* (scrambled eggs)."

A modest budget meant Cama Baug, *motto* otlo; a shoestring budget meant the *nallo* otlo. The middle class went for Allbless Baug;

the upper middle and above for the Colaba *Agiary*. The venue had to be booked months in advance, as all wanted certain auspicious days. Amongst caterers, the no nonsense Kaikhushru Bhoot slugged it out with the genial Navroji Patel and his enterprising wife. In the late 1960s, a Rs 10 *paatra* was drooled over, but you could bargain for a bare minimum of three rupees and eight annas. The Godiwalla juggernaut had not then arrived. In the towns of Gujarat quite a few *mobeds* turned part time caterers, sometimes with disastrous results. Decades ago, there was an eccentric *mobed* known as Nariman Dagri in Navsari who undercut his competitors to secure plum jobs and invariably ran out of food. In the first sitting, mutton cutlets were served with tomato gravy. In the subsequent sittings, the gravy would go missing; then the cutlet served half; and finally, a fried egg would be dumped on one's *paatra*. Woe betide those who protested. Dagri would glower and then abuse you as if you were Oliver Twist.

On the other hand, some hosts went overboard in laying out a feast for their *parohnas* (special guests) at each of the 18 meals during six days, including one after the marriage. From gluttonous breakfasts running into five courses to out-of-the-mainstream delicacies like *dodhi ma gosht* (mutton with bottle gourd), *aleti paleti* (mutton and chicken offals), *khichri né vengna tambota no* patio (yellow rice with tomato and aubergine gravy), *papri ma kabab* (field beans with mutton kebabs) and *bhaji ma bheja* (spinach with goat's brains) for lunch. We knew of an honest and hardworking gentleman who blew his life savings for his only daughter's marriage, which was remembered decades after in admiring tones by the *parohnas* who did not know that the man and his wife literally starved for the rest of their lives.

A live band was de rigueur. The wealthy preferred the portly Goody Seervai playing the accordion. Later, his competitor was the feisty Nelly Batlivala, a young widow who brought up her children by playing music. Phil Davar was affordable for the middle classes. The *masoor paavs* (hoi polloi) preferred Dara and his Darling Orchestra who belted out numbers like "Number 54, the house with the bamboo door" and current Bollywood hits. Dara's sons, Pervez, the veteran Parsi theater actor, and the late Marzban, the official community crooner, regaled Parsi audiences. It was quite a class event. In the towns of Gujarat, there would be the *naan khatai* band of uniformed ragtags creating an awful cacophony beating tin drums and blowing desi clarinets. The better off of Navsari invited the *takorkhana* (brass band) from Surat, who would play some doleful music, totally inappropriate for the occasion. As the marriage house would be bustling with activity, the *takorkhana* would be housed in the portico of a neighbor, who would feel privileged at the honor. During those days, the entire *moholla* belonged to the hosts. The news of a death in the *moholla* would be suppressed if it were to occur on the wedding day. We remember seeing a young boy slapped by his irate mother and being called a liar for loudly shouting that Pervin's grandmother had just died. After dinner, men and women joined in singing songs and dancing garbas, including some bawdy ones abusing the groom's family. This would be supplemented by old ladies attempting to sing in the Indian classical style for a measly fee; and most listeners wanting to throttle these inflictors of pain. *Taro* (a holy bull's consecrated urine) had to be consumed under the eagle eye of the officiating priest, who was at times known to turn glad at the time of giving *nahan* (cleansing bath) to the bride, particularly if a young *mobed* got his terms of reference wrong.

In the 1970s, the towns of Gujarat started to empty. The first of the navjotes began to be celebrated in the ball room of the Taj Mahal hotel followed by Rs 100 a plate buffet on which the Parsis gorged as if they had just broken a seven-day fast; and then cynically complain that they missed the *paatru*. The invites became commoditized and indistinguishable from invites of other communities. There were no six-day feasts. Goody and Nelly and Dara Mehta were gone. Music systems blared out popular songs or some Catholic band from Bandra played no Parsi numbers. There are no longer any wedding processions in the *moholla* which has a solitary Parsi house. *Madavsaro* has been replaced by mehendi and the *takorkhana* has gone silent.

Anyone interested in reviving these rich cultural traditions should plan a destination wedding at Udvada.

Parsi wedding

Crockery, cutlery and class

Utensils and origins are inextricably linked

Have you always eaten your meals at a dining table? Have you sipped hot tea from a saucer? Have you cooked your food in aluminum vessels? Do you know how to operate a primus stove? Have you slurped on a *goor-ni daa* (marrow spoon)? Can you drink water without touching the brass pot to your lips? If your answers are mostly in the negative, then you are a NCPA (National Centre for the Performing Arts) Parsi. On the other hand, if your answer is a resounding yes; then you are an authentic *masoor-pav* Parsi.

Parsis do not generally equate wealth with class. Ultra high net worth boors abound, and some impoverished ones are very proper. Like Jane Austen ("an English spinster of the middle class; who knew a lot about the amorous effects of brass"), you can be classy, though not necessarily rich.

Decades ago, this writer, as an applicant for the Rotary International scholarship to read law at Cambridge, was asked by a formidable looking interviewer as to how proficient he was with knives (at the dining table, of course). The response was a stupid smiling nod (which meant nothing), but was taken as a confident answer. The formidable one then boomed, "Of course, I forgot you are a Parsi! Of course, silly of me even to ask!" We still wonder as to whether we would have got the scholarship had we candidly confessed that not only were we most uncomfortable holding a knife, leave aside distinguishing between a knife to cut bread and a knife to apply butter, but at the relevant time, we were just getting used to a dining table at home.

Strange though it may sound, Parsis, who migrated from Gujarat to Bombay during and after the Second World War (1939-45) continued with the traditional way of life for decades thereafter. A large coir mat would be spread on the living room floor and the family sat cross legged, to partake of meals. Food was cooked in aluminum pots and pans (few knew then of its alleged link with Alzheimer's). Stainless steel was a luxury, reserved for heating milk. The name of the head of the household was engraved on all utensils. Barring stuff which could not be picked up with the fingers, cutlery was not to be seen. A fork was used only to scramble eggs and a teaspoon to stir sugar in tea. Knives were for carving raw fish and flesh; the only exception being the table knife to apply butter. One ate with one's hands (Ayurveda lauds this as excellent for health); fingers deftly rolling a *ghaoon ni roti* (wheat chappati) around a *masoor ma botoo* (chunk of meat in lentils) – only the poor then ate *jowar, bajra* and the like. It was an art form, the manner in which one converted the dal sodden rice into a sushi like morsel (called a *book* in Parsi Gujarati), not at all unseemly or indecent. Did someone say soup? It was seldom on the menu. Also absent were steak or meats requiring to be carved or sliced or cut. Mutton was very popular and so were pomfrets; chicken, though, was a luxury. One was expected to pick up the meat stripped bone and suck the marrow within. Marrow which was too deeply embedded in the bone would be extricated with a *goor-daani*.

Cheap white crockery was purchased from roadside vendors lining Colaba Causeway, and of course, Crawford Market. A slightly chipped cup was not immediately replaced - anyway, one poured tea in the saucer and drank it with a relishing slurping sound onomatopoeically called *sarrappo*. We have seen tea being similarly drunk from saucers in other East Asian and Arab countries. If one really wanted to feel satisfied, one had to eat with one's fingers; and enjoy tea (no déclassé tea bags then) best from a saucer. Even the anglicized Parsis would condescend to eat the sticky, gelatinous *khariya* (trotters) with their fingers. A rather pretentious loud mouth lawyer had once told us that his mother-in-law was so aristocratic that even when she was compelled to eat *khariya* with her fingers, she would ensure that only her first phalange was soiled.

The meals would be washed down with boiled water strained through a glass cloth and stored in a *matloo* (red earthenware pot). When refrigerators arrived in the late 1950s and early '60s, cold water was savored in the sweltering summer. Priestly families and other orthodox never touched the *katli* (brass receptacle) holding the water to their lips. Glasses were a late entrant and many felt that water did not taste as well as it did from the *karasyo* (metal drinking utensil).

The early migrants, who had then assimilated with the British rulers, eagerly adopted the English lifestyle. Wedgwood ware dining and Waterford tea sets, imported from England, without payment of customs duty, were prized possessions, not only of the rich but the anglicized upper middle classes. It would adorn the table on festive occasions or to impress guests, who would breach etiquette by slightly turning the plate over when out of the host's eyeshot, to ascertain whether it was indeed Wedgwood or a cheap Japanese imitation (today's China). Cutlery had to be Sheffield. The "boy," as the serving attendant was called in Parsi households, was familiar in the art of arranging the knives and forks in order for the courses planned for the dinner. The "mistry," as the cook was called, was equally well versed in selecting the appropriate serving dish. The landed gentry would exchange a polite snigger or two, if their *nouveau riche* hostess displayed ignorance of the crockery-cutlery code of conduct.

The dining bell, or the silver gong, compliments of Wedgwood, was a ritual religiously observed, even if Sorabji and Goolbai were just a few feet away from the dining table.

Freshly brewed tea, with mint leaves floating, from a Royal Albert teapot, ensconced in a Pemberley tea cosy, strained through a silver Royal Doulton strainer, poured into an exquisitely thin bone china cup with its subtle floral design, sugar (always white) stirred with that familiar tinkling sound - all so subtle and heavenly.

The classic Parsi kitchen would have been so aghast to see mugs, toasters, mixers, tea bags, microwaves, sweetener sachets, jostling diners at soulless buffets, port wine and sherry in champagne glas*ses* and unbreakable Chinese plates.

If NCPA Parsis were given a choice between modern invasions and the *masoor-pav* way of life, they would have opted to sit crossed legged on the coir mat and eat with their hands.

Parsis like to use good crockery like old country Roses China

Dadar Parsi Colony's sub-culture dissipating

The Dadar Parsis are losing their uniqueness

Pesi was hugely irritated with the untimely ringing of bells in St. Joseph's Church, on the outskirts of the Mancherji Joshi Dadar Parsi Colony. His complaints to the Archbishop of Bombay went unheeded. Pesi then wrote to His Holiness, the Pope himself, who sent a personal reply to an elated Pesi. The bells rang less and the famous railing of the colony's Five Gardens instantly christened him Pesi Pope. The truth of this implausible story will be verified by almost all senior inhabitants of the colony.

The railing, in its heydays, was imposing, cruel, funny and unsparing. The rally driver, causing his terrified passengers to involuntarily relieve themselves in the Fiat, when being driven to Lonavala after midnight in an hour-and-a-quarter (remember there was no Expressway then), was called 'Rocket.' The kind-hearted, podgy manager of the Central Bank of India (Khodadad Circle Branch) was called *'Bun pao.'* A Mae West look alike was 'Nagoo Doll.' There was a *'Bafaat'* and a 'Mike' and a 'Chocolate.' Almost none escaped the mandatory rechristening à la Anthony Burgess' dystopian novel - A Clockwork Orange. There were three or four railings but *'Lokhan ni railing'* was the meeting point for authentic *haadaas* (an untranslatable expression for crude, unsophisticated louts and loutees) every evening. Nothing was sacrosanct and no reputation remained unscathed. Every eccentricity was celebrated and every idiosyncrasy pilloried.

Expletives were as ubiquitous as pigeons. Even inanimate objects like the daily newspaper, a bottle of milk or a cricket bat were routinely accused of having illicit relationships with their close female relatives. The Dadar Parsi was tough, macho and not exactly sophisticated. And they mostly were, and are, obsessively fond of their bikes and their Colony.

The Colony, of course, being a collection of unconnected 100 odd plots, most with a ground and three-storeyed building, having a single commonality - the Parsis-only covenant. This covenant was legally challenged in a bitterly fought litigation in the Bombay City Civil Court many decades ago. The Parsi Central Association (PCA) succeeded in upholding the covenant (thanks to the brilliance of noted lawyer Nadir Modi who appeared gratis and a somewhat sympathetic Judge Rego). The colony also has several non-covenanted plots, mostly of Parsi ownership. Much against our liberal instincts, we must confess that this covenant has helped in preserving the quaint sub-culture, notwithstanding that the Parsi-only buildings are now sandwiched between cosmopolitan apartments, after most have been mounted upon by additional floors on stilts.

As is inevitable, in the covenanted buildings Parsis have married non-Parsis and there are several flats having non-Parsi spouses and children. What is jarring is that the PCA has begun to flex its muscles against Parsi women introducing their non-Parsi husbands and children into these covenanted flats. PCA's policies are counter-productive and may well backfire if one of these aggrieved ladies challenges once again the validity of the covenant, in the changed circumstances.

Like all Parsi institutions, the once bristling and strident Dadar Parsi Colony is fast mellowing. When we came to reside in one of the buildings (non-covenanted, of course), two decades ago, the warm and popular Yezdi Daruwalla (who soon died young and was much mourned) informed us that the colony was a very secure place ("before you can scream *chor, chor* (thief), men with sticks will rush out of their hou*ses*"). All that has disappeared. Most have a look of resignation around them. Of course, the colony does come alive during the Jamshedi Navroz spring festival, and if you are keen to hear authentic, original Parsi, and almost lyrical, abuse, you can still visit the Dadar Parsi Gymkhana (a worthy competitor to the Dadar Parsis in this field were some Navsari *mobeds* we encountered during our *navar* ceremony).

Are the Dadar Parsis largely orthodox? Maybe, though not in the WAPIZ (World Alliance of Parsi Irani Zarthoshtis) sense of the term. They are more inclined to preserve Parsi properties in Parsi hands and more comfortable to relax and share laughter with fellow Parsis, preferably also from the colony.

While adventurers abound, with the passing away of old hands like Rustom Tirandaz, the colony now lacks a charismatic personality to lead and electrify its 6,000 inhabitants and to gracefully preserve the unique heritage of this village like oasis with its gorgeous trees (all numbered) and its nostalgic lanes.

Unlike a Parsi baug, the colony, being a collection of scattered buildings, is fast losing its Parsi character. The numbers are eroding, the people are ageing. The bikes don't backfire at midnight. '*Bafaat*' has made his last faux pas. 'Mike' has been silenced. 'Nagoo Doll' does not look like Mae West anymore, or vice versa. 'Rocket' does not drive now. The railings are full of people, but not Parsis. The church bells ring again, more than they ought to, but there is no Pesi to write to the Pope.

Unveiling of Mancherji Joshi's statue at the entrance of MJDPC
Photo: Katrak Studio

Our culture is being carpet bombed

While the Udvada Atash Behram is engulfed in Parsi warmth, the same does not hold true for Navsari

Our annual pilgrimage to the Navsari and Udvada *atash behrams* made us pensive. Although it was not one of the "big days" of the Parsi calendar, there was no sitting space at Iranshah. Occupancy at the hotels and the recently spruced up sanatorium is high. Sales of mawa cakes at the local Irani Bakery are brisk. Thanks to our Prime Minister, the roads leading to our holy site are excellent. Udvada Village is buzzing with positive energy and looks very Parsi.

The other *atash behram* at Navsari, though charming and vibrant as always, had only a few worshippers. A solitary young priest is around. Ever expanding Navsari is about to have a municipal corporation heralding its official transformation from a large town to a city. Three-and-a-half thousand Parsis constitute little under one percent of its population, the Jokhi's Ava Baug having attracted several Parsis to the town. The *Atash behram*, founded in 1765, and massively restored in 1925, sports a new donor plaque, thanking the Navajbai Ratan Tata Trust for its two crore rupees donation in 2011. Soon, it will celebrate its 250th anniversary. The prayer hall surrounding the sanctum sanctorum is more impressive than the one in Udvada (we may, of course, be biased, as its founder was a direct lineal ascendant/forebear). The holy fire, divinely charming, faces a marble wall where, a few decades ago, a distinct impression of the first Dasturji Meherjirana (who was invited to Akbar's court) mysteriously surfaced and can be seen even today. Over the years we have heard many first-hand stories from the *boiwalas* tending the fire about a powerful guardian spirit dressed all in white silently moving in its environs. Just across the *Atash behram* is the *Mobed* Minocherhomji Daremeher. Few know that this *Agiary* was founded in 1687, that is, 78 years before the *atash behram*.

This *Agiary* has a rich and fascinating history. Restored in 1954, and recently renovated, things now look very quiet. An elderly priest sitting in an armchair in sudreh-lengha and reading the *Gujarat Samachar*, hastens to put on his *jama* and place the sandalwood sticks onto the fire. This 327-year-old *Agiary* is an inherent part of the great Zoroastrian heritage. As we bow before the holy fire, we hear some FM radio station blaring Hindi film songs. Other communities have bought over most of the houses encircling the *atash behram* and *Agiary*. As we walk down memory lane in the *moholla* we see the few remaining Parsi houses derelict, locked or dilapidated. Not more than just 30 years ago this *moholla* had a distinct Parsi character with not a single non-Parsi house.

Advocate Dara Deboo (who has done a superb job modernizing Sorab Baug's rooms for visiting devotees) shares with us the history of each house or vacant plot. Death, migration, poverty and greed have all played their role. We ask him about the whereabouts of a solitary spinster, and just then she walks down the road, adding to the collective pathos which engulfs the place. The erstwhile family home of a Bombay High Priest now has a nameplate which says "Raziya Palace," with some Urdu inscription beneath. Defeat is writ large on the faces of the surviving neighborhood Parsis. A way of life has disappeared. Somebody has carpet bombed our culture.

While the area surrounding the Udvada *Atash behram* is engulfed in Parsi warmth, the Navsari precinct is not. As if to resist the irresistible, Dinshaw Tamboly's WZO House, modern and spanking, stands like a lone warrior near the *Atash behram*. We enquire from Deboo the possibility of acquiring one of these houses or vacant plots to build a Zoroastrian Heritage Center, to preserve and protect the *Atash behram* and *Agiary* from even more difficult times to come. An acre costs a crore, he says. Such a heritage center could function like a mini museum, artefacts shop and also send a constant update on the situation to Bombay. While the city center of Navsari is too large to be reconquered, it is not impossible to culturally revive the *mohollas* surrounding the *Atash behram* and the *Agiary*. Unfortunately, unlike Udvada on the sea, dusty and polluted Navsari is no vacation or weekend stop. Despite this, if 10 Parsi houses can be acquired in this small area, we would be creating a protective shield around our spiritual inheritance. Until 50 years ago, Navsari was regarded as "*Dharam no tékdo* (support/pillar of the religion)." Today, it is culturally annihilated. In the years to come more such bastions will fall. Shall we resignedly accept it as destiny, or shall we somehow manage to reset the clock just before midnight.

The consignment dilemma

Forsaking the Towers of Silence still wrenches the heart

After a great deal of reluctance, our 92-year-old mother has opted for the Prayer Hall at Worli. Ever since this facility was inaugurated, the number of Parsis opting to be cremated has increased. All post death religious rituals and ceremonies, as at *Doongerwadi*, are performed in this Hall, a substitute for the '*Cremate-ni-bungli*,' made possible with the active involvement of Dinshaw Tamboly, chairman of The Prayer Hall Trust (TPHT). Nearly a dozen priests are now available at this new Prayer Hall whose environs are clean and pleasant. A stone's throw away is the public electric crematorium. The process is speedy and seamless.

On the other hand, the Towers are still faulty. The solar panels, though operated at high intensity, are not functioning optimally. During the monsoon months of June to September, the panels are terribly dysfunctional. Across the road, residents complain of stench. Disposal is still grisly, gory and gruesome. The crusading zeal of Dhun Baria, who exposed the state of affairs at *Doongerwadi* a decade ago, is dimmed by age and frustration. Other reform initiatives have also lost steam. Many have watched the gut wrenching video recordings of the horrors inside the *dakhmas*. Unworkable plans like building a vulture aviary have been shelved. There is an almost universal conspiracy to remain silent lest this priceless property is lost to any unholy nexus between politicians and builders.

Despite the gnawing discomfort of knowing that the bodies of those consigned are often recognizable for months thereafter (particularly, during the monsoon months); and despite the availability of this new Prayer Hall, why do most Parsis still prefer the Towers? Maybe, a man likes to exit in the same manner as his forefathers. And the Towers do have many endearing features.

Parsipanu can be seen and felt in the environs of the *bunglis*. Time, literally, stands still. The collective vibrations of the thousands of *geh sarnas*, *uthamnas* and *Sarosh*, intoned during the last few centuries, can still be felt by the sensitive. An aura of protection exists from the occult circuits in the ground, created throughout *Doongerwadi*. As soon as the *Doongerwadi* hearse winds its way uphill to the *bunglis*, within seconds one is transported from the cosmopolitan traffic jams of Kemps Corner into an exclusive oasis of silence.

The pall bearers bathe the body and call you to tie the *kusti*, for the last time, round the body. A priest gently mumbles prayers before the body lying in rest as the sandalwood and incense laden breeze wafts through. You quietly reflect upon the life of your loved one which has just ended, as countless Parsis before you have done, exactly at the same spot and exactly in the same manner. This is indeed so cathartic. Throughout the night, the pin drop silence is punctuated by a solitary dog barking.

So is the ritual of the mourners walking in pairs, limply clutching a white handkerchief; the face of the deceased being exposed for a final goodbye on a marble platform just outside the *dakhmas*; the mourners silently waiting for the pall bearer to clap thrice to signify that the body has been consigned; the recitation of the short prayers to the *dakhmas* followed by a cleansing kusti; offering a sandalwood stick to the *dadgah* fire; and then quietly making your way downhill to the *bungli*, when you may spot a dancing peacock. All this simply cannot be replicated.

Of course, if you are a dispassionate stoic, you may dismiss all this as sentimental claptrap and argue that the central purpose - disposing the dead - is not being achieved; and hence, the new Prayer Hall is the only option. However, for most, handling death delicately is very important.

Strangely, this dilemma can be resolved with ease. The optimal solution is to have an electric crematorium at the Towers. At first blush, this may appear radical. However, in the months when the solar panels work (and we are reliably told that they are operated now at considerable intensity), the body is dehydrated, with wisps of smoke emanating, within 48 to 72 hours. This is nothing but a solar powered crematorium. Technology is now available in India to set up a solar powered crematorium which can work on stored solar power, and thereby, even during the monsoon months. If a referendum is conducted on this issue, we believe that the community will overwhelmingly support the proposition. The present trustees of the Bombay Parsi Punchayet do have the resolve to make this move. Better than sitting on a time bomb of a public health scandal, which is too unpleasant even to imagine.

If this proposal is implemented, the traditional way can be seamlessly merged with state of the art technology. The sun will continue to remain as the energy which dispo*ses*, exactly as the scriptures dictate. The post death soothing will not be denied to anyone. Perhaps, TPHT will then be too happy to dedicate the premi*ses* to our sister communities.

The prayer hall for those cremated, at Worli, Mumbai

A story of two funerals

What lies ahead for the Towers of Silence?

After considerable thinking, it was decided to consign my 93-year-old mother's body to the Towers of Silence. From the same *bungli*, where my 55-year-old father's body began its last journey some 42 years ago, the priests of the oldest Bombay *agiary*, Banaji Limji, recited the *geh sarna* prayers for my mother. Some traditionalist groups sent me congratulatory messages for what they exultantly termed as my "correct decision." Several reform minded friends remained silent but wondered as to why she had not been cremated, despite the availability of the Prayer Hall at the Worli crematorium.

Fifty years ago, in his weekly column, *"Parsi Tari Aarsi,"* in the *Bombay Samachar*, which he also edited, my father provided ample space to the diminishing number of vultures. Community activist Dara Cama had circulated photographs showing undisposed bodies with partially recognizable faces. Dr Aspi Golwalla, then chairman of the Bombay Parsi Punchayet (BPP) and an eminent physician, had entered the *dakhmas*, along with another trustee and a leading lawyer, Shiavax Vakil, to assess the true state of affairs. All three, Cama, Golwalla and Vakil, were abused, threatened and vilified. Golwalla was the personal physician to the Camas of *Bombay Samachar*, while Vakil was my father's close friend. They corroborated Dara Cama's horrific album. Dervish Irani, the legendary caretaker of the Towers confirmed that the situation was worsening by the day. Eight years later, my father, diagnosed with terminal cancer, had sufficient time to contemplate the possibility of cremation. He was a peculiar blend of a devout, daily praying Zoroastrian, an ordained priest, yet a devotee of Shirdi Saibaba and a witness to many interfaith marriages, which required courage those days. In his final hours, he said that he preferred to exit the way his forefathers had.

All the traditional prayers were performed in the Hodiwala *Bungli* starting with the *bhoi pur nu bhantar* (prayers recited by a *mobed* seated before a *ruvaan* (corpse), from the *sachkar* (ritual bath) to the beginning of the *gah saran*) which began at dusk till the early hours of next morning. Throughout the night the experienced *mobed*'s mellifluous tone, rising and falling in a crescendo, over the flickering sandalwood fire fed with frankincense in the dim lighting of the *bungli*, helped his dearest to come to terms with their grief. The body, wrapped in white and placed in a rectangular space, a zone of protection created by many elaborate occult rites, lay in state, relieved of its earthly pains; a solitary *divo* (oil lamp) flickering near the head. The almost total silence, according dignity to death. Then in the morning, the memory erasing *gah sarna* prayers, from the *Ahunavad Gatha*, sung in an amazing synchronicity, by a pair of *mobed*s used to each other's rhythm, ending with the emphatically pronounced *Avestan* power mantra, *Nemascha ya Armaitish izha-cha*, thrice. The resulting silence broken by the shuffling of feet of the mourners bowing before the body, one by one. Moist eyes, stifled sobs, the realization of the fleeting nature of human existence, all mingled together, as the procession went past the many non-Parsis lining the road on either side.

Uphill, the iron mesh bier was placed on the marble platform, the face exposed to the encircling mourners for the last time. They later, awaited the cue of the *nassessalar* clapping thrice to signal that the body had been placed in the well to begin praying *Namaskar dakhma no* from a tiny book. Some peacocks wailing their distant protest at the clapping. The ritual of dipping your finger in the consecrated urine of an albino bull (some seasoned mourners deftly avoiding the urine dispenser), the *kusti* and then bowing before the *Sagdi* fire. I saw plenty of vultures when his body was consigned.

Those days, the death certificate was issued by the BPP itself from its office near the *Sagdi*. I collected the crisp, green certificate certifying my father's consignment to the *dakhma*; a strange feeling of catharsis at the death of the person you loved most, as I made my way downhill to be consoled by those not permitted to join the funeral. Two nights later, the *uthamna* before dawn before that empty rectangular space and the still flickering *divo*. The Dog Star Sirius (*Tir Yazad*) above the *bungli*, brightly shining in the summer sky as the manthric vibrations of high energy resonated within. The family made their way up to the *Sagdi* fire where the priest recited a powerful intonation to the soul which had just crossed the bridge of judgement by striking the bell 12 times and uttering the name of the departed. However traumatic or young, death may have been, most went home with an overwhelming sense of peace.

In the intervening four decades, many a crusader, including this writer, passionately wrote about the failure of *dakhmenashini*. None more effectively than the fearless Dhun Baria whose videotapes were shown on national television. A former qawwali singer under the stage name Mahajabeen, the feisty Baria shook the establishment as never before. Her response to midnight callers threatening death was so original that they soon realized that Baria was from a different planet. With nonsensical plans of the BPP to breed vultures in captivity failing spectacularly, the solar panels operating at high intensity dehydrated the body in three to five days with wisps of smoke emitting, except during heavy rains. Ozone dispensers were deployed to mask the occasional stench. Bones and undisposed remains gathered and buried more frequently than before. Baria and I nearly wangled a *cremate ni bungli* at *Doongerwadi*. Dinshaw Tamboly succeeded in establishing the Prayer Hall for Parsi crematees.

My mother and I debated at length the disposal method she wanted for herself. Public crematorium is not clean, she observed after attending her brother's and nephew's cremations. Can we not have a crematorium for Parsis only? she asked. Like her husband, a daily praying Zoroastrian and a fervent believer in the efficacy of after death prayers, she was not too impressed with the new Prayer Hall. Does not have the same ambience and atmosphere, she twitched her nose. Her ambivalent approach continued until her last days, being super alert mentally. Do what you think fit, she smiled. Just before dawn, as she peacefully breathed her last, with her head cradled in my arms, I dialled a surprised Hoshedar *Panthaki* of Banaji *Agiary* to arrange for the prayers and then called for the *Doongerwadi* hearse.

I wanted her to be protected by the consecrated circuits of the *dakhma* connected with the fire temples through lines in the earth. I wanted her to have the same prayers and rites performed as she had done for so many of her loved ones. If this sounds like mumbo jumbo, so be it. My father was right. There is nothing more beautiful than exiting in the same manner as your forefathers did. Perhaps in the not too distant future, there will be an electric crematorium in the *dakhma* to ensure spiritual protection and expeditious disposal at the same time. Almost certainly, a few years later, non-Parsis will be permitted inside the *bungli*. The Towers will continue to dispel grief and soothe broken hearts.

My mother's funeral and other ceremonies were an identical rerun of my father's funeral more than four decades ago. Her favorite priests, whom she patronized throughout her long life, prayed for her with passion. After the pre dawn uthamna, the Sagdi bell was struck 12 times and Sirius shone above the Hodiwalla *Bungli*, exactly as before.

A young Berjis Desai with his parents Minoo and Mani

Great doctors, strange patients

The community may be mildly hypochondriac

The Parsi penchant for litigation has a serious competitor - our propensity to be hospitalized, at the first available opportunity. Decades ago, a legendary Parsi physician, even though in robust health, would check into the Parsee General Hospital (PGH), to enjoy a free annual vacation, undisturbed by ubiquitous night calls from paranoid patients. His wife would solemnly inform the caller that the doctor himself had been hospitalized. The grateful hospital management, for their prized patient's valuable services throughout the year, would pamper him with king-sized meals, rivaling Oliaji's hotel in Daman. In the evening, a loyal ward boy would massage his feet, as the doctor downed a whisky or two.

It is no secret that Parsis prefer Parsi doctors and the reason may not be entirely communal. Only another Parsi can appreciate the peculiar constitution, habits and idiosyncrasies. Being pregnant and not consulting Dr Rusi Soonawala was sacrilege; and who could understand our unique Kyaani *tokham* better than Dr Farokh Udwadia. These legendary medicine men are only a notch below the *Ameshaspands* (angels) in the Parsi consciousness.

A Parsi lady of aristocratic lineage became obsessed with dolls. She possessed more than a thousand dolls of various shapes and sizes; and with some of them, the good lady shared a rather intimate relationship. Apparently, her dolls had a propensity to run high fever at midnight. The feverish doll would first be dabbed with cologne water sponges, and despite this, if the temperature remained high, the old lady would phone one of the community's best doctors and fervently plead for a home visit. Such was the influence of this dowager that the tired doctor, trying to recover from a hard day's work, would pick up his medical case and drive down to the lady's bungalow. In all seriousness, the sick dolly would be examined thoroughly and occasionally injected (at which point, the old lady would look away, in distress). Next morning, the doctor would receive more than five times his normal fees for a night visit to examine less malleable patients.

We knew two Parsi sisters, again of aristocratic lineage, who were extremely pleased with the services of their young general practitioner but rather distressed at his "dismal bed manners" ("He actually sat on my bed!"), and insisting on addressing his patient as "Aunty" ("I do not think, doctor, that we are related. Please call me Miss W"). One of these sisters had to undergo a cataract operation and consulted one of India's best ophthalmic surgeons (Parsi, of course) hailing from a family of eye specialists. The surgeon explained the do's and don'ts for the surgery, after which the doltish sister enquired whether she can wear her bra during the surgery. "Darling," said the smarter one, "he is operating on your eyes, not your boobs."

This famous eye surgeon has a great sense of humor but a rather short fuse. While examining a middle aged Gujarati lady, post her surgery, he was extensively questioned by the patient's husband as to what were the dietary restrictions for his wife. Initially, the doctor patiently answered his questions ("Can she have tea?" "Yes!;" "Can she have coffee?" "Yes!" "Can she have milk?" No answer. "Can she have cow's milk?"). The last question resulted in the good doctor, who has a slight American accent, shouting the forbidden swear word at the stunned Gujarati couple, who made a hasty retreat.

The ultimate eccentric doctor though was Dr Hormusji Mehta, resident medical officer of the PGH, ex-police surgeon, eminent forensic expert and toxicologist, who ruled that institution for many years. According to his fans, he built a first class Hospital and ensured that Morarji Desai (when he was chief minister of Bombay State) did not grab the additional land for secular use. To his critics, he was a bully who treated the hospital as his backyard. He managed to oust the entire managing committee of the hospital barring Sir Dinshaw Petit, by packing the electoral college. We have seen him manhandle a Parsi faith healer in the corridors of the hospital, and then himself trying to hypnotise a rooster, with the bird, in great discomfiture, between his knees.

One of our acquaintances, who enjoyed robust health and merged his *ravaan* (soul) with Ahura Mazda at 96, was a classic hypochondriac. Unlike today, when there is a glut of hospital rooms, those days securing admission was not easy. He was a voracious eater ["*Gaikalé raatè mè ék* dozen oysters *afaari kaarya* (I walloped a dozen oysters last night)!"] and believed that every bout of indigestion he suffered was either a cardiac episode or serious food poisoning or galloping cancer.

He would be in and out of hospitals every other month. I love the antiseptic smell of hospital corridors, he told us. If he was bored of PGH (late evenings, he sneaked out to Scandal Point to polish off some *bhaiya-ni-bhelpuri*, and upon his return, make a few chicken drumsticks vanish) it would be Masina hospital (he regretted that he couldn't be admitted to the *Tehmulji nu suvavarkhanu* or the Parsi Lying-in Hospital) or Breach Candy or the St Elizabeth Nursing Home (hop, skip and jump from my house, *dikra* (son). A gentleman of leisure, with a tidy fortune, he spent a considerable portion of his wealth on hospital stays. He knew every doctor's birthday and which town of Kerala every nurse hailed from. On Jamshedi Navroz he distributed *malai na khaaja* (fresh cream puffs) and Parsi Dairy *sooterpheni* (white candy floss) to the cleaning staff of the PGH who would anxiously wait for his return. As he was a liberal tipper, many unnecessary enemas would be administered unto him, which he said, he enjoyed immensely.

Then there was this aunt of ours, who spoke so rapidly that she was breathless mid-sentence. A mild diabetic, she loved to undergo blood sugar tests every month (in those days, no pathologist came home and there were no easy blood sugar detection jabbers). She had lost her father on Hormazd *roz* and mother on Bahman. Every month thus, she visited the *agiary* on these first two days of the month for the *aafringaan-baaj* prayers for her parents who had departed during World War I.

And then, on the third day of the Parsi month - Ardibehesht, she went for her blood sugar test to PGH's out patient department. As soon as the sample for her fasting sugar was taken, she would open a huge tiffin containing *papeta pur eendu* (eggs on potato), a cup of *malai* (fresh cream), half a ball of Edam cheese, Polson butter on three or four small *paavs* (home baked bread), a quarter kilo of Mohanlal Mithaiwala *ni barfi*, Kissan jam or Dippy's *dodhi no murrabbo* (sweet made from bottle gourd). No prizes for guessing her postprandial sugar reading. She died in her 80s and required six pallbearers on her final journey. Believe it or not, she passed away on the fourth day of the Parsi month — Shahrevar. That is what you call timing, *dikra*!

Natak nostalgia

The punch in Parsi plays is missing today

At this year's New Year play, we saw the editor of a Parsi publication holding a largish novel and exiting the auditorium after the interval. He was reading the novel, sitting on a chair in the foyer of the theater. Most of the audience must have envied him. The so-called musical revue, a la Adi Marzban, was even below our modest expectation. And some may say that we are being uncharacteristically polite. Most of the skits and gags were dated or poorly executed. One handsome lawyer belted a few Elvis numbers and the audience politely clapped. Music had miles to go. Not a single authentic Bawa joke. The only thing which elicited laughter was a rather stout lady in the front row cackling away at every sentence including the announcement of the interval.

Our expectation this year for this revue was based on some new talent on display. A well-known counsel, a seasoned actor in

Marzban's English plays including a memorable performance in Ah, Norman!, was the compere. He did a highly efficient job without faltering for a second but was a pale imitation of the maestro, who would be the perfect fall guy for the inimitable Jimmy Pocha or the natural comedian, Dinshah Daji. Adi would never smile, be barely audible, appear thoroughly exasperated and pretend to be harassed by the frequent intrusions on stage by the other two, and yet enthral the audience. Maybe, a difficult act to follow but we thought that he would have a go at it. He preferred perhaps to do it his own way.

The other great talent we were looking forward to, was another, senior solicitor and partner in a large vintage law firm who did a brilliant cameo act. We thought more would follow but that was all. If only he would have rendered his Pathan selling shilajit (for the uninitiated, an aphrodisiac) at Victoria Terminus railway station act, the audience would have rolled in the aisle, even if it had to be slightly censored so as not to offend the sensibilities of the few politically correct *non-handas* in the theater. There are other highly gifted Ripon Club high table diners who can start a laugh riot with their rendition of bawdy Parsi songs of yesteryears. Perhaps, they may be encouraged to perform in the larger interest of our community.

Barring one nonagenarian, there was no old talent on display. A few months ago, when the vintage Marzban cast, all senior citizens, did a retrospective, the community was thrilled. In recent years, Parsi histrionic talent is rather inadequate, to say the least. One can only nostalgically recall the great talent Marzban could muster — thespian Piloo Wadia as the old battle axe; Pocha as the unhappy queen *Taramati* in Parsi Harishchandra; Daji's cackle itself being so funny; laughter on entry star, Pheroze Antia as Behram in *Behram ni Saasu* (Behram's mother-in-law) and its many sequels; the greatly talented pair of Dolly and Bomi Dotiwala; Burjor and Ruby Patel, heartthrobs of the audience - the list is endless. Marzban died rather young, by far the greatest showman of the Parsis, and with him, Parsi theater. Post the maestro, Homi Tavadia, Hilla and Nader Nariman, and playwright, Dorab Mehta valiantly persisted but the Marzban magic could not be replicated. The audience is still very much there for Parsi comedies, not only Parsis but Gujaratis and Bohris too. They love Dinyar Contractor, perhaps the only man after Marzban to have a mass following, and a natural comedian. For some reason, Contractor prefers these days to stage Gujarati comedies with only a little Parsi color, but despite his great stage presence, Parsis prefer to see authentic Parsi and not shudh (pure) Gujarati melodrama.

Those outstanding amateurs, Dr Jehangir Wadia-led Parsi doctors, no longer perform their hilarious plays - politically incorrect, loaded with double entendre, narrowly skirting the acceptable limits of bawdiness - but simply brilliant. Dr Jimmy Sidhva, the noted radiologist, singing in operatic style about his *mèlo léngho* (dirty pyjama) was unforgettable. Shakespearean tragedies morphed into Parsi comedies like Hormusji Hamlet turning into riotous plays where actors were encouraged to ad lib while carefully planted assistants in the audience would complete profane limericks, which the actors themselves would be censored from uttering. We urge the senior solicitor referred to earlier, to take the lead and form an amateur group to perform some of these old plays whose tapes and scripts are available. Otherwise, the editor of that publication will have to buy another novel next Navroz.

Parsi actors rendering a bawdy quawwali

Panchayet tales

BPP trustees have always been interesting human material

They say that Muncherjee Khareghat was the best ever trustee of the Bombay Parsi Panchayet (BPP). Few will dispute his impeccable record of service. We know exactly the thought passing in your mind. No, we are not in a position to name the worst ever. Like Lord Byron and the Queen, not that we won't, but we can't. So many vie for this position that it would be unfair to disappoint. Almost everyone has a tale to tell about their favorite candidate. Even Solomon would be hard pressed to decide. We will, however, narrate a few of these tales without naming those who are living [considering the countless '*mari jai muo*' (die, wretch) uttered by the beneficiaries, they must be truly blessed to be insulated from these cur*ses*], for the dead cannot be defamed.

When this writer was 14, he impulsively shot off a letter to the Kaiser-e-Hind about how the youth ought to replace the blue blooded geriatric trustees clinging to the rusty throne of power (in Gujarati, the letter sounded even more melodramatic). That very evening, BPP trustee Erach Nadirshah and his wife arrived at our tiny flat unannounced. Father gave us an irritated look not about our penning the letter but because he had to endure their presence on a Sunday evening. Even on that sultry May evening, Nadirshah was dressed immaculately in a three piece suit. His wife, after spurning the offer to have tea, imperiously announced how disturbed her Erach had been since morning. Whereupon Nadirshah fished out the newspaper cutting of the letter and held it up like a rat he had caught for the municipality (he retired as the chief hydraulic engineer from the BMC and that is another story but of no direct relevance) and asked our father whether his son had indeed penned the offending letter. We smilingly nodded, which incensed the trustee saheb no end. He launched into a diatribe about the lack of respect for our *akabars* and how our father ought to have prevented the publication of the letter. Our father simply said that he had no control over Kaiser-e-Hind or his son (he was then editor of *The Bombay Samachar*). After the couple departed, we innocently asked why out of the seven trustees only one had protested. Our father said something which is unprintable.

The trustee was equally incensed with his brother-in-law, Minoo Nariman, who wrote several Parsi comedies including a hilarious one about his old aunt who met Hitler and introduced *kera pur eedu* (eggs on bananas) to the dictator and how that spurred him to gobble up Poland. Nariman invited Nadirsha to be the chief guest at a Parsi New Year play which he had written. Nadirsha discovered to his utter horror that the play titled *Houdaas Choudaas* (corrupt) was a satire on the BPP. He and his wife had to endure the catcalls of the audience. A few years later, the BPP honored the then about to be deposed Shah of Iran at the Taj, when the Shah told Eruch that he was a 'Shah' too. The Nadirshas were delirious with joy, as if the purpose of their incarnation had been achieved.

This trustee stayed in the same building as B. K. Boman

Behram (BKB), his co-trustee. BKB was a cool cat and perhaps the most controversial trustee of his times. If the Nadirshas had pretensions of being aristocratic, BKB was a people's man, polite, diplomatic and suave. As an independent municipal corporator, he managed to get himself elected as mayor of Bombay with the help of 40 Shiv Sena corporators. Somehow, after this election, his popularity in the community dramatically dipped. Allegations flew fast and furious, with that doyen of Parsi solicitors of the yesteryears, Rustom Gagrat, calling him all sorts of names in the Press. BKB wrote in the Evening News that he was not bothered by the rantings of "some Tamarind Lane solicitor;" to which Gagrat retaliated by calling his bête noir a 'Meadows Street lawyer.' Rarely though did BKB's veneer come off. He was a liberal at heart and truly secular, though, like many today, he projected himself as orthodox, particularly after he allied himself with Dr Nelie Noble in the BPP boardroom. He was extremely popular with the Kannadiga community and chose to unwind in their religious festivals by donning traditional attire, dancing and playing the violin. Apart from those merry jousts, he was keen to adopt an orphan boy called Chinappa. BKB never married.

Murmurs about all not being kosher with housing allotments started when BKB was at the helm. In the late seventies, under the  editorship of Jehan Daruwalla, the Mumbai Samachar ran a long campaign against BKB's acts of omission and commission in the BPP, and just stopped short of alleging lack of probity. This was the catalyst for the CER (Committee for Electoral Rights) movement when the very thin cucumber sandwich eating elite took to the streets and won all but one seat in the electoral college. BKB and Noble naturally did not recontest and Jamsheed Kanga of the CER was elected unopposed. BKB, slightly bitter, faded away from municipal and Parsi politics.

Noble, a spinster, was known for her sternness even while a student at the Grant Medical College. Her integrity was never in doubt even during those BKB-Nadirsha years. A diehard fanatic in religious matters, she believed in Minocher Pundole, a self-proclaimed Ilm-e-Khshnoomist scholar, and his many miracles including conjuring up the exact number of mutton cutlets from the refrigerator of an Udvada hotel for his hungry disciples, even though he preached vegetarianism. To make sense of the last sentence, you require *akuri* with masala logic, which Noble amply pos*se*ssed. She was instrumental in the creation of an additional *agiary* at Udvada, causing consternation to the non-Pundolite traditionalists who detested her. At BPP elections (those days, elections were a very tame affair), she managed to capture some registers in the then electoral college with sponsored voters and a mild display of some muscle by one of her brothers until 1980, when Dinshaw Mehta made her realize what a rank amateur she was.

Just imagine Nadirsha, Noble and BKB in the present BPP boardroom. Noble would have wilted like a daisy upon learning that MC does not mean master of ceremonies. Eruch would have fainted in his three piece suit upon seeing chairs being flung. Perhaps even BKB, a veteran of many a fight in the legislatures and the courts, would have felt a trifle embarrassed. Hope you got your answer.

Tribute to a traditionalist

Though the late Adi Doctor's views were esoteric, committed Zoroastrians of any hue are comrades in arms

There was poignancy in the tributes paid to Adi Doctor in the latest issue of *The Parsee Voice*, the newsletter of the *Ilm-e-Khshnoomists*, the ultra orthodox group. Doctor, a bachelor, who died recently at Bombay, was a bank official, Western music critic, a writer and speaker, a professor, and most importantly, a lifelong exponent of *Ilm-e-Khshnoom* (IeK). He was a vocal spokesman for the hard core traditionalists. A defeatist undertone was evident in these tributes, as Doctor's disconsolate followers conceded that without their leader, The Parsee Voice may not survive.

This writer never had occasion to interact with Doctor, though we had crossed pens over the last two decades. For Doctor, we were the *din dushmans* (enemies of the faith), religious "deformists" and heretic scum. We returned the compliment by terming him and his brethren as fruitcakes who constituted the lunatic fringe of the community (rather strangely, The Parsee Voice, in its obituary for Doctor, seemed to regard these terms as evidence of their being protectors of the faith). At its peak, the debate grew shrill and strident. For Doctor, persons like the editor of this publication, Dinshaw Tamboly of the World Zoroastrian Organisation Trust Funds, the Wadia brothers, Kerssie and Vispy of ARZ (Association for the Revival of Zoroastrianism), the late Jehan Daruwalla, editor of *Mumbai Samachar* and this writer, were anti-Parsi and pernicious. The din dushmans retaliated by arguing that Doctor and his tribe were spewing racism and putting off the youth by their Taliban-like tactics.

By all accounts, Doctor was honest, kind, led a spartan life and dedicated himself to the cause he espoused. Unlike the mainstream orthodox, he was not a politician. He used to say, "I'm not orthodox. I'm ultra orthodox." We wonder if he ever felt any self-doubt about his lifelong views, as he witnessed the traditional citadels falling one after the other. The increasing proportion of interfaith marriages, the dramatically desolate demographic trends, a liberal high priest and the ever shrinking number of authentic traditionalists must surely have distressed him. However he continued to espouse his views against organ donation, making Udvada a world heritage site, admitting even the children of interfaith married Parsi men into the faith, renovating *agiaries*, providing prayer hall to cremated Parsis, extra religious worship, World Zoroastrian Congres*ses* and cremation. Preserving racial purity was his credo. Probably, Doctor coined that memorable

Adi Doctor: unflinching faith

phrase - "*Tokham ni jalavani né boond ni paasbaani* (preservation of racial/genetic stock)" - much lampooned by the reformists.

Doctor was never shy to espouse unfashionable views, however preposterous they sounded to liberal ears. He was convinced that the esoteric writings of Behramshah Shroff and the Chiniwala brothers, Framroze and Jehangir, exponents of IeK like him, were the only truth. Though even he steered clear of the controversial Minocher Pundole, a latter day IeK exponent, and his many "miracles" including reportedly conjuring up the exact number of mutton cutlets for his devotees in an Udvada hotel (even though Pundole preached vegetarianism!).

Doctor propagated that the sahebs of *Demavand koh* (mountain) in Iran supervised the affairs of the faith and the community's future was secure. Doctor's unflinching faith did not, however, lead him to suggest that the sahebs were also looking after Bombay Parsi Punchayet affairs, which were presumably beyond even their extraordinary powers. Doctor did not exactly love the World Alliance of Parsi Irani Zarthoshtis (WAPIZ) but nevertheless supported them to keep the din dushmans at bay. By keeping its membership open to children of interfaith married Parsi men, WAPIZ greatly disappointed Doctor. For a purist like him, any such concession would only open the gates of our faith to marauding barbarians.

Doctor believed that every Parsi was duty bound to protect the faith and its traditions. The slightest deviation from *tarikat* (strict observance of religious diktats) would upset the balance of nature and was a cardinal sin. None could deny that Doctor had the courage of his convictions. The liberals may call it xenophobia, but for Doctor even the slightest opening of the doors of our religion to non-Parsis was sacrilege.

While we may have been rough with Doctor on occasions, we were always conscious that persons like him, despite their seemingly barmy views, had the same goal as the reformists he so deplored, namely, preserving the faith and the community. Hard core traditionalists like Doctor and the reformist opposition are both concerned about what happens to the community, unlike the silent majority who are either indifferent or only mildly curious. To an honest, compassionate and committed Parsi, with whom we violently disagreed on everything under the sun, farewell. We sincerely hope that *The Parsee Voice* continues to be published and soon sheds its poignancy and regains its stridency, without which life would be so boring.

Discovering the magic of the faith

An unorthodox solution to trigger a community revival

Just the other day, this writer was stunned to learn that there are only 37,000 Parsis in Mumbai. Our community institutions are increasingly inefficient and crumbling. The so-called leadership is a combination of prickly egos, enlarging prostates and diminishing minds. Most Parsis are utterly indifferent to the fate of the community. This atmosphere of doom and gloom may, perhaps, be dissipated by discovering the magical aspects of our religion. A religious revival may then trigger a socioeconomic and demographic revival.

Zoroaster was one of the greatest prophets, his faith is replete with many magical qualities. Most of us find little meaning in mechanically reciting prayers in a language which we do not understand. While there is much to be said about the *manthric* vibrations of the prayers and the spiritual energy they unleash, the indifferent require to be enthused with some magical results. Color has to be infused in humdrum rituals, rites and recitations. We have to raise the rhythm of our spiritual practices.

Much is written in occult and theological literature about the Lost Word. The Rosicrucians and the Theosophists believe that the Lost Word is to be found in the *Avesta* prayers of the Zoroastrians. Recite the Lost Word with concentration and a clean heart for creating positive energy. It also acts as a shield against negative or malevolent forces. This word is oft repeated in several of our *Yashts*. The Rosicrucians teach as to how each syllable of the Word is to be recited on each day of the week, for awakening and cleansing the *chakras* or psychic centers in the body.

Sufis, members of the only esoteric sect of Islam, believe that the continuous recitation of any divine phrase or name, like '*Allah*' is highly beneficent. They call this practice '*Dhikr*,' literally, remembrance; akin to the tradition of counting rosary beads among Catholics or chanting '*Hare Rama, Hare Krishna*' or '*Om Namah Shivaya*' amongst Hindus. Reciting the Lost Word or one of the 101 names of Ahura Mazda, in similar fashion, is a practice well known to Zoroastrianism. According to legend, the Prophet was assassinated whilst praying with his beads in an *atash behram*, his last act in life, which underscores the importance of this practice. Our grandmothers prized their *kerba ni mala* (rosary of amber stones) known  throughout world cultures for its many magical properties. Many miracles are associated with the intonation of the *Ahunavar* or the *Yatha Ahu Vairyo* capsule prayer. Chanting the Lost Word with a *kerba ni mala* can manifest dramatic results.

After Zoroaster, the most powerful magician - healer - king was Shah Faridoon, composer of an extremely potent nirang (prayer) to ward off disease, black magic and despondency. The little blue booklet containing this prayer, in Gujarati, was published many decades ago and is a collector's item. You grasp the right hand thumb of the afflicted and intone the Nirang, with the oft repeated potent formulae - *Fè namè yazad, ba farmaane yazad; baname nik Faridoon e gaav daye.*' This writer has witnessed some amazing results which confound rationality.

The daily rituals performed in an *agiary* only interest a micro minority. However, many even with a faint interest in religion, will throng to perform a personalized ritual like lighting a *divo* at the Bhikha Behram well and making a wish; or seeking a cure for sunstroke or jaundice or migraine or piles, through recitation of Zoroastrian prayers; or be counselled spiritually by someone like the late Ervad Nadirsha Aibara of the Cusrow Baug Karani *agiary*.

The hard-core orthodox are doing their cause a disfavor by writing and speaking on esoteric issues in a highly pedantic style. Few will come to attend a lecture by a 90-year old at the Bharda New High School, at 4.30 p.m. on a Monday, on the "Significance of Varasiaji in post-Zarthost Cosmology." They further put off people by expressing rabidly communal, sexist and nearly fascist views on ethnic superiority and the like. If their energies are utilized to share esoteric knowledge, as a solution for daily issues, many can be made to take interest in community matters.

According to Theosophists, the Prophet, like other great initiates (Rama, Moses, Orpheus), has an aura, wide enough to fill half a country. Interlocking your mind in his great consciousness, for selfless reasons, can inspire you to do something for the community and the religion. Aspirants on the path often carry out visualization exercises at dawn like Zoroaster's radiance lighting up their home or workplace; or praying near the sanctum sanctorum of their favorite fire temple, as if they were physically present. Such simple spiritual exercises enable the practitioner to raise the consciousness of those around him. The universality of the Prophet's teachings can break down artificial barriers and pave the way for reform. The stranglehold of the fundamentalists over community institutions can be broken if the hitherto indifferent are inspired to serve.

The situation demands unorthodox methods to revive the interest of Parsis in their faith, and through it, in the community. The rationalist must learn not to dismiss everything as mumbo jumbo. If people visit the Banaji *Atash behram* on Monday evenings or pray in a small attic room in one of the oldest agiaries in Fort, do not mock them. We require every ounce of interest and energy to generate a demographic revival, by all possible means. And, yes of course, the Lost Word is *Mathrem* (pronounced 'Ma,' short for mother; 'threm,' to rhyme with frame). Get hold of a *kerba ni mala* and start chanting it.

Jiyo cynicism

The cheeky advertising campaign is cute, smart, but little more

The *Ilm-e-Khshnoomists* dismiss all talk of demographic decline as alarmist and maintain that the second coming of the Lord, as Soshyos, will reverse the trend. Soshyos has apparently inspired some smart Parsi copywriters from Madison Advertising to produce the Jiyo Parsi campaign to make Parsis produce more babies. Jiyo Parsi is the Rs 10 crore project of the Government of India and Parzor, a Zoroastrian think tank, to increase the Parsi population.

Some of the advertisements in the campaign are passé, but a few are brilliant. When the world is being urged to use condoms for safe and responsible sex, the campaign urges Parsis not to do so. When survival is at stake, who is worried about HIV? Like the Vatican, we too must frown upon condoms, albeit for different reasons. Not using condoms will not increase fertility rates. When you are firing blanks, bullet proof vests are hardly needed. The haplessness of our situation is evident from the fact that the same government which has been crying itself hoarse to limit the family size is now partner in an initiative to abjure family planning. Non-Parsi readers, unaware of our demographic decline, will be baffled to see the Ministry of Family Welfare urging Parsis not to use contraceptives.

The campaign wants the Mumma ob*sessed* Parsi boy to look at other women. But Mumma herself is not too unhappy at her Rusi not marrying. Daughters-in-law are such a pain, aren't they? Mumma cooks great, never nags, does not like shopping or vacations, is not bothered about her son's indifferent personal hygiene and loves him unconditionally. Why would Rusi ever listen to the Jiyo advertisement's exhortation to break up with mummy? The campaign decries the propensity of Parsi girls to look only for highly successful Parsi boys. If you are Nergish Chargeman, then don't imagine you are Nicole Kidman, the advertisement seems to suggest; aspire for Ratan Khambatta, not Tata. This appears to be the single largest factor for rejection, according to the matrimonial bureaus. Girls are not ready to even look at boys who earn less than fifty thousand a month. And boys who do, find non-Parsi girls to be less aggressive and better marriage material. What can the poor copywriter do about this mismatch of aspirations?

Not surprisingly, the most brilliant advertisement has caused the maximum consternation. A Parsi girl, standing outside the *Agiary* at Dadar, stares at a road sign which reads Hindu Colony. Your comfort zone will be invaded by strangers soon if you don't procreate. Communal, xenophobic, in poor taste, crossing the line, say the critics. Not really. The advertisement plays on primal fears that this most cherished Parsi enclave will lose its ethos and character. Somewhat insensitive, maybe. The advertisement could have avoided the road sign and yet sent out the same message. However, individual

decisions are not made out of collective fears. What will certainly work is economics. Help to the extent of five lakh rupees for IVF treatment is truly tempting. Add liberal subsidies for a second child and one will see results.

The campaign does not sufficiently play on behavioral economics. Plan your pregnancy without worry, we shall finance the process and the product, is what the campaign should convey. Should this campaign be restricted to only the Parsi print media and online is the question. We exist to be fair sport for our neighbors. There is no harm if the advertisements appear in the mainstream print media. Parsis will be perceived as cuter, unique, vulnerable and deserving — to be preserved like valuable artefacts. This may result in greater goodwill for the community. The exercise may not result in extra babies or more Parsi marriages. Nevertheless, it will make us stop and think about what we are up against. The situation is so grim that even the most incorrigible optimist will give up. Perhaps that's why even the *Ilm-e-Khshnoomists* spend their nights poring over esoteric tomes trying to decipher when the Lord will come again, instead of doing something about it themselves. Thank God, they are a micro minority. Jiyo optimism!

The other fire temple

Explaining our shameless bias for the Navsari Atash Behram

A part from the hotly contested annual boat race and the position in the university league table, the alumni of Cambridge and Oxford never tire of condescendingly dismissing "the other place." A similar rivalry exists between the residents of Udvada and Navsari about their respective fire temples. Navsari is obviously less visited, concede the Nausakras, but is more profoundly peace bestowing. As a diehard Navsari fanatic, this writer is convinced beyond doubt of the Nausakras' claim. There are multiple reasons for this bias: historical, personal, sentimental, spiritual and rational.

Every summer vacation, our grandmother, a no nonsense disciplinarian, would take us to Navsari. After the Gujarat Express had left Vasai, the second class compartment would impromptu turn into a dining car of sorts. The old lady would imperiously untie a straw container (called *karandiyo*) and serve a breakfast of *brun pao* (hard bread) — those days, an eagerly awaited import into Navsari - liberally plastered with Polson butter together with a plain vanilla omelette (not containing anything except the eggs – not the deep fried, onion laden reddish brown Parsi *poro*). At Navsari station, the coolies would barge into the compartment to grab your luggage, as if their life depended on it. You settled into a *ghora gari* (horse driven carriage) which meandered through the narrow dusty lanes until Tarota Bazar when you would get the first glimpse of the magnificent *Atash behram*. As you reverentially bowed, the horse hoofs would resound on the cobbled streets of Desai Vad [then, not having a single *juddin* house – gosh! we sound like WAPIZ (World Alliance of Parsi Irani Zarthoshtis)!). The next morning, scrubbed and shining, we would amble across to the *Atash behram*, armed with a thin sandalwood stick and a 10 paise coin to be placed as *aashodaad* (offering). At times, we saved the coins for an illicit purchase of blushing pink hand-made Kolah's ice-cream, an unauthorized diversification of funds [indicating our early potential to be a Bombay Parsi Punchayet trustee].

Post the worship, we dutifully carried the *rakhiya* (holy ash) to the aged relatives residing in the *mohalla* (locality) to be rewarded with multiple breakfasts, a secret from our grandmother. This daily gluttony for six weeks of the vacation ensured our mother's look of utter disgust at her rotund child. We would never enter the *Atash behram* from the main entrance but a small side entrance having a wrought iron door, close to the *dar-e-meher*, the Vazir (prime minister) of the Holy King. This practice has been followed by us for the last five decades, not only on the annual visit to the fire temple, but in our daily visualization exercise.

Close the wrought iron door carefully, kiss the parapet of the well, dunk the *karasyo* into the brass water pot to clean our hands and face (*padyaab*), prior to the kusti. [Talking of *karasyo*, we must rather unsublimely digress to narrate the story of a Navsari *agiary* worker called Burjorji (long deceased) nicknamed '*Bai Bai karasyo*,' due to his lady employer who, during the *muktad* days, shouted at him from the toilet about the missing *karasyo* — those days, there were no cleaning faucets - whereupon the overtly enthusiastic man rushed into the toilet with the *karasyo*, saying "Bai, Bai, karasyo"]. Occasionally, a divo would be lit by us to assuage the guilt of having deprived God to pay Kolah.

A few decades ago, the *Atash behram*, including the sanctum sanctorum, was majorly renovated with the holy fire temporarily housed in the dar-e-meher. Post this renovation, on the marble wall exactly opposite the sanctum, an impression of a priest praying with folded hands surfaced and became more prominent over the years. Many devout believe this to be a picture of the saintly first Dastur Meherjirana who attended Emperor Akbar's court and whose descendants have been, till today, the High Priests of Navsari.

Early morning or at dusk, when there are few worshippers, the silent attunement with Him, a visibly living presence, will make a devotee out of an atheist. Iranshah, being busier, rarely provides the same opportunity to meditate before the holy fire. Many *boi*walas (*mobeds* tending to the fire) have narrated stories of seeing a tall figure, clad in white, whisking across in the wee hours of the morning. None have experienced fear but only protection from the guardian angel.

The *Atash behram* was constructed by our direct lineal ascendant, Khurshedji Bapa, as he was popularly known and the interesting marble plaques narrate the history of successive contributions over nearly three centuries. The Desai Vad and the other mohallas near the *Atash behram* were all Parsi as late as the 1960s, giving great character to the precinct. Sometimes xenophobia is tolerable. On the other hand, as the fiddler on the roof would say, non Parsis often stand outside the *Atash behram* with bowed heads seeking the blessings and protection of the holy fire that they will never see. They request Parsis to place their sandalwood sticks and money. The circuit of devotion is palpable.

A quick day trip to both the *Atash behram*s can conveniently be planned by boarding the Gujarat Express at 5.45 a.m. (have breakfast only if your metabolism is unusually robust), hopping into a hired car at the Navsari station, having a quick bath at Jamshed Baug which is a stone's throw from the *Atash behram*, offer prayers, dash across to the cute little dar-e-meher, drive to the Iranshah in less than an hour, worship, lunch, and be back in Bombay by early evening. Spiritual batteries recharged for the year.

After five decades, little has changed around the Navsari *Atash behram*. The same little wrought iron gate opens with the same creaking sound, the same feeling of peace instantly descends upon you as soon as you enter the compound, the same experience of protection and peace when you gaze reverentially into the holy fire; time standing still forever. The Kolah shop still sells ice cream but with rather pretentious flavors. Both the *Atash behram*s are pillars of our faith and, to protect these, our most precious heritage, many a Parsi would gladly perish; just as our forefathers did, centuries ago, in Persia, to guard the Guardians from the marauding Arab hordes.

Pirojbai Cawasji Modi Dar-e-Meher in the Navsari Atash Behram compound

The pilgrim's choice

Why tiny Udvada scores over sprawling Navsari

Navsari and Udvada share a rather uneasy relationship. After all, the Iranshah, before He was enthroned in Udvada in 1742, had been in Navsari, for three long centuries (1419 to 1740) until the *Pindhara* (plundering tribe) menace forced His migration. But for this quirk of history, Udvada would have been one of the faceless 18,225 villages of Gujarat, observe the *Nosakras* sardonically. He has been with us too for nearly 300 years, and will continue to do so till eternity, counter the *Udvadias*. Giant Navsari (population, 163,000; 2011 census) is a district; tiny Udvada (5,897) is a hamlet. However, ask Parsis in New Zealand and Nova Scotia - all know Udvada but only a few are as aware of Navsari. After all, it matters where the King presently resides.

Like both his parents and all of his grandparents, this writer would have been born in Navsari (if his mother's water bag had burst

10 hours later). He spent every school vacation in the dusty *mohollas* (neighborhoods) of Navsari and was ordained as a priest in the Vadi Daremeher where he learnt everything except religion (that is another story). Despite our bias, over the years, we have become sufficiently dispassionate to evaluate the places fairly. For the last few years, we do our annual pilgrimage to both the *atash behram*s on the same day, which sharpens the perspective.

Its many Parsi *mohollas* (like Dastur *Vad* and Kanga *Vad* and Baria *Vad*) divided into two sections of the town, called Motafalia and Malesar (the former was slightly elitist and snootier), made Navsari a bustling Parsi town. Most hou*ses* in the *moholla* were Parsi occupied. A non-Parsi occupied house stood out distastefully like a sore thumb. If a Parsi died, the *moholla* was cordoned off to prevent any *juddin* entry during the *paidast* and *uthamna*. During the four days (sometimes six) celebration of a marriage, the non-Parsi service providers were, of course, permitted (to serve food, to play the horrendous '*Naan Khatai* ' band or the slightly less offensive '*takor-khanu*' from Surat, and engage in other such menial activities). You could have spotted a black swan but not a non-Parsi guest. The other communities implicitly and non-grudgingly accepted the superiority of the Parsis (even a Parsi transgender was elected as municipal councillor defeating a highly respected Gujarati lawyer - that too in the 60s).

And then suddenly in the 80s, things crumbled. Like Pompeii, Parsi*panu* in Navsari was destroyed. *Mohollas* still retain their names, but have lost their character. A Parsi occupied house now stands out like an arthritic thumb. No *moholla* is cordoned, and there is hardly a marriage to celebrate. Deaths, of course, are many - of lonely, old spinsters and childless widows. Parsis are regarded as harmless eccentrics; the social superiority has long since dissipated. Some Parsi community housing complexes do exist, but are hardly distinguishable from the jungle of apartment buildings, spawned all over Navsari as a result of unregulated development. The *vadis* (mini orchards) of *Lunsikui* - where every evening, at impromptu clubs, old

Parsi men poured 'prepared' tea from large aluminum kettles into modest looking glas*ses* and dunked humungous *batasa* biscuits in the glass, along with salacious male gossip, and where many decades ago, the venerable Sir Pherozeshah Mehta had stayed at the '*Dhadaka-no-bungalow*' to defend the honor of a fellow advocate called Merwanjee Vakil, in what came to be known as the 'Lamp Case' - have now been replaced by semi attached row hou*ses*, without any personality or trees, all in a highly polluted environ.

Udvada, on the other hand, is frozen in time. The precinct around the Iranshah remains very much Parsi. An exclusive little conclave. Unlike the cacophony outside the Navsari *atash behram* (though sublimely peaceful within), there is a respectful silence around the Iranshah and the row of all Parsi owned hou*ses* in the adjoining lane. Even the vendor on the cycle, selling home made ice cream, markets his produce in hushed tones. The largish housing complex, constructed by a Parsi builder for Parsis only, is quiet. In the monsoon, the swell of the Arabian Sea looks sinister, from the balcony of one of the buildings in this complex. If you walk in a straight line on the beach, you can reach Nargol or even Valsad. From this balcony, you can see the ruins of a demolished building, which was once the Majestic Hotel known for its sea views and sumptuous breakfasts. The family, which owned it, dissipated; a lonely matriarch in her final days lost her mind in a tragic end to a bustling hotel. One of its competitors, the King's Hotel, also on the beach, vanished similarly. The Globe, owned by the Sidhwa family, survives with some of its gargantuan rooms and fried *boi* (river fish). We remember a middle-aged Bapsy Sidhwa instructing us to rub off the *rakhiya* (holy ash) from our forehead, lest some *juddin* see or touch it. The upstart Ashishvangh Hotel is the Globe's only competition, if you exclude the spanking new Sir J. J. Dharamshala. If you desire a break from the heavy duty carnivorous feasts, you can obtain a tiffin containing the most delicious Gujarati meal. The same establishment also sells home ground spices at rock bottom prices (what on earth is GST?).

Navsari, on the other hand till recently, never had a single decent hotel. Jamshed Baug and Sorab Baug are, of course, great value for money and kept quite neat and clean; but no competition to the famed Parsi hotels of Udvada. Only once, we were compelled to spend a very uncomfortable night in some horrific Navsari *juddin* hotel after dumping the bedsheet and the pillow cover which had retained various remnants of the previous occupants. In its heydays, Navsari had the small Tarota bazar near the *atash behram*, and the larger market, 10 minutes away, where the Kolah clan, competing within, sold ice-cream, *sarko* (vinegar), pickles including *garabh nu achaar*, sandalwood, and other items of rural cuisine; along with many other Parsi service providers, all of whom have disappeared.

Udvada is firmly embedded in the community consciousness as the mandatory pilgrim place for paying obeisance to the Iranshah. The Navsari *atash behram*, despite its more splendid architecture, is a distant second. More critically, Navsari has lost its Parsiness. In Udvada, it is palpably evident. Elementary, my dear Watson, says the traditionalist. Uniqueness can be preserved only in an exclusive ghetto; otherwise, in a large set-up, one's identity is bound to be obliterated. In our old age, we have to sheepishly agree.

Around the Iranshah, Udvada

Something is very fishy

But it is also healthy and does not stink

There are Parsi fishes, and *juddin* fishes. If you salivate over pomfrets but spurn smoked salmon and tinned sardines, you are a true Parsi. If you savor grilled lobster with only a slice of lime added, you are an indifferent Parsi. If the rich aroma of river fresh *boi* (mullet) being fried nauseates you (fresh fish never smells), you are a reluctant Parsi. Even diehard vegetarians by choice, like this writer, may be repulsed by meat but often secretly envy their fellow diners relishing fish. Just the other day we were compelled to cover our steamed rice with a gooey mixture of dal and *dodhi* (bottle gourd), barely managing to resist the temptation to garnish our rice with *kolmi* (prawns)-*ni-*curry, without the *kolmi*, of course.

The temptress above mentioned is enjoyed best when it is warm, but not immediately off the stove. Both the Parsi and Goan curries are coconut based (grated, ground coconut, never coconut milk), but the latter is watery; unlike the Parsi version which acquires full body with tomatoes, ground peanuts, chickpeas and garam masala together with blended garlic-ginger paste and fresh *curry patta* (curry tree leaves). It is a cardinal sin to add *boi*led prawns after the curry is cooked; they must be an integral part of the process from the very beginning so that the essence of the prawn can permeate the texture of the curry. The size of the prawns is critical to its culinary success. Rather tiny shrimps, derisively called *jhingla* in Parsi dialect, are to be avoided. However, the greed to use very large ones will result in rubbery prawns unable to absorb the curry's flavor. With a mean green chilli enhanced *kachumbar* and paper thin fried papads as accompaniments, *kolmi-ni*-curry is guaranteed to make your palate orgasmic.

Like the ragas in Indian classical music, each type of fish has its fixed time of the day for optimal consumption. A gargantuan Parsi breakfast of yesteryears comprised fried eggs, mutton *kheema* (mince) and the much desired *boi*. While on the kitchen table, raw *boi* looks rather displeased with itself (unlike the happy looking pomfret bearing a silly grin). However, it undergoes a divine transformation when it is fried after being marinated with a light dash of spices. Its sweet flesh, ensconced in the warm hug of the *ghaoon-ni-rotli* (ghee laden, multi-layered Parsi version of the paratha), titillates your taste buds. In the Parsi consciousness, *boi*, which is seldom available in Bombay, is associated with the Udvada Parsi hotels (the now defunct Majestic; and the vibrant Globe and Ashishvangh) serving them at breakfast, before you pay homage to the Holy Iranshah (unlike Hindus who fast before visiting a temple).

Bombay's answer to *boi* as a breakfast fish is, of course, *boomla* (Bombay Duck). Coated in a batter of *rava* (semolina) and lightly fried golden brown, the flesh just melting in your mouth. Rice flour *rotlis* and *gor-keri-nu-achaar* (sweet-sour mango pickle) are permissible companions; though the purist would like to eat the *boomla* by itself, after jettisoning its single soft bone. One such purist was the jovial director of the *Mumbai Samachar*, the late Rustomji Cama - a man of much joie de vivre and great girth - who would polish off a few dozen *boomlas*, not from a plate but from a *kandiyo* (container made of woven straw); lifting four or five together with his podgy fingers. Some prefer to have *boomlas* with beer, midmorning. We recollect the *boomla* courting controversy, decades ago, about its propensity to contain undigested worms (you pressed the raw *boomla* and a few worms would wriggle out); this did not, however, deter Cama or thousands of other Parsis from relishing it.

During our Navsari summer vacations, we came across yet another little known breakfast fish called *levta* (mud hoppers), wriggling live in the container and even a couple escaping - little black unattractive looking devils - cooked on a black *thikra* (a black flat griddle) with a little oil. It was an acquired taste; sort of crunchy. Some made *levta no patio* too.

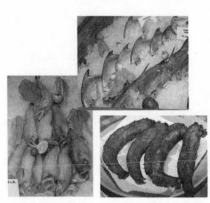

(Top): pomfrets; uncooked and fried Bombay Duck
Photos: Jasmine D. Driver

Fisherwomen in the towns of Gujarat then made home delivery, early in the morning. Sharp tongued and witty, they would match their bargaining skills with their Parsi customers. The latter had a sharp eye for scarlet red gills - a guarantee of freshness - and would unabashedly press their thumb on the fish to rule out softness, and, therefore, staleness. Sometimes things got vicious but otherwise there was bonhomie with the fisherwoman, as also with the *boo* (female mutton supplier), which is yet another story.

The cheap and wholesome era faded many years ago and now the dearest fish in town is, unfortunately, the pomfret, endearingly and uniquely called *chhamno* in Parsi dialect. Even five star hotels of antiquity serve the farm bred basa instead of the expensive pomfret;

and Parsi wedding caterers charge a hefty premium on the *paatru*, if pomfret is to be served. Undoubtedly, *the* Parsi fish, pomfret is delicious in its myriad avatars - lightly fried, steamed after wrapping in leaves and coated with green chutney as the famed *paatra-ni-macchi* or in the mouthwatering sweet and sour white *saas* (sauce) with the ubiquitous cherry tomato, fillets or cutlets for those allergic to bones, and in fish pies. Our late aunt, who was a theater actor in Adi Marzban's comedies, used to bake the most divine fish pie made with pomfret, cheese, mashed potato and white sauce (there were no ovens those days in middle class homes, so it was baked in an aluminum vessel covered with glowing charcoal on top - a slow laborious process, during which the juices from the pie's ingredients would seamlessly intermingle). The aroma of her fish pie still does something to our neural network.

A few Parsis enjoy *rawas* (mango fish or Indian salmon), *surmai* (seer fish) and *bangra* (mackerel). These are less popular, though cheaper, as the flesh is coarser or there are too many bones (which even nimble fingers cannot pick). One Parsi fish which merits mention is the *bhing* (shad), popular in the Bharuch area; sold wrapped in a small *saadri* (mat). Baked *bhing* was quite delicious.

For those with a taste for the exotic, there is dried *boomla* (they smell to high heaven) in a *patio* or pickle; *garabh* (fish roe) - quite awful, to be honest - though its pickle is exported even to North America and the UK.

This completes our list of Parsi fish. Those fish whose navjote cannot be performed are smoked salmon, black ink emitting squid, shell fish like mussels, scallops and oysters, the evil looking eel. Almost all designed for the subtle European palate. *Kolmi-ni*-curry, please take a bow!

And finally, it would be unfair not to mention this quintessential Parsi fish. It is cute, shapely and white; with bright red eyes and silvery fins and a perfectly manicured tail. Super sweet creamy flesh, with not a bone. Even Jains relish it. The *mawa-ni-machhi* from the Parsi Dairy Farm looks so much like the real thing that one vegan acquaintance would not have it on her dining table. We believe it would be sacrilegious to suggest gift wrapping it in a miniature sudreh and kusti to make it look more endearing.

Sweet memories

If you are fed up with bitterness in the BPP, savor Parsi sweetmeats

L ike American writer Mark Twain, the owners of the Parsi Dairy Farm (PDF) recently asserted that reports about their imminent demise were exaggerated. At its peak, PDF was the community's favorite institution. On account of its obvious association with happy and auspicious occasions, it was a vendor of joy. Years ago the octogenarian solicitor Burjor Antia, representing PDF in a family dispute, chastised us for accepting a family disputant's brief, expressing dismay as to how our client could sue an institution feeding *mithai* and *malai* (sweetmeats and fresh cream) to the community.

At dawn, the ubiquitous PDF *bhaiyyas* (delivery men), clad in blue shirts, balancing aluminum milk containers on their head with ballerina skill, would fan all over the city (for Parsis, the city ends at Dadar Parsi Colony). Frothy full fat milk gushing out of the container tap into the customer's stainless steel utensil was received in exchange for a prepaid coupon. Costlier, but more wholesome and purer than competing milk. Believe it or not, being a PDF customer was at one time a status symbol and there was a long waiting list. Next morning, the refrigerated milk would be covered by an inch thick layer of cream to be eaten with fresh white bread (not whole wheat or toast) after sprinkling it liberally with sugar. The cream would unclog one's arteries, the sugar excite the pancreas and the white bread make one slim. The cream was, therefore, literally to die for. The remaining cream was then boiled down to produce ghee, which one could buy readymade in tins from PDF. It was distinctly different in taste than the famous Porbandari *gai nu* ghee (cow's milk ghee).

In the winter months the *bhaiyyas* delivered doodh na puff (sweetened creamy milk froth cooled by the dew in the open). In those days to call their *dahi,* yogurt would have been sacrilege. Set in earthen pots, the mildly sweetened *dahi* (not the oversweet *mishti doi*), sprinkled with good quality pistachio and thinly sliced almonds, was so thick one could cut it with a knife. The tongue would be instantly orgasmic.

From their buffalo farms onwards, the vertically integrated dairy farm processed the milk products to produce mava molded into the traditional sweetmeats like *pendas* (yes, not *pedas*) and barfi, which was shaped sometimes into a unique fish form called *mava ni machhi*, with its red candied eye and cutely shaped tail. The fish looked so real that our then neighbor, an old Jain lady, immediately wanted it off her table. Their signature sweetmeat, however, was *sutarfari* [in *shuddh* (pure) Gujarati called *sutarpheni*], white candy floss circularly threaded, best enjoyed with a large slurping spoon after dunking it into cold milk. The *mawa ni machhi* dunked in frozen milk was reborn as PDF kulfi, circular and wrapped in butterpaper, the palate cleanser of sorts, after Godiwala's *lagan nu bhonu*, at weddings.

However, when it came to *malai na khaja* (flaky pastry filled with fresh cream), Parsis preferred a Bohri sweetmeat vendor called

Lookmanji. The *malai khajas* carried a label reminding one that they had to be eaten fresh lest the cream turn sour, unlike the more durable mava na khaja. These delicious cholesterol cakes were to be eaten along with lightly brewed tea laced with fresh mint leaves and lemon grass. Like the khajas, Lookmanji was and remains a favorite with the community for that quintessential Parsi sweet, *agharni no laarvo*, dubbed by Adi Marzban as "pregnancy balls." Distributed on the occasion of baby showers, these are nothing but conically shaped laddoos, meltingly soft when fresh. The tip is reserved for wannabe mothers, guaranteed to deliver better results than any IVF (in vitro fertilization).

PDF's range of offerings included *halwas* - the rubbery ones, loaded with gelatine, and the so-called "ice-cream" variety. No amount of lethal washing powder could possibly remove the grease formed on the *mithai* trays, which were licked by an army of cats, to make cleaning easier.

Traditional Parsi sweetmeats, not available commercially, included *sadhana* (slightly sourish crepe made of toddy marinated dough); *popatji*, the butt of many double entendre jokes in Parsi comedies, a deep fried pastry with a small protruding beak (and its crispier cousin, the *karkaryu*); *varadhvaroo*, a hard crusted cake with a softish interior; the *agiary* triplets of *malido, mehsoor* and *koprapaak*, the latter two Parsi-style; and *kumas*, a kind of honey flavored soft cake. In the towns of Gujarat, Parsi ladies earned their livelihood by making these sweets on festive days as well as weddings. RTI (Sir Ratan Tata Institute - nothing to do with the Right To Information) outlets do sell some of these sweetmeats. *Dar-ni-pori* and minced sweetened coconut dumplings called *khaman na laaroo*, also qualify as Parsi sweetmeats (the latter made on the day a toddler takes his/her first steps or a child is given the first bath after recovering from chicken pox).

Today, the PDF brand is shared. As a part of a family settlement, one branch operates independently under the same brand.

The *bhaiyyas* distribute the milk in pouches. The *dahi* comes in soft and slippery plastic containers and can now safely be called yogurt. Doodh na puff is a distant memory and *varadhvaroo* is extinct. *Sadhana* is confused with a Bollywood heroine of yesteryears. Nothing can now be gorged without guilt. Except, of course, nostalgia, the staple diet of a dying community.

Delicious is never dirty

Flirting with the patru can be hazardous to health

A friend, who had undergone a kidney transplant six months ago, enquired whether it would be 'safe' to have dinner at a Parsi colleague's wedding. We politely tried to dissuade her but failed to dampen her enthusiasm for the delicious *lagan nu bhonu*. I am willing to abstain from eating any 'problematic' dishes, she promised. Would you consider opting for the Gujarati thali, we hesitatingly asked, and received a look of utter disgust. So we set about identifying cour*ses* for her to abstain from.

Our friend was rather puzzled at our excessive concern. Parsis are so hygiene focused, she remarked, several suffering from OCD (obse*ss*ive compulsive disorder). Like Lady Macbeth, many Parsi mothers indulge in compulsive and excessive washing of hands - their own and their children's - not due to any guilt complex, but out of fear of dust, grime and bacteria in a tropical country. Never sip from a straw, our aunt used to injunct, what if a fly settles on excreta and then upon an exposed straw, your digestive lining can go for a toss. A housemaid may do all other chores but never cut a mango. Matronly ladies prefer sitting on the edge of a taxi seat or other public transport, ensuring that their talc powdered forearm never brushes against the window glass. Using public washroom facilities was out of question, nephrological complications notwithstanding. An uncle used to examine his domestic's nails every morning when there were no air oxidisers, hand sanitisers and jet sprays to clean the larger auricles.

However, we explained to our friend that, strangely and suddenly, this great sense of hygiene stands suspended at communal feasts. As a community, we suffer from a mass amnesia, once we see a *patru* (plantain leaf) before us. Our collective sense of comfort at wedding and navjote dinners or at the so called *gahambar* feasts is an inexplicable phenomenon, when deliciousness overwhelms dirtiness. It cuts across clas*ses* and countries. The *masoor paavs* and the NCPA (National Centre for the Performing Arts) Parsis (our coined term for the hoi polloi and the elite) both are oblivious to the cleanliness factor. The visiting NRIs from overseas are equally unaffected. A cousin in Boston will not let her child eat coconut chutney with idlis in an Udipi restaurant but the child can go bananas (literally, on the *patru*) at Albless Baug.

Cooking commences rather early for large public feasts, almost at dawn. The pomfret pieces are cut and then allowed to sunbathe on old newspapers, enjoying the affectionate lick of the many canines, felines and rodents roaming the site. Towards the evening, they are dipped in *boi*ling water and then the famous green chutney paste (made by adding many bottles of imported Evian mineral water, of course!) is lovingly applied to the fish, which is then wrapped in leaves, lying in a dump, and the Cinderella moment arrives, as you dig into the famous *patra ni macchi*. Its cousin, the *saas ni macchi* (fish in tangy white sauce) with a little cherry tomato enticing you, has undergone somewhat similar culinary indignities. Forget the fish, we tell our disappointed friend.

Carry a napkin from home and scrub the *patru*, as it usually has water on it. Wipe the cutlery clean or use your fingers. Avoid the innocent looking *rotli*, as it has been exposed to flies. Same goes for the evil looking *achaar* (carrot and dry fruit pickle) stored in vats visited by lizards and cockroaches, both during manufacture and later. You may have the *sarias* (sago chips), we concede. Eat whatever is piping hot, as it minimizes risk, provided you don't mind the aluminum vessels in which the food is cooked (a proven link having now been established between Alzheimer's and aluminum vessels). Try not to look at the serving pots and pans, we believe that they are the secret of the great taste.

With items cold, you are flirting with trouble, so no pumpkin *murabba* or lagan nu custard, and certainly not those divine paneers dunked in water of suspect origin, glistening and velvety due to the rennet derived from the stomach lining of a duck. And please ignore the servers, a few inebriated after downing some hooch; surely, you do not expect the caterer to have their fingers manicured? Actually, the servers add to the ambience and are a marked contrast to overtly attentive waiters hovering around you in a five star hotel.

Imaginary fears, snorts our friend, dismayed at the prospect of her highly truncated menu. Have you known of any episode of mass food poisoning, with the B. D. Petit Parsi General Hospital running out of beds? She queries. No, we say, but perhaps Parsis have acquired immunity over decades of food bristling with salmonella and bacteria. Maybe our Kyaani blood or some celestial angel protects caterers; there has to be one, as evidenced from the following true stories.

A budding caterer obtained an order to serve at a navjote of some corporate bigwig, whose South Indian boss went into raptures savoring the *sali murghi* and demanded a second helping, when he noticed that the texture of the chicken was very rubbery and strange. Upon closer scrutiny, it was found that it was a rat whose head, limbs and tail had been carefully severed by a saboteur in the service of the budding caterer's more established competitor.

The second story is even more authentic. Our aunt visited the caterer to settle his invoice, when she noticed a freshly baked lagan nu custard with currants liberally sprinkled on it. When our aunt protested about why her custard had been deprived of the currants, the caterer simply flicked his fingers to the many 'currants' who flew away to settle elsewhere, perhaps on the *patra ni macchi*.

Columnist's statutory warning

Reading this piece may be injurious to your appetite for *lagan nu bhonu*.

Who ate the malido?

Before you think otherwise, the subject is temple cuisine and not charity trustees

Our family friend, the late Ervad Framroze Panthaki, head priest of the oldest *Agiary* in Bombay – Banaji Limji near Akbarally's, Fort, was a liberal soul, secular and far ahead of his times. He would begin the day with a sonorous recitation of the jashan prayers in his spic and span *Agiary* – the holy fire credited with many a miracle - and end by playing the *manjira* (small cymbals) at a *bhajan mandali* (a group singing Hindu hymns) in some bylane of Kalbadevi. Every year, on his spiritual Master's birthday, he conducted a jashan, open to non-Parsis. Post the jashan, the disciples of the Master displayed more than the usual desire to partake of the *chaasni* (the consecrated eatables) which included the most divine *malido* in the Milky Way. Golden yellow, smooth and slightly warm, dripping with pure cow ghee, not having the slightest aftertaste of the million eggs which had perished in making it, sprinkled with finely sliced almonds, pistachio, raisins and *charoli* (a small round nut which if eaten alone is insipid, but on the malido, simply inspiring). The container (called *'lungdi'*) would be empty before one could say *"Khshnaothra Ahurahe Mazdao."* (praise be, to the Almighty!)

The malido was accompanied by *papri* (a deep fried, savory, salty, thin crusted bread of sorts). Ervad Framroze's papri, on that special day, was light, crisp and non-oily. A dollop of malido on the top of a piece of papri and a Parsi would feel that he had just crossed the Chinvat Bridge on the day of judgment and entered *behest* (heaven). *Humdins* cleansed their palates with chopped apples, bananas, pomegranate and melons.

The papri is quite similar to the famous Sindhi breakfast item - *dal* (lentils) *pakwaan*. If Mirchandani and Batlivala were blindfolded, they would not be able to tell papri from pakwaan. Indeed, we had once mischievously served pakwaan to a priest visiting us *"Gannij sojji papri chhè - Kai agiary ni chhè* (excellent papri, which *agiary* is it from)?" he enquired. We, of course, did not tell the good *andhyaru* about its Sindhi origin.

Barring the traditional Zoroastrians, most would let non-Zoroastrians eat the chaasni, except its most sacred item, the *daroon* (a hardened, rice flour chappati – equivalent of the 'bread' in church communion). We can assure our non-Parsi friends that they are not missing anything. Despite its high spiritual status, daroon is tasteless – though, on that special day, even the daroon tasted soft and divine. We must hasten to add that daroon may be consumed by cows and goats (normal practice in Navsari and Udvada), though not by non-Parsis. The discrimination is somewhat similar to the dog (but not non-Parsis) being allowed entry in the *bunglis* at *Doongerwadi* to witness the funeral ceremony. If Ervad Framroze was capable of conjuring up Michelin starred temple cuisine, at least on special days, routine temple cuisine is almost inedible: The malido, sickly pink in color, hard as a pebble, made out of jaggery and vanaspati oil, without eggs, sugar or dry fruits. Devoted behdins, out of respect for their deceased ancestors, would try to swallow it, wrapped in rubbery hard daroon. The papri would be capable of cutting the insides of your throat. The *bhakras* (an indigenous cookie), if eaten by a daring soul, would instantly remind you of your pending root canal treatment.

Every large *agiary* has a kitchen attached to it. Apart from serving food to the practising *mobeds*, these kitchens produce temple cuisine - almost uniformly pedestrian - as offerings to the deceased at *baaj* and *stoom* prayers. The stoom (popularly pronounced as satoom) involves offering a full meal to the soul of the dear departed. We have heard a portly behdin lady telling the harassed panthaky of the *agiary* that he was to place only chicken drumsticks, and not wings, in her late husband's satoom offering, as the deceased simply deplored chicken wings.

On the last day of the *muktads* (all souls' days), when the flower vases and vessels are finally lifted, the *agiary* would send to the behdins a full meal as chaasni comprising a rather anaemic omelette, pieces of dry chicken and fish, wheat chappatis and french beans, generally, so awful that it would be surreptitiously given away to the non-Parsi servants. In the good old days, Navsari temple cuisine was exotic and delicious. On 'big days,' old ladies would freelance as temple chefs and conjure up mouth-watering *sadhana* (not to be confused with a popular heroine of the yesteryears, famous for her haircut). The Parsi sadhana is a steamed cake made of fermented rice, very light on the palate, if rightly made. Then there was *kumaash* (a kind of Persian sweet cake) and the yummy *varadhvaroon* (also made for pre-wedding feasts in the moffusil). The varadhvaroon looks like a huge bhakra but is very different in taste. It has a hard exterior, which crumbles to reveal a soft and sweet inside. The dough would be marinated overnight with slightly fermented toddy (an alcoholic drink made from the sap of the palm tree) and buttered sugar added to the concoction, which would be deep fried in *sojju* pure ghee, the next morning - a delicious accompaniment to the mint and lemongrass flavored Brooke Bond tea.

We cannot end this column on temple cuisine without narrating this endearing anecdote. Almost four decades ago, when this writer was a cub reporter with *The Bombay Samachar* and assisting the venerable Jehan Daruwalla in his Parsi column on Wednesdays called "Parsi Prakash," he penned a piece on an episode in a Bombay *agiary* relating to temple cuisine. The panthaky's son, now deceased, usually a well liked and affable fellow, demanded a piece of freshly made *koprapaak* (a sweetmeat made of coconut and spiced for flavor) from the temple cook. The cook, a pious man, told him to wait till

the koprapaak was first offered in prayers, which were about to begin. The son, furious at this denial, hit the cook's back with the *chamach* (a large cooking spoon) used for making the sweetmeat. Industrial action by temple workers was narrowly averted. We thought this episode fit for publication and titled it as "*Kissa koprapaak ka*" (in those days, a popular political thriller film *Kissa Kursi ka* had been released).

(Clockwise from top left): sev; ravo; malido; and papri

A few days later, the enraged gentleman barged into Daruwalla's cabin and wanted to meet this writer. Since we did not want to be similarly hit by the temperamental gentleman, we politely suggested that we would be glad to publish his clarification, a journalistic ploy to further the controversy. In the next column, a clarification appeared, with the gentleman's smiling photo so that he could be easily identified, stating that the gentleman was apologetic for the slight hurt caused to the temple cook; and, in any event, it was not koprapaak, but *mehsoor* (another delicious sweetmeat). Of course, the title of our column said: "Sorry, it was not koprapaak, but mehsoor".

Aambakalyo and Oomberioo

Parsi rural cuisine is eclectic

In wintery dawns, you go out into the backyard (*paachloon baar*) and bring those dew-cooled glass*es* of *doodh* (milk) puff indoors. Hopefully, you have brushed your teeth with crushed neem branches, placed your index and middle fingers deep on your tongue and spat out the bile. Soothe your roughed up throat and mouth with the light-as-air, frothy cream, slightly sugared and rose petaled, with a little cardamom, which occupies three-fourths of the glass and then drink the cold milk left behind. A resounding burp and the lady serves you a railway glass of tea (big, thick fellows in which the Gujarat Express served tea), milky with fresh mint leaves and lemon grass (*lili chai*); use your index finger to remove the layer of *malai* (cream) and stick it on the outside of the cup, pour tea in the saucer and drink it with a huge slurping sound, but not before you have dunked some *batasa* biscuit from a Surat bakery into the concoction. Pour a few *karasyas* (mugs) of scalding hot water heated in a *bumbo* (cylindrical brass heater energized by wood or charcoal), apply some *chana no aato* (gram flour) in the various crevices, viscous Brahmi hair oil on your scalp, and you have worked up an appetite for the rustic breakfast.

Duck eggs with ghee sodden *ghaoon ni rotli* (wheat chapatis), thick enough to give an inferiority complex to the paratha; *khurchan* (offals and potatoes in thick gravy); and crunchy *levtas* (mud fish) fried on a black *theekra* (griddle), some of them jumping of live from the pan onto the floor in a death defying feat. How about some *vengna ni akuri* made by adding tender pieces of brinjals in the spiced up scrambled eggs.? The last mentioned being a recipe from *Vividh Vaani*, a Gujarati cookbook published in 1926, written by Meherbai Jamshedji Wadia before she succumbed to bubonic plague in her 31st year. Two thousand one hundred and eighty recipes, mostly European puffs, pies, pastries and pancakes, but also some priceless nuggets like the above mentioned aubergine-egg mix up.

Parsi rural cuisine, as is common in agrarian communities, was robust and spartan. No part of an animal or bird was too inferior to be thrown away; *patio* (thick, spicy, sweet and sour gravy) was made out of peeled skin of vegetables; ghee was homemade, as oil and butter were costly, and so was charcoal; hence, food was cooked in novel ways. The ubiquitous *oomberioo* was a prime example. Fresh *papdi* (green flat beans), young unpeeled baby potatoes, not-so-young sweet potatoes, small onions, mini brinjals were all thrown in a clay pot with a dollop of salt and garam masala added. The pot was sealed and placed on red hot charcoals, in a small pit dug in the ground, which was covered with earth, overnight. The next morning, the veggies had simmered. Most were ecstatic to consume this delicacy in the winter months; others found it insipid. *Oomberioo* retained the natural flavors of the vegetables and was best relished with fresh toddy tapped from palmyra, until the urine drinking Morarji Desai prohibited the vending of toddy.

Differently shaped molds of yore and (right) Meherbai Wadia

On the other extreme was the *aambakalyo*, made towards the end of the mango season when the fruit is a bit overripe, and usually not out of Alphonso mangoes. Kilos of sugar caramelized with lemon juice or vinegar, to which were added cloves, cinnamon and cardamom, formed the base for cooking the fruit over a painfully slow wood-fed stove. Gooey and pancreas challenging sweet but with a slightly sour and tangy taste, *aambakalyo* was hard enough to be sucked like a toffee, and then chewed by Parsis not having dental cavities. It was commonplace to have it at breakfast with chapatis in Navsari homes. Unlike the annually made *gor keri nu achaar* (not to be confused with the bacteria infested *lagan nu achaar*) and the crimson red *murabbo*, the fragile *aambakalyo* could be preserved only for a fortnight, in the absence of refrigerators.

Our maternal grandfather, Behramji Baria, more popularly called Behramji Popat, due to his house always having a green parrot in a cage hanging at its entrance, was a legendary caterer of authentic rural cuisine (the *Jam-e-Jamshed*, in his obituary, said that "*marhoom ni chamach vakhnayali huti*; literally, his cooking spoon was praised;" though it sounds like an awful double entendre from an Adi Marzban farce). His *bhoojan* (sort of barbecued liver, kidneys, testicles and other exotic goat parts) delighted many Parsi palates. He also had a secret recipe for masala dal, with tomatoes, brinjals and gourd added, simmered over a wood fire. Smokey like single malt (though he downed some locally distilled stuff with *mahuva* flowers, every evening) with a dash of *desi* ghee and deep brown fried onions sprinkled on top, his dal was the ultimate triumph of rustic cooking. Its accompaniment was a *sookka boomla no patio* (SBP, dried Bombay Duck patio). Like caviar, the SBP was an acquired taste. His wife swore that SBP was the prime cause for her dry eczema, though we never understood why she continued to eat it. *Paani nu achaar* (raw mangoes marinated in salt and brine water for a few months, resulting in the mango looking like a wrinkled old face) strips did a *jugalbandi* with Behramji's masala dal.

Sekta ni sing (drumsticks), *guvar ni sing* (clusterbeans), *garabh* (fish roe) were standard ingredients of rural cooking. Cheap, available in large quantities, maybe a little rough on the palate but filling, were the key considerations. The urban palate, accustomed to the creamy and crusty, may not always take kindly to the rough, rural cuisine, like a wearer of silk donning khadi; however, it had its own aficionados.

Varadhvaroo, kumaash, saadhna, coconut milk filled *popatji* were the Parsi village sweetmeats. Deep fried with kilos of sugar, yet melting in your mouth. Not surprisingly, the intrepid Wadia, in her magnum opus, also provides a recipe for '*Marda ni faaki*,' a home remedy for diarrhea or persistent loosies. Crush cardamom with *khadi saakar* (crystal sugar) — better than any antibiotic, to provide relief to the overburdened rural gut.

Nothing minimalist about this

Parsi furniture is an elaborate affair

The salesperson of the real estate company expected squeals of delight from his potential customer, a pedigreed Parsi gent. The apartment on display, ready for moving in, was in minimalist style. Expensive Italian marble - Statuario Venato with Rosa Travertine cleverly contrasted; one sitting area had oddly contoured chairs from Milan (more for staring at, than sitting on); refurbished 1932 French sofas in blood red leather; electronically operated curtains slithering without a whisper; a delicate white marble top dining table surrounded by deceptively fragile looking chairs; very low snow white beds merging with snow white walls. Too sleek, his customer sneered. He then volunteered to explain what constitutes quintessential Parsi furniture.

Marble is for mausoleums; the floor should be wooden or parquet. Art deco sofas, tastefully restored. Curtains should be lace;

no need for extra clever gadgetry - in an office, maybe, not in a residence. The dining table late Victorian style in mahogany or red walnut with sturdy chairs with the solid base often ornately carved. The oak sideboard, also profusely carved, Jacobean (circa 1800) with its corniced top and thick set panel doors matching the dining table. Coffee to be served on the oval shaped rosewood oak table.

"My granduncle Pestonjee pos*sess*ed the loveliest sofas," elaborated the Parsi. In a corner of his living room, he had a French painted Louis XV style sofa with yellow floral tapestry and rather dainty arms and legs. Along with it was the Hepplewhite mahogany chair back settee, serpentine fronted. Though outwardly fragile looking, these two pieces did not creak under the weight of Pestonjee's gargantuan spinster sister, whom food, and not thyroid, had rendered large.

Of course, the traditional Parsi easy chair (known as the fornicator), offering extendable wooden surfaces on which both pairs

of arms and legs may unabashedly lounge, is a non-negotiable item. Parsi gentlemen of leisure, attired in *sudreh* and *lengha*, reclining at a 45 degree angle on the easy chair, their legs spread-eagled on the extensions, with the *Jam-e-Jamshed* in their hands (when it was not tabloid size), was a common sight. This posture was akin to the *pawanmuktasana* (releasing wind) in yoga and must have facilitated the *dhansak* laden digestive tracts to expel any noxious gas. Ancient solicitors can be seen snoozing on these easy chairs at the Ripon Club and the Petit Library even today.

Sketch by Manjula Padmanabhan

The traditional Parsi bedroom had huge mahogany four-poster beds made in the George III era. The beds were covered with mosquito nets (*machhardani*) at night to prevent any airborne creature from transgressing into the space and were expertly folded during the day. One felt ensconced and safe in these four-poster beds which simulated the warmth and comfort of the mother's womb. The ever popular George V's (*aapro paanchmo* George) reign witnessed the manufacture of beds in art deco style, book matched burr walnut veneer, with fruitwood cross banding and inlaid mother of pearl detail. These beds were often brought by the Parsi bride as part of her dowry and became the *lagan no dholiyo*. The beds were so comfortable that they induced instant sleep and are perhaps a contributory factor to the declining population.

Enormous mid Victorian ash chests with long drawers stored the linen and other home textiles of the Parsi household. Nineteenth century pedestal wine tables were ideal at which to savor vintage port or cognac after dinner. Teetotalers used these tables to display bronze figurines. All very British; the Continent was, of course, for lesser mortals.

The community's taste in furniture raises some interesting questions. Are we simply unable to shrug off the hangover of all things British or are we trapped in a time warp which prevents us from going modern and chic? Antique furniture reminds us of our days of glory, of our proximity to our English masters, of that feeling of inherent superiority over the lesser natives, of an era of exclusivity and pomp. A glorious past allays the fears of a not too bright future. One can sense grandpapa sitting in that easy chair and mother sipping her mid-morning coffee from that wine colored coffee table having that extraordinary patina. The modern and minimalist is for the nouveau riche. We are, after all, the *ancien* Régime.

One of our aristocratic Parsi lady clients had gifted us an antique rosewood kidney shaped table for our study with a green leather upholstered chair, because her strained cash flow did not permit her to pay us a dime in fees.

At her opulent residence, we had seen an excellent Victorian burr walnut duchess dressing table (mid Victorian period), made from solid walnut with walnut veneers. The oval shaped mirror, which swung back and forth, was rather small for our client's large visage. She also possessed the quaintest stools of all kinds, an obsession in many Parsi residences. The Queen Anne style stool with red upholstery, a pair of children's stools, and of course, we must mention the adjustable revolving three-legged piano stool with glass ball feet. The 12-inch diameter of the seat though was adequate only to house one half of the abundant posterior of the noble lady while she played the German piano.

Cowsie, the friendly ghost

Zoroastrian cosmology does not countenance poltergeists

Somewhere outside the small dakhma in *Doongerwadi*, there is a platform, upon which none dare sleep at night. Late Dervish Irani, the uncrowned king of the pallbearers, who devoted his life preserving *Doongerwadi*, was the only one to do so. Anyone else was flung from it with great force and suffered severe fright. We have corroborated this story from Irani himself and other staff at the Towers of Silence.

The Grand Paradi buildings and a row of bungalows overlook the Bombay *dakhmas*. Crows and kites deposit remains plucked from the undisposed bodies lying in the *dakhmas*. Decades ago, when we were on the editorial staff of the *Mumbai Samachar*, an enraged resident had complained that when he was having breakfast on his balcony, his eggs Florentine were garnished with a Parsi index finger. The then trustees of the Bombay Parsi Punchayet (BPP) had dismissed the story as poppycock. Be as it may, bizzare suicides of such a disproportionately high number have happened from the Grand Paradi buildings that they cannot be dismissed as coincidence. About 12 years ago, we were deliberating on purchasing one of the Grand Paradi bungalows which garden has a common boundary with the *Doongerwadi* lands. We were surveying the garden, just after sunset, with a pleasant February breeze blowing, when most of us experienced a distinctly eerie feeling. Of course, it can be dismissed as conditioning, though one of us observed that she could smell death in the air.

This writer spent most of his summer vacations in the mohallas of Navsari (then still retaining their Parsi character). Power supply was weak and yellow bulbs shed their light dimly. After dinner, we were compelled to make our way alone to the bedroom on the upper floors. As you lay on the four poster bed with the

machhar daani (mosquito net), fat lizards perched on the walls eyed you warily. The coconut trees in the backyard cast strange shadows on the wall. A hungry dog cried plaintively. Cursed with a fertile imagination, we slept transfixed on the bed, fervently hoping for our stentorian grandmother's entry into the bedroom. If we dared to express fear of the unknown, she admonished us by stating that "Parsi *koi daharo bi bhoot nahin thay* (there are no Parsi ghosts)." Little consolation, we muttered to ourselves, what about the non-Parsi ghosts whose existence she was implicitly confirming.

If you did your kusti before going to bed and recited "*Srosh asho, tagi, tan-farman, shekaftzin, zin-awazar, salare damane Ahura Mazda berasad,*" no ghostly fear could haunt you at night, advised our granduncle, who was an *Ilm-e-Khshnoomist*. Years later, we must admit that this incantation does ensure that there are no nightmares. Though one such evening in Navsari, we saw, at the window of the house across, an old Parsi gentleman, whom we had never seen before, giving us a sweet smile. We must have been all of eight years. After dinner, we narrated this to our grandaunts and uncles, who froze in silence. We could not understand the conspiratorial whispers that followed. Years later, our grandaunt on her death bed, told us that her uncle had lost his young wife, a six-year-old daughter and an eight-year-old son in the 1935 Quetta earthquake. Overwhelmed with grief, he committed suicide, from the same window where we had seen him, about 25 years before our sighting. Uncle Cowsie adored children, our grandaunt said.

Zoroastrian cosmology does not countenance poltergeists, ghosts that make strange noi*ses* and cause objects to move. The *geh sarna* (funeral) prayers, when intoned with concentration and sonorously, are designed to wipe all earthly memories and connections of the soul. Pregnant women are forbidden from attending as they are known to miscarry. Coupled with the equally potent Srosh prayers, the soul lo*ses* any incentive to haunt. This belief is quite firmly embedded in the collective consciousness, as evidenced by this bizarre incident, a century ago in the dakhma of either Navsari or Surat. The body of an old lady, consigned to the dakhma after *geh sarna*, stirred, sat up and asked for water. Elders and priests were hastily summoned to deal with the situation, caused by some quack who had certified her dead. Once the geh sarna is completed, the body cannot be brought back, was the verdict. How the verdict was implemented is too sordid to record.

Although traditionalists do not interpret Zoroastrianism as believing in reincarnation, they do emphasize the continued existence of the soul and its journey till the final Day of Judgement (like all other religions 'of the book'). During muktad, the souls of the departed are supposed to be pleased with the flowers, sandalwood and frankincense offered to them, as also with those, on earth, who lovingly remember them in prayers. There is no evidence though to suggest that the aroma of chicken drumsticks and crisp *bhakras* placed in the *stum* ceremony can still entice the soul of Sorabji who gorged every alternate day at the Kentucky Fried chicken outlet, when alive.

The poltergeist phenomena of moving objects, unexplained sounds and smells, troublesome spirits and apparitions are to be distinguished from rare appearances by spiritually advanced souls or angels or what is termed in Theosophical literature as the "deva Kingdom," to help a human being in distress. In some of our agiaries and *atash behram*s, several attending priests have testified to the presence of a guardian angel, clad in all white, sailing through the corridors of the fire temple, as if keeping vigil.

The protection of prayers will not be fully effective, unless the body is consigned to the dakhma, say the orthodox. The consecration rituals of the dakhma create an electro-magnetic field through an elaborately constructed circuit to ensure that no dark forces tinker with a Zoroastrian soul until the dawn of the fourth day from death when it cros*ses* the famous *Chinvat bridge* and enters the Great Beyond.

Geh sarna for those who are cremated is therefore no insurance against the deceased turning into a spook. The hard core contend that a Parsi is risking much by refusing the sanctum of the dakhma. On the contrary, snorts the liberal, rotting undisposed bodies are more susceptible to spiritual abuse. A crematorium in the dakhma to take benefit of the circuit can resolve the issue for both sides. In the meanwhile, we will continue to believe in the comforting thought that Parsis don't become *bhoots* though a Bhoot can be a Parsi (decades ago, there was a famous wedding caterer called Kaikhushru Bhoot who provided his services at our navjote).

Rearranging the furniture

Good old haandagiri is back

Decades ago, Parsi public meetings were often stormy and boisterous. "*Bau khursi oochri* (plenty of chairs were tossed about)" was a common observance. The fights were either between the orthodox and the reformists or between strong opposing personalities. Those were the days of political incorrectness. Name calling was rampant and *haandas* (boorish louts) roamed the streets.

Eminent jurist, late Homi Seervai, a man of saintly integrity and true nobility used to recount the story of his colleague, a senior partner of a venerable law firm, and later, chairman of the Bombay Parsi Punchayet (BPP) who was aghast to read in the Jam-e-Jamshed a tribute published by his opponent in Parsi politics, who christened his dog with the lawyer's initials The article was titled: "*Maro vafaadar kutro, - ; Ooth kéhvoon tau oothé, né bès kéhvoon tau bèsé* (my faithful dog, stands if I command him to stand, and sits if I command him to sit)." The lawyer was dissuaded by the sagacious Seervai from suing the party for defamation, since he apparently had the right to name his dog. Perhaps, the dog could have sued.

The *Kaiser-e-Hind* (with Queen Victoria on its masthead, even much after Independence) espoused the liberal cause and was more acerbic than the then orthodox supporting Jamé. Adversaries in Parsi politics would routinely trade insults in the columns of these newspapers, avidly read by the community. We recollect a public meeting at the K. R. Cama Oriental Institute, where the radically reformist Dastur Framroze Bode (who performed the Vansda navjotes) along with Kaiser's editor, Jal Heerjibehdin, pleading with the crowd to stop pelting them with eggs (those days, we had mostly desi, not 'English,' eggs) and Quink ink bottles. The crowd apparently did not believe in freedom of speech and after a few chairs were broken, the learned speakers escaped through the backdoor and the gathering dispersed.

It was an accepted practice to heckle speakers, manhandle opponents, hurl rotten tomatoes, publish scurrilous advertisements and use language which would make a *goonda* (hooligan) blush. Speaking of goondas, a report in the Saanj Vartamaan (a defunct Gujarati eveninger), describing a Parsi public meeting which was raucous, was headlined: "*Parsi kom ma goondagirié, fari ék vaar oonchkéloo mathoo* (Goondagiri surfaces once again in the community)." It went on to say how some prominent Parsi goondas (names mentioned) had disturbed the meeting and torn the dugla of the wretched speaker. Saanj Vartamaan was promptly issued a legal notice by the prominent goondas who said that they were defamed, as the Bombay Goonda Act (a legislation which still exists on the statute book) applied only to hardened criminals. Unchastised, the eveninger penned another editorial terming their leader as a "*jaaro, kaaro Parsi goondo* (a fat, black Parsi goonda)." Such fun and games were prolific.

After the days of the legendary Lt Col Rustam Kharegat, Lady Hirabai Jehangir was perhaps the last of the aristocratic trustees.

With the arrival of Boman K. Boman-Behram (former Mayor of Bombay), Parsi politics acquired a new flavor. The story of his rise and fall will occupy much space. At some point, he joined hands with the fundamentalist Dr. Nelie Noble and together, they controlled the Anjuman Committee, the cabal which elected BPP trustees. Noble's

1975 BPP election victory of Jamshed Guzder

brothers owned a cycle shop and they were tough, in a very Parsi sort of way. Their reign ended rather unceremoniously with the rise of the Committee for Electoral Rights (CER). The Nobles could have easily terrorized the urbane, very thin cucumber sandwich eating CERians, but for Dinshaw Mehta with his wide experience in making his father Rusi win successive Bombay municipal elections, for nearly 30 years, from the tough red-light district and drubbing the then aggressive Muslim League. Parsi politics suddenly became serious. On the first day of the 1981 elections which gave CER a bone crushing victory over Boman-Behram and Noble, a Committee of United Zoroastrians (CUZ, a group opposing CER) supporter tore down a poster. He was a giant of a man who thought the CER was full of sissies. The late Zal Contractor, compassionate and helpful to all, and a genial man, delivered a knock out blow to the CUZ giant who fell on the ground unconscious.

A decade earlier, reputed solicitor Shiavax Vakil defeated Nanabhoy Jeejeebhoy in a closely fought election (salacious details as to why he lost). Vakil entered the *dakhmas*, with co-trustee Dr. Aspi Golwalla, to examine the state of affairs, and earned the ire of the fundamentalists. They threatened to throw acid on Vakil. Brave though he was, Vakil was fed up with Parsi politics and resigned within two years. In the 2011 universal adult franchise elections, there was an interesting skirmish between Jimmy Mistry's bodyguards and Mehta's family, at Rustom Baug. *Haandagiri* and *methipaak* (clobbering) have thus a long history. It is wrong, therefore, to say that the BPP trustees have reached "a new low," when the chairman tried to rearrange the furniture in the board room (practitioners of Vaastu, feng shui are convinced that this building is jinxed, and it is better for the community, if its landlord, Sir Jamsetjee Jejeebhoy VIII is successful in the eviction suit filed by him against the BPP). Quite a few non-Parsis were amused at this episode, though a little disappointed with the trustees, at the Anglicized abuse used by them instead of the authentic Parsi *gaars* (abuse).

We have heard from the grapevine that in the BPP boardroom, all chairs have now been fixed to the ground, tea will be served in paper cups with plastic cutlery, and no pencil or pen will be permitted (anyway, there is nothing much to record). Four police constables will be stationed throughout the meeting and all entering the hallowed room will be frisked. It is certainly not a new low, it is, on the contrary, a new high. All those lamenting the demise of Parsi theater will now take hope that a bumper season of fun and frolic awaits the community in the next trusteeship elections. Gentlemen, please don't disappoint us.

Tossing those pills away?

Parsis have been known to resort to unorthodox methods of healing

The orthopedic specialist has grimly pronounced that you must lie flat in bed for three weeks, not bend down or lift weights for the rest of your life. The disc has truly slipped. As you lie forlorn, staring at your false ceiling, ruing the postures you can no longer adopt, a Good Samaritan prom*ises* a magical, instantaneous cure. Groaning in pain, you stand before a large, mustachioed Parsi gingerly eyeing you. In the style of security guards at the airport, he frisks your fragile spine with his farmhand fingers and locates the source of your woes while his two helpers hold you back to keep you from running away should you have a last minute change of mind. The healer taps your back lightly with his foot twice or thrice before nonchalantly delivering a hard kick on the offending vertebra with laser precision. Momentarily, you are unable even to cry and then the man commands you to get up. Hesitatingly, you do and discover that your pain and stiffness have disappeared, instantly. You walk away smiling. The healer charges no money and you go home happily, thinking of the alternative employment the orthopedic doctor will soon have to find.

The legendary founder of this kick school was Manchersha Madhivala, a rough diamond. He cured thousands and never took a penny. Visitors to his simple home in Madhi village, a few miles from Navsari, were not allowed to leave without partaking of a spartan meal of coarse rice, dal and dried Bombay duck. It was believed that he had been given this magic touch by a sadhu. Madhivala imparted his method to Jal Amaria, Keki Kotwal of OK Wafers and Eruch Avari of Colaba, all of whom served selflessly and all now deceased. Kayomarz Patel continues the tradition. There were no horror stories of a kick landing wrongly or puncturing a kidney or lung.

Parsis suffering from back and neck problems also visit a Gujarati businessman at his modest residence in one of Bombay's western suburbs. He does not kick but manipulates vigorously. In the Jain tradition, his *sadhana* (discipline undertaken in pursuit of a goal) has resulted in a *siddhi* (a power) from Mataji, a female deity, enabling him to deal with the muscular skeletal system for the last 35 years.

Allopathy provides relief but no cure for common hepatitis or jaundice. This writer, when 12, suffered a bad attack of jaundice and the doctor was concerned with the rising bilirubin level. An old *chasniwalla* (fire temple worker) was approached, bargained hard for his fees, concluded the arrangement, took a bowl of water, mumbled a prayer, blew on the water and dipped the patient's finger in the water which slowly turned yellow. Later that evening, the blood test showed normal bilirubin and the coffee colored urine turned pale yellow. The utter revulsion for food or even its aroma was soon replaced by a gargantuan appetite. The doctor just shrugged his shoulders.

A century ago, in the state of Baroda ruled by Sayajirao Gaekwad III, a granduncle working as an engineer during day would cure scorpion bites after nightfall. The villagers brought the writhing victim, suffering from excruciating abdominal cramps, to him in a cart. The Parsi said a short prayer and the victim would gratefully get up and walk away, blessing the healer. Nothing was taken in cash or kind. Having been taught some spell by a roaming dervish, the Parsi had to stand in chest deep water in the river at midnight on one particular day in the year, virtually like a refresher course in toxicology. The Parsi did not pass on his powers to anyone. Migraine cured by eating a piece of sweetmeat at dawn; sunstroke cured by passing a stainless steel *thali* (plate) filled with water, stones and a few other things, all over the body; piles cured by consuming a cup of mild black tea blessed by a gentleman residing in a bungalow at Bandra - these are cures that have been witnessed by this writer over the years.

For those trusting only in Zoroastrian prayers, the powerful Ardibesht Ameshaspanda Nirang followed by the equally potent nirang of the legendary king of yore, Shah-e-Faridoon, a great white magician and healer, destroyer of all evil, have been found to be miraculous not only in curing ailments but for exorcising evil and mental disorders. The healer holds the right thumb of the patient while sonorously uttering the intonation: "*Fénaamé yazad ba farmaané yazad, banaménik Faridoon é daavgayé* (Faridoon commands Evil to be frozen)."

Manchersha Madhivala: a kick in time

Not all Parsis take kindly to alternative healers. Decades ago, one Sunday evening, we remember seeing a resident medical officer of a community hospital throwing out a Parsi healer reciting prayers before a young lad afflicted with a brain tumor. The doctor bellowed in a stentorian voice across the lobby that he would summon "the Gamdevi" (police). Strangely, himself an expert on forensic science and toxicology he was reportedly often found sitting in his cabin trying to hypnotize a rooster trying its damnedest to escape the iron grip of the good doctor.

Horoscopes hardly horrify

The community's belief in astrology has diminished

Goolbai had been forewarned by her trusted family astrologer that her only son Homi's life was in imminent danger. Goolbai fervently pleaded with Homi not to report for an Air India flight, as senior purser. Homi ignored his mother's repeated entreaties but, at the last minute, he relented and missed the flight. The next morning, on January 1, 1978, Goolbai woke up to read in the newspapers that the flight had indeed crashed near Bombay and there were no survivors. She rushed into Homi's bedroom, only to discover that her son had succumbed to a massive cardiac attack. Homi's post mortem estimated his time of death within minutes of the crash. This is a true story, with names changed. The astrologer died a year later.

Parsi households in Gujarat were avid believers in astrology. Within a week of a child's birth, a rather preliminary horoscope, called *Janam chitthi* (literally, a birth note), would be cast to determine if the child's *pagloo* (entry) was auspicious for the father (mother, those days, did not matter). Around navjote, a detailed horoscope would be cast indicating the position of the planets, Sun, Moon, Rahu and Ketu (the last two being imaginary nodes of the Moon accorded planetary status in Hindu astrology) in the 12 hou*ses* of the Zodiac. Myopic eyes would then pour over dusty almanacs to as*sess* the strength of a planet in a house, as determined by the exact time and place of birth. The periods and sub-periods of the planets over the entire lifetime worked out including the dreaded '*sadesati panoti*' (a seven-and-a-half year period relating to the placement of Saturn). It was believed that if you were the only son, there was a good chance of losing your father during a *sadesati*. The permutations and combinations were infinite - benefics and malefics; planets in square, trine and conjunction to each other; the exotic '*parivartan yoga*', where planets were lords of each other's hou*ses*, the wealth bestowing '*gaj kesari yoga*' and a thousand other such yogas. For a pittance, the family astrologer (rarely, a Parsi) would laboriously collate; all of which can be done now, literally in two minutes, and free of cost, on your smartphone or Ipad.

It was an era of arranged marriages and the *Kaajwali* (matchmaker) would first demand the candidate's horoscope. A strong *Manglik* (position of Mars in certain hou*ses*) would 'swallow' (kill) the spouse, unless the spouse too was a Manglik. Your marketability shot up, if you had a non-Manglik horoscope. Horoscope matching before matrimony was almost mandatory amongst the Parsis then.

Gradually, the liberals began to dismiss astrology as unZoroastrian. How can a religion which advocates *Vohuman* (the right mind) and free will believe that birth, death and marriage are predestined? they argued. They were wrong. Perhaps, Zarathushtra founded astrology, say several respected scholars. According to the Roman historian Pompeius, the prophet was the founder of the science of foretelling the future from the stars. He was the ultimate Magi.

The *Qisse-i Sanjan* refers to Zoroastrian high priests consulting astrological charts to determine the safest pathway for Zoroastrians fleeing Iran. Firdowsi's *Shahnameh* speaks of Persian kings consulting the priest-astrologers about the future of their first born son. The ninth century Zoroastrian text, *Dinkard* refers to 'star-readers' foretelling events from a horoscope. Of course, the most famous Zoroastrian astrologer was Jamasp, prime minister of King Vishtasp and one of the first disciples of the Prophet. He wrote the *Jamasp Namah* or Jamaspi, a Nostradamus like collation of predictions of things to come in the centuries ahead (The English translation by Dr. Jivanji Jamshedji Modi is quite fascinating).

In the early part of the last century, Parsis from Gujarat consulted Hareshwar Joshi who also had the Gaikwads of Baroda as his clients. His grandson, late Dr Vasant Kumar Pandit, a Rajya Sabha Member of Parliament, and a renowned astrologer was quite popular amongst Bombay Parsis in the 1970s and '80s. Behram Pithavala and Ervad Eruchsha Karkaria were both serious students of the subject, but only as a passion. The style of operating of these yesteryear astrologers was quite different from the lighthearted predictions of the likeable Bejon Daruwalla who delivers them in his inimitable, breathless style on television. Of course, the bylanes of Bombay had quite a few Parsi astrologers (one old gentleman called Tehmul, who stayed all his life at the Petit Sanatorium, accurately predicted when his clients would acquire a residential flat; and a middle aged spinster at Tardeo, who voluntarily phoned us to warn that we ought not to cross the street ahead of any red vehicle including a fire brigade-*no-bumbo*, during a particular fortnight).

It is erroneously believed that since Zoroastrianism emphasizes a final day of judgement for all souls, there is no place in it for reincarnation and karma. Astrology makes little sense, if you dismiss repeated rebirths. If it is true that one's entire life is predetermined by past karma then your free will kicks in only to determine how you react to your life situation, which, in turn, will decide the fate of your future incarnations. As the above mentioned Tehmul had explained to us, if you were destined to live up to 90, you may booze to your heart's delight and survive (which he did). However, for the sin of abusing your body, you may get cirrhosis of the liver in your next incarnation, even though you may then be a teetotaler. Bloody Mary unfair!

There were Parsis obsessed with astrology who would not leave or enter the house during 'Rahu-kaal' (a period of 90 minutes each day, during which commencement of any new venture would invite misfortune). The *Jam-e-Jamshed*, years ago, commissioned one Swayamjyoti Maharaj - a Jesus look alike - for his weekly forecasts according to the Moon sign (position of the moon in the horoscope). He was a hit amongst the *Masoor-paav* Parsis, who revered him ['we have stopped eating Dhansak on Sunday, as our Swayamjyoti Maharaj has said that Rusi's Sun is debilitated, and would be pleased (that is, the Sun, not Swayamjyoti Maharaj)if we remained vegetarian']. Unlike the Hindus, few Parsis got *pooja* (prayer rituals) performed for propitiating a malefic planet; though we recollect a Parsi collegemate who released a tiny serpent made out of silver in some river near Nasik to relieve herself of the ill effects of *Kaalsarp dosha* (serpentine defect of having all your seven planets sandwiched between Rahu and Ketu in your horoscope), and successfully shed her spinster status, soon thereafter.

Like our dramatically declining numbers (only 57,241 in India in 2011; current estimate 55,000), the belief in astrology has considerably diminished. The Ilm-e-Khshnoomists (a Zoroastrian occult group who are ardent believers in reincarnation, vegetarianism and astrology, inspired by the late Behramshah Shroff) - confidently predict a second coming of the Lord - Saoshyant or Soshyos - who will revitalize our faith and community. It is all written in the Zoroastrian cosmology, they assert. For once, let us hope that the Khshnoomists have got it right.

The monarchs of Mahalaxmi

The community continues to contribute to every aspect of thoroughbred racing

A single statistic tells the story. Although 60,000 Parsis constitute an infinitesimal part of India's 1.3 billion population, a huge majority of owners, trainers, breeders, jockeys and administrators — 'connections,' in horse racing parlance - are Parsis. Beyond any doubt, Parsis are the first community of horse racing. Dr Cyrus Poonawalla - Forbes billionaire; creator of the 100 billion dollar Serum Institute of India, the world's vaccine powerhouse; envied owner-to-be of Lincoln House which earlier housed the American Consulate in Bombay; savior of the nearly abandoned 2013 World Zoroastrian Congress; chief sponsor of the Iranshah Udvada Utsav; host to many a community *gahambar* - is also India's foremost racing personality by a mile. He successfully organized and led the Asian Horse Racing Conference (a misnomer for the world racing conclave) in Bombay. After Ratan Tata, Poonawalla is perhaps one of the most well known

Parsis. Despite his stellar achievements in many non-equine fields of endeavor, he is proud to be known as the undisputed monarch of Mahalaxmi. After all, it was Sir Cusrow Wadia who donated land for the Mahalaxmi race course.

Poonawalla is not the only Parsi to be the chairman of the Royal Western India Turf Club. (How it has managed to still retain 'Royal' in its name in Maharashtra is a minor mystery. Perhaps the social stigma attached to racing has prevented some political leader's name being fastened.) His brother, Zavaray has been the chairman, and so was Khushru Dhunjibhoy-seven times. All of them are breeders of thoroughbreds, having stud farms near Poona, just like Shapoor Mistry and Dr. Farokh Wadia. Fierce contests are fought not only on the turf but also during the annual Club elections with the usual cocktail of anonymous letters, allegations and counter allegations, wooing voters with lavish food and booze and gifts of flowers, dates, chocolates, shawls and even massage oils. Out of the nearly 2,000 odd voters, 250 are Parsis.

In the good old days, when Mahalaxmi was the preserve of royalty, film stars and celebrities, after the English trainers departed, many leading trainers were Parsis. Some were colorful and most were notable eccentrics. One gentleman, who could hardly get his equine wards past the post, would rise every morning at four, visit all agiaries from Colaba to the race course, perform *kusti* near the winning post and only then commence training. Alas Ahura Mazda did not deem it fit to bestow any success upon him. The other, a man of all seasons, painted a class one horse black and ran him as a class five horse who naturally hacked the field. As the trainer was gleefully counting his ill gotten gains, it started raining at the Poona race course, resulting in the color of the horse and his scheme both coming off in full public view. Not to be daunted by this mishap, he quickly spirited the poor horse, killed it, cremated it and buried its remains. He was banned for life. His off course activities were equally colorful. In a particular village near Poona, many claimed before the land revenue authorities that the trainer was their biological father and that they had a claim to his land. He proudly claimed, only in half jest, that the secret of his libido was his consuming live a large queen ant, which kept him as fit as a stallion in his prime.

Even presently, there are as many as 15 Parsi trainers. Five have saddled Indian Derby winners — the legendary nonagenarian Rashid Byramjee for a record 11 times, followed by the heart throb of the yesteryears, Bezon Chinoy (four); with Cooji Katrak, Dallas Todywalla and Pesi Shroff, saddling one each. In the recent past, allegations by and between two Parsi trainers of doping the rival's horse have been investigated by the civil and criminal courts as also the economic offences wing of the Bombay police. Being co-religionists has not prevented the sordidness. We do exist to be sport for our neighbors to laugh at.

Parsis have been top jockeys too. Proving the dictum that after skiing, horse racing is the most dangerous sport, Karl Umrigar, nearing the peak of his riding career, fell off his mount and had his lung punctured by another horse. He gamely battled for seven days, recovered, and then suddenly succumbed. His untimely and tragic death did not deter his cousin, Pesi Shroff, from becoming one of the country's top jockeys and saddling eight Derby winners (a ninth win was annulled when his mount Saddle Up later tested positive). Shroff had the rare distinction of riding for virtually every leading owner including Poonawalla, Vijay Mallya and the recently deceased turf baron from Madras, Dr M. A. M. Ramaswamy. After hanging up his boots in 2004, Shroff has emerged as the champion trainer winning all the Indian and regional classics. Though a distance away from Shroff, other notable Parsi jockeys include Zervaan Suratia and Malcolm Kharadi.

The other stakeholders in this game are the bookmakers (popularly, bookies) both licensed and unlicensed, who generally manage to come on top; and the hapless punters who live their life dreaming of that elusive jackpot. There are about five Parsi bookies but an army of Parsi punters. Unlike other communities, not much social stigma is attached to race goers. The sport is a great equalizer, with noted doctors, lawyers, architects and chartered accountants happily rubbing shoulders with the hoi polloi from the First Enclosure. Animated discussion starts from Saturday night when the unofficial odds are announced up to the post mortem of every race. Mahalaxmi is a dream factory. AD, a clever Parsi punter, won a couple of crores in the 70s and lost every cent in the next two seasons. D. P. C. Kapadia, a Parsi gentleman who died at 100, owned a horse called Pyare Mia which never won a single race in its career except the Indian Derby! Dreams are made and shattered within seconds as evidenced by a pioneer Parsi breeder, Wadia, founder of the Yerawada Stud Farm. He witnessed the rare spectacle of the Derby winner, the runner-up, the third and the fourth horse – all bred by him but his overjoyed heart brimming with pride, stopped beating within minutes, in the paddock itself.

Parsi punters are, by and large, responsible gamblers. We know of a bachelor, S, now in his seventies, who proudly states that he has never done a decent day's work in his lifetime but eked out a modest living from attending every single race day and generally betting on 'Parsi' hor*ses* (owned, trained or jockeyed by Parsis). Like our mother who always enquired whether the doctor treating her is a Parsi or not, S too first ascertains before punting whether "Parsi-*no-ghoro chhè kê* (Is it a Parsi horse)?" The traditionalist concern for genetic purity apparently extends to equines too.

Special race for the 10th World Zoroastrian Congress 2013

Selective sense of hygiene

Maku Macbeth does not always wash her hands

The infamous 'railing' where the *hoipolloi* of the Dadar Parsi Colony met christened her as Maku Macbeth. She was much more though than Shakespeare's compulsive washer, Lady Macbeth (who felt guilty for killing the King — 'all the perfumes of Arabia will not sweeten this little hand'). Not only did Maku wash her hands repeatedly, she clipped her nails every morning and changed her underclothes in every *gah* (staying near an *agiary* helped, as she could hear the bells resonate to mark the beginning of a *gah*). Of course, she and her sister Freny never contemplated matrimony; aghast at the idea of touching another being; to put it mildly. They repeatedly checked whether the front door was locked, as if they were guarding Fort Knox. It did not require a genius to conclude that they suffered from OCD (obsessive compulsive disorder), a difficult psychiatric condition to cure. Unfortunately, the community has a disproportionate number of Maku Macbeths and Fastidious Frenys. Are we genetically predisposed to OCD, or do we have a selective sense of hygiene?

While the cau*ses* of OCD could be many, at an ethnic level, it could be deep insecurity. Even though more than 1,200 years have passed since we sought refuge in India, some of us still have a strange sense of unbelonging in a foreign land. A collective guilt, perhaps, of not making enough effort to go back to the motherland. Also, the feeling that we are somewhat superior to the natives - cleaner, more hygienic, better organized. A simpler explanation is that we are plain eccentric. Whatever the reason, many Parsis have an exaggerated sense of hygiene.

As children, we were not allowed to sip a cold drink through a straw. A housefly settling on an exposed straw (in those days, straws did not come in sealed paper pouches) could upset one's digestive lining for weeks. Banish the thought of tucking into some *variyali* or *saunf* (fennel, aniseed) from a bowl in a restaurant; tiny cockroaches could have laid their tinier eggs there overnight. There were a laundry list of prohibitions - *paani puri* (did you see how dirty the bhaiya's nails were, as he punctured the puri to fill it with spiced water? Un*boi*led and bristling with germs, of course); *bhelpuri* at Chowpatty sea front (the ink from the newspaper comes off with the watery chutney); freshly cut fruits (did you notice the thin layer of rust on his knife, and the flies buzzing nearby?)

Nakh pur makh nuthee bestee
A fly can't sit on the nose
Arrogant person

Apart from hygiene, there is also this obsession with

orderliness. One of our clients - we will call him Jamshedji - would rise from his chair in the midst of an important meeting to minutely correct the angle of the photo frame on the wall, much to the amusement of his *juddin* colleagues. "I feel giddy at seeing a crooked frame," he would whine. We had an aunt who singularly contributed to the sales of Tata's eau de cologne, a bottle of which would be found those days in almost every Parsi household. Apart from being liberally applied to matronly necks and hands, cologne water, as it was popularly called, was used to revive those who had fainted; a few drops consumed in water was supposed to cure nausea. Years ago, an aristocratic Parsi lady client would carry a bottle to official meetings and suddenly summon her Man Friday to liberally slap the liquid on her sleeveless muscular arms, ostensibly to repel mosquitoes [("Bamboat! *Jaldi*, cologne water *lagaro*! (Bamboat! Quickly apply the cologne water!)].

Another acquaintance, a well heeled gentleman of leisure, bitterly complained to us about the exorbitant charges of doctors paying a home visit. We solicitously enquired the reason for the home call. "You know, I suffer from piles," he said, "I called him to apply antiseptic cream, and he charged me 800 rupees!" "Why did you not apply the cream yourself?" we asked incredulously. "Never!" he exclaimed, "*Mané soog laagé* (I feel yucky)!"

In the late 60s, an old Parsi hotelier and his daughter ran a lovely little hotel at Deolali (the desserts were simply divine). One of the rooms facing a large garden was permanently occupied by a Parsi spinster known throughout Deolali and Nasik as the Eucalyptus Queen. If you walked on the verandah (porch) of the hotel to digest a sumptuous breakfast, the salubrious morning air of unpolluted Deolali was replaced by the pungent odor of eucalyptus oil. She stored hundreds (no exaggeration) of bottles of the oil in her room; generously sprinkled it on all her clothes, bedsheets, towel and even the curtains. Maids suffering from a severe cold volunteered to clean her room, so as to open their blocked sin*uses* instantly.

Until her knees turned arthritic, Goolbai preferred the Indian style toilet. One's posterior did not have to touch any foreign object nor was it subjected to the indignity of water splashing from the toilet bowl. Water faucets had not then arrived, so Goolbai put on thin surgical gloves. Using a public toilet, be it in a five star hotel, was out of question. Hence, she shortened her public engagements, including leaving the theater during the interval. To visit her son in England, she would abjure direct flights at night lest she was forced to use the first class loo. All her laundered underclothes would be wrapped in butter paper, the kind one u*ses* not to soil a plate. Every day she would unwrap a fresh cake of soap, which would be dumped in the dustbin, as she could not bear the thought of her servants using it. She had a perpetual frown of disapproval on her rotund face, like an angelic being shuddering at the dirty world.

This extreme sense of hygiene, however, disappears, when it comes to partaking meals from a *patru* at weddings and navjotes. So do we unconsciously distinguish between Parsi dirtiness and *juddin* dirtiness? The former being incapable of offending our selective sense of hygiene, we turn a blind eye to the conditions under which feast food is prepared and served. After stuffing herself with *saas ni macchi*, Maku Macbeth perhaps does not feel like washing her hands.

Being cutely cuckoo

Some reflections on our mental health

Our famed ability to laugh at ourselves emboldens others to slip in a few nasty ones about our mental health. Nine out of 10 Parsis are nearly mad, and the 10th one is mad, goes one jibe. All Parsis are mad but Homi is a mad Parsi, is another. The world often perceives those who are different, as mad. Are we just outstanding eccentrics or are we cutely cuckoo? Do most of us appear pleasantly mad to other communities, like some funny looking harmless aliens still trying to assimilate, for the last thousand years, in the land of their refuge.

We are not talking about the disproportionately high prevalence of neurological disorders in Parsis due to intense inbreeding and other obvious cau*ses*. Clinical insanity is sad and arou*ses* compassion. Being an oddball is fine, but does the buck stop there? Intense eccentricity can degenerate into madness when one stops living in the real world and occupies fantasy land.

Our demographics are horrific. The widening chasm between deaths and births every year; more than half of us being single; very late marriages; poor fertility; much of the community being senior citizens - a deadly cocktail indeed. Lonely old bachelors and spinsters desolately staring at their grandfather clocks chiming unnecessarily every quarter, as life slowly ebbs out each day. The youth no longer enjoy the head start of yesteryears when just being a Parsi was a guarantee for a job, respect and adoration by other communities. No wonder then that mental health issues abound.

Most of us take refuge in the abiding faith in our agiaries which recharge our drooping spirits and provide hope. The atheists and agnostics prefer, of course, to lie down on the psychiatrist's couch. We are often not even aware that we are subtly depressed. Increasingly, the external environment appears hostile and mocking. Some respond by forsaking the communal identity and prefer not to be seen as Parsis. Most take solace in the emotional cocoon that a baug or a colony provides. We create little fortresses of xenophobia, a morbid dislike of strangers. Others adopt the ostrich approach of digging their head into sand and pretending that all is cosy and secure.

The deteriorating mental health is reflected in increasing stridency and cantankerousness in public affairs [Bombay Parsi Punchayet (BPP) trustees washing dirty linen in the media and the courts]; hotly contested cases in the Parsi matrimonial court (even amongst couples in their late 60s); inability to tolerate any dissent or a different viewpoint (bitter fights over petty issues like whether to allow advertisers to shoot in colony precincts); occasional outbursts of violent behavior with *methipaak* (beating) administered to liberals and other heretic scum (roughing up of the Russian *navar*-aspirant at Sanjan and rearranging the furniture in the BPP boardroom); a burning desire to excommunicate (banning of priests, and crores of public funds lost in defending the ban); an obstinate refusal to reform or innovate in a fast changing situation.

In the 1960s, many Bollywood films depicted the ubiquitous '*bawaji*' (dressed in a *dugla* and *pugree*) to evoke a few good natured laughs. In the '70s, Hrishikesh Mukherjee's comedy *Khatta Mitha*, sweetly cherished the community. The tone suddenly changed in the '80s and we had films like Pestonjee, depicting, though with empathy, the sadness, loneliness and isolation of a micro community. Later, Percy, on a similar disturbing theme of being trapped in a time zone. More recently Being Cyrus and Little Zizou; on the surface, light-heartedly lampooning our idiosyncrasies but also highlighting the creeping sadness of a dying community.

Many will disagree. What about our infectious laughter, our gregarious spirits, our joie de vivre, being the soul of the party, our sense of humor, our compassionate charity? they ask. Aren't these evidence of our mental robustness? We have always enjoyed juicy and salacious details in the Parsi matrimonial court [some senior citizens spend their entire day there along with their *bhona no dabbo* (lunch box)].

Life would be too drab without a dash of Parsi madness. A screw may be loose here or there but we are not about to knock collectively on the doors of a lunatic asylum. We are not even bothered that we are a dying community. Why worry when you won't even be there? Let us all laugh uproariously on our way to the solar crematoria. The sane are often sadder than the mad.

Sedate, sober and classy

The taste of the community in jewelry remains impeccable

The ships, owned by the Parsi merchant princes, laden with opium and spices, sailed to China. They returned with silk and bamboos and South Sea pearls. The world's most valuable natural pearls were near round or baroque. Silky silver or champagne in color, sometimes with deep golden tones. They soon adorned aristocratic necks from the first families - Petits, Jejeebhoys, Wadias and Camas. In family portraits, these pearls enhanced the effect of the purple Chinese gara, with its thick flowery hems. The penniless refugees from Persia had at last come into their own, and heirlooms were slowly being built.

Soon Burmese rubies became hot favorites with the Parsi rich. Even today, the most expensive gem per carat, the best of these rubies were 'pigeon blood' red in color and had a strong fluorescence. After the Great Mutiny of 1857 had been quelled and the British grip firmly established over India, nomadic groups from Burma were able to travel as far as Surat to sell these rubies. Wrapped unceremoniously in small pieces of muslin cloth, housewives in the dusty lanes of Navsari would haggle for a pair of larger rubies for making earrings, and half a dozen smaller ones, to be embedded in gold bangles to be worn at weddings and festive occasions. There were no certificates from gem councils and assurance labs; cheating was still absent from the world's DNA. There were no discussions on cut, color and clarity. Eye contact between the purchaser and seller established trust and made way for repeated purchases over the years. Though, at times, spinel, another semiprecious red gemstone, was mistaken for ruby.

Red was an auspicious color for the Parsis, like the red *tilo* (mark) on the forehead to signify married status and to conceal the third eye from unwanted male gaze. Upon widowhood, the ruby encrusted bracelet would be preserved for the daughter or daughter-in-law; a plain vanilla gemless, solitary gold bangle replacing it, until death. Belief in astrology was then all pervading. The planetary configuration in your horoscope determined whether you could wear a particular gem or not. The family jeweler, though not himself an astrologer, confidently advised on the suitability of a gem. It was considered (even now, in most families) perilous to wear the blue sapphire (*neelam*) without ascertaining the position of the natural malefic, Saturn, in your birth chart. Parsis recounted tales of the *neelam* making or breaking fortunes. Its cousin, the yellow sapphire (*pukhraj*) associated with the benefic, Jupiter, was regarded as somewhat benign. Burmese vendors also sold these yellow sapphires to Parsis in Gujarat and Bombay.

Our grandmother purchased one, sometime before the First World War (1914-1919) in Navsari, and our father wore it in a gold ring on his first index finger until his death in 1975. It lay hidden for decades in the cupboard until, upon a whim, we decided to wear it; with some spectacular results. After more than a 100 years, this octagonal shaped gem looks as if it was bought yesterday. Seasoned jewelers have looked at it with awe and proclaimed their inability to obtain such a yellow sapphire for love or money. The gemstone touches the nerve ends on your index figure. It is supposed to absorb beneficial vibrations from its ruling planet and transmit, via those nerve ends, into your system. Dismiss it as unscientific claptrap or enjoy the feeling of enhanced protection. The choice is yours.

Along with rubies, Parsis loved emeralds. Wise old ladies visited the family jeweler in early afternoons to ensure maximum sunlight under which their eagle eyes would examine the pure verdant green hue and transparency of the emerald. Those days, emeralds were not 'treated', like now, and its many faults, called inclusions, were visible to the naked eye of these astute Parsi purchasers. Middle-class households invested in tiny emeralds and rubies for bracelets and bangles; the wealthy flaunted the larger gem, like a dozen green flashers on a very fair neck, as a sign that they had truly arrived. At weddings, envious ladies were transfixed by this green power. In the later years, some Parsi business families (more of the Johnny-come-lately type) purchased emerald jewelry from distressed royals, after the privy pur*ses* and privileges of the latter had been abolished by Indira Gandhi.

Diamonds were a relatively late entrant. Though, after Independence in 1947, jewelers like K. Wadia, who specialized in diamonds, prominently figured in *Jamé* and *Kaiser*, and were patronized not only by the Parsis, for their qualities of trust and integrity. Like the sapphire twins, and unlike the benign pearls, rubies and emeralds, diamonds too were blamed for many a misfortune descending upon some of the acquirers.

On Dhanteras (two days before Diwali, when the goddess of wealth, Mahalaxmi, is worshipped), the senior of the Parsi household would ask all members to deposit their ornaments of daily use, which would then be washed with rose petalled milk and prayed upon. This ritual is followed even today in traditional Parsi households. On Dassera and Diwali, Parsi ladies bought gold guineas (coins of one quarter ounce of gold minted in the then home country, Great Britain, from 1663 to 1814) including half and quarter guineas. Queen Victoria and George V guineas are still available in large quantities with most Parsi households. On the birth of a child, or at an engagement ceremony or navjote, these guineas are gifted in tiny red pouches.

The Parsi taste in jewelry has always been conservative, sedate and sober. Fingers flashing five carat solitaires are looked down upon, so are Parsi men looking like Goldfinger (there is this not so apocryphal story about a certain gentleman from Cusrow Baug, who rose from rags to riches, often shouting to his wife to throw from the window his gold cufflinks and gold rings, which he had 'forgotten' to wear to office). Seldom will you see Parsi families in over-glitzy jewelry shops poring over gold and diamonds. Even today, they patronize nondescript shops of old jewelers who conjure exquisite designs, and it is sacrilege to even ask if the jeweler is sure of his carats, quality and price. In the Parsi consciousness, it is the ultimate crime to be a jewelry exhibitionist. Carry those South Sea pearls in a sedate necklace gracefully; wear that hundred-year-old ruby encrusted bracelet daintily; and put on an old emerald (not too large) ring denoting class. Like a delicate swan with a light pink ribbon, not a gold crusted shining hippopotamus.

Wearing exquisite jewelry: (From l-r): Sakarbai Bolton and Parsi Lady in Blue Sari, from Parzor's Everlasting Flame exhibition

Large hearts and small minds

Our attitude and approach towards charity is warped

To the world, a poor Parsi is a misnomer. Such giant charities - land and cash - are surely adequate to ensure that no member of this minuscule minority suffers from any want. There is a disconnect between this external perception and the ground reality. Parsi farmers in far-flung villages of Gujarat, in debt and penury; the old and the indigent not being able to afford healthcare; the long retired who have run out of savings but are too self-respecting to seek help; widows in sanatoria making do with a single meal; those living under leaking roofs and fear of a house collapse. The largesse is not reaching all of the deserving. Of course, there are poor Parsis; and each one of us should be ashamed.

Parsi pioneering merchant princes were magnanimous and munificent. Their great desire to do charity arose mostly out of compassion towards poor relatives and comrades whom they had surpassed manifold. Also maybe to salve their conscience for selling opium to the Chinese. Decades later, a dowager, in a moment of pique against her interfaith marrying children, transferred the ownership of the housing colonies dotting Bombay to the trustees of the Bombay Parsi Punchayet. Survey the mega charities of Bombay and find an astonishing percentage having been created by Parsis, quite a few for secular user too. Hospitals, with exclusive ones for pregnant women, children and animals, orphanages and girls schools, art and architecture colleges, the racecourse, convalescent homes for the old and infirm, morgues and dispensaries. Parsi charity is the stuff of legend. In the last hundred years, new charity, mostly from overseas, has continued to flow. These donors, however, would not be pleased with the state of affairs today.

The fault lies not only with the charity managers but also with the approach and attitude of the beneficiaries: "Our hospital is being sold to a Muslim business group." "Money is exchanged under the table for allotment of flats." "A builder is being allowed to encroach upon the *Doongerwadi* land." Each of these statements is alarmist and false. However, many are ready to believe and spread the word. Factionalism is rife in virtually every large charity. These factions love to denigrate each other by encouraging whisper campaigns. This deters the competent and the honest from becoming trustees unless they are thick-skinned. Without credible evidence, it is unpardonable to allege lack of integrity. An idiot is not necessarily dishonest.

Most of us have been conditioned to believe that charity is our birthright. Even when we have prospered, we continue to avail of charity. Perhaps it is too much to expect those who have done well later to voluntarily surrender their charity residence. However, it is distressing that many who have moved out or migrated, keep their hou*ses* locked and unused. Crores are lost in litigation and some even enjoy a post lunch visit to the court like a digestive. If all behaved honorably, not a single Parsi will be on the waiting list for housing. Warring trustees obtain frivolous stay orders on super technical grounds so that scores can be settled and artificial shortages keep the electorate beholden to the bestower of favors. A Sicilian approach to charity.

The average age of trustees in many large trusts hovers near 70. Often a single trustee rules the roost and others follow. And they bicker and snigger. Emotional intelligence, a must for charity management, is poor. Add to this cocktail called gerontocracy, the ingredients of crass stupidity, prickly egos and a six-inch vision. Contrary to popular belief in baug circuits, there is hardly any corruption any longer, but there is oodles of favoritism, bias and mismanagement. Several beneficiaries are ill informed, selfish and undeserving. Undoubtedly, matters have improved in the last 50 years; but not commensurate, considering the resources of the community. Of course, there are beacons of hope like Dinshaw and Bachi Tamboly, wiping many a tear from the poorest in the hamlets of Gujarat in a highly organized and scientific manner.

Considering that we have no reservations in colleges, the assistance provided to students, even from cash rich charities, is inadequate. We forget that there are huge resources for the benefit of the fast shrinking few. Educational help is obviously the most vital for the future of the community. Being miserly with other people's largesse makes for a bad trustee. There are exceptions, of course, like the A. H. Wadia Charities, which sanction liberally once a cause is identified. The mindset generally is to provide assistance, much below the legitimate requirement.

Coordination between Parsi charities is non existent. Decades ago, the Liaison Committee was formed, some of whose members reportedly arrogated to themselves the right to barge into poor homes and examine the food cooked ("You are able to afford to eat mutton and yet you have applied for help? Shameful!"). Shameful, indeed. A few beneficiaries continue to abuse the system to seek help from multiple trusts.

Several charities distribute hampers, during Navroz, containing mostly food items. Many recipients are delighted to taste butter and cheese after a long time. Some community organizations distribute monthly ration to the poor which is the survival kit for many Parsi families. It is healthy to feel guilty about these folks the next time you wallop on lobster thermidor.

Facility for the community elders in Navsari

Is Gujarati no longer our mother tongue?

Parsi Gujarati may become extinct much before the Parsis themselves

If you were a non Gujarati speaking student at the venerable Bharda New High School in the 1960s, there was a reasonable probability that you were unable to follow what was happening, at least during a quarter of the time. Retirement age was an alien concept and Parsi teachers in their sixties and seventies lapsed into Gujarati every second sentence. Trying to explain an equation, x=y=z, a math teacher called Mr Khori used to say, "*Maathoo dholiya ni aai bajoo muko, ké péli bajoo muko, gaan to vacchej aavani* (whether you put your head on one side of the bed or the other, the arse will remain in the middle)." Gujarati and Bohri pupils could comprehend the proceedings, save some hard core Parsi Gujarati. Scant regard was paid to the English medium of instruction, as most teachers, who also taught in the Gujarati medium, often forgot which class they were addressing. The stray Maharashtrian or Sikh or South Indian child could have as well been in a school on Mars. Almost all Parsi pupils belonged to the lower and middle classes and Gujarati alone was spoken at home. Parsi Gujarati, of course, was adored by the Gujaratis and Bohris as sweet sounding. The same story it was, with all Parsi managed and owned schools like Sir Jamsetjee Jejeebhoy and Byramjee Jeejeebhoy and Master Tutorial; and to a somewhat lesser extent with Bai Gamadia and Bai Bengalee.

Barring the initial migrants into Bombay — Petits, Jeejibhoys, Wadias and Camas — the nucleus of the fast Anglicized Parsi aristocracy, most later migrants from Gujarat thought, fought, swore, exclaimed in fear after a nightmare, all in Gujarati. You do all this only in your mother tongue. Many of these first generation migrants were schooled in Gujarati and fluently wrote, or at least read, the language. *Jamé* (then a daily) and *Mumbai Samachar* were read by most Parsis. An English prayer book in an *agiary* was a rarity, as almost all could read Gujarati. Even the rich Anglophiles were comfortable conversing in Gujarati. Most *mobeds* barely understood a few English words and *behdins* instructed them in Gujarati. The original side of the Bar at the Bombay High Court was dominated by Parsis and Gujaratis; and too bad if you did not follow the language. The political correctness of apologizing for an accidental lapse into Gujarati had not then arrived. Same was the story with the Bombay Stock Exchange and the then thriving Parsee General and Masina hospitals and the consulting rooms of eminent Parsi doctors. Most Parsis spoke atrocious Hindi with a much lampooned accent, except the late Parvez Katrak who enthralled Hindi speaking audiences with his mellifluous rendition of Kabir's dohas. But nearly all Parsis then spoke decent Gujarati, and most managed to praise the *ganga*'s (domestic help's) good work in faltering Marathi.

A micro minority spoke what was somewhat derisively termed as *shuddha* (pure) Gujarati. Strangely, these *shuddha* speakers would seamlessly switch over to the Parsi dialect, depending upon the listeners and the occasion. Our father, as editor of *The Bombay Samachar*, would converse with his colleagues in pristine Gujarati, and joke with his brother-in-law at home in Parsi Gujarati. We ourselves acquired this ability without any effort. The *Jamé* and *Kaiser* used Gujarati which was a mix of the pure and the Parsi version. Novelettes, serialized by both these newspapers were written by Parsi amateurs (Piroj Mau and Aloo Rusi Dodhi were quite prolific), avoiding bombastic Gujarati words, beyond the comprehension of the lay Parsi reader.

About four decades ago, the decline of Parsi Gujarati began in Bombay. Marathi replaced Gujarati as the second language in schools. Parents conversed increasingly in English with their children. The *Jamé* ceased to be a Gujarati daily and turned into an English weekly. The *Kaiser-e-Hind*, like its namesake, disappeared. *Khordeh Avesta* copies in English proliferated. Parsis began to think, fight and exclaim after a nightmare, in English; the only exception was that Parsis continued to swear in Gujarati, at the dogged insistence of the Dadar Parsi Colony ("Where is that f_____ newspaper?" simply does not sound as sweet as "Where is that *madar*_____ newspaper?"). In the High Court, now

He's a part-time umpire too

Wicket puree guyee
Wicket fell
Died

Illustration by Hemant Morparia
Reprinted with permission from Parsi Bol

hardly anyone lap*ses* into the native tongue. *Mobed*s receive service orders for *afringaan, farokhshi* and *baaj* (different rituals) online in English. The modern practising *mobed* is comfortable, if not fluent, in English. Just the other day, we heard a pallbearer at the *Doongerwadi* grumble to another, "The body was too heavy, boss." Unlike the olden days, nur*ses* and junior doctors at the Parsee General give a blank look if the attendant to the patient says that "*évan né chhati ma bahuj dookhéch* (he has severe chest pain)."

As for the Bharda New High School, not a single teacher and not a single of its 1,500 students is a Parsi. *Su dahra aayach* (and we won't translate this one)!

Gall in the family

We fight our relatives with vigor and venom

If we may be pardoned an unscientific generalization, Parsis fight with their relatives - spou*ses* and siblings, parents and progeny, aunts, uncles and cousins - more than members of other communities. While money and marriage are the major reasons, allergy, eccentricity and simple dislike also lead to courts and police stations. The orphan Mako, who lost both his parents when the state transport bus to Valsad overturned, was brought up by his spinster *maasi* (maternal aunt) who doted on her rather healthy ward. *Maasi* was secretly overjoyed at his resolve never to contemplate matrimony until she discovered him with the maid in their tiny bathroom. His decent wages, as a booking clerk with Air India those days, bankrolled *maasi's* house and put him in a commanding position. Mako did not permit *maasi* to terminate the domestic's services thereby threatening *maasi's* dominance.

Great affection was soon replaced by great hostility as aunt and nephew declared war. The dining table was agreed to be divided into two equal parts demarcated by a rope. *Maasi* would send Mako's *doodh ni tapeli* (utensil holding milk) flying off the table if it dared to trespass upon her section. In retaliation, the nephew would lock her in the bathroom, the original battle ground, and leave the house. They routinely filed criminal complaints against each other, and one Friday night the harassed sub inspector locked both up for two nights until Mako, who had a phobia about lizards, fainted in the lock-up.

In the very early days of our impoverished legal practice we foolishly agreed to mediate between two middle-aged sisters staying together in Cusrow Baug, both spinsters of course, and both working for the same bank. Their exotically wild allegations and counter allegations would have made Harold Robbins blush, and even 35 years later, publication of their allegations would be deemed obscene. Neither would let us recuse from the mediation and taught us the virtue of infinite patience. Years later, one of them sent us half-a-dozen Lookmanji's *malai na khaja* (a fresh cream filled philo sweetmeat), with a note saying that our services as the mediator were no longer required, as her sister had died the previous evening.

Jury box at the Bombay High Court
Illustration by Manjula Padmanabhan

Like Westerners, Parsis believe that divorce at any age is acceptable. After decades of unpeaceful coexistence, Parsis sue their spouses for divorce before the matrimonial division of the Bombay High Court aided by the so-called delegates of the "jury system." Most of these geriatric delegates cut a sorry picture before an audience of regulars who come armed with a *bhona no dabbo* (tiffin box) to be devoured in the recess after enjoying the salacious details of matrimonial lives made public. The Parsi Marriage and Divorce Act does not recognize irretrievable breakdown as a ground for divorce. Many cussedly do not agree to divorce by mutual consent to prevent the spouse from remarrying, which results in contested cases lasting for years. Those who have been married long, take longer to divorce. Often the non-Parsi judge hides his exasperation with the litigants, exacerbated by inane comments from the delegates, behind a polite countenance, out of deference to the collective goodwill for the eccentric community.

Shapurji, a gentleman at large, who spent his life between the courts and Ripon Club, refused to settle a dispute with his cousins regarding some old furniture worth Rs 17,000, and thought it very unsporting of his cousins who refused to appear in court, thereby denying Shapurji the pleasure of a contest. He gladly paid his solicitor's bill for Rs 70,000. We recall his quaint little solicitor, in his late 80s, taking a goodly 30 minutes to finish the arduous journey from his easy chair at the Ripon to the washroom, and ambling back.

We were also privy to an acrimonious dispute between three Parsi Irani brothers in the bakery business. Every morning, they baked fresh bread and also fresh disputes, mostly banal. The eldest, who suffered from Parkinson's disease, insisted that we reduce our fees and that he would soon "please" us. Our doorbell rang at 5.30 in the morning, and there was our client with a huge walnut cake, shaking violently, for our gustatory pleasure. His middle brother, who had an uncanny resemblance to the hero of *Taras Bulba*, applied ginger paste on his sweating bald pate to keep it cool and saunter into the High Court, setting a hundred noses twitching. The youngest brother complained to us that our client's wife was so jealous of his wife that when the latter had her hysterectomy performed by a noted obstetrician, the former too went to the good doctor with a request that he perform her hysterectomy too.

In the Parsi DNA, there is an as yet unidentified litigation gene which is transmitted from one generation to the next. For these families, filing a suit is as common as having breakfast. Consent terms are for cowards; settlements are for sissies. Parsi ladies and gentlemen of leisure litigate for sheer pleasure. In their unending quest for justice they care not if their opponents are their own blood. Mako died prematurely before his *maasi* who sobbed every day and honored her errant nephew's memory by refusing to untie the rope which divided their dining table, after dismissing the offending maid.

The early libertarians

Like semi ripe mangoes, the sweet sour tales of Navsari are worth savoring

A 100 years ago, Navsari (a town in Western Gujarat) was pristine pure Parsi. Though orthodox and proper (an interfaith marriage, even 50 years ago, was as sensational as a bank dacoity), its many *mohollas* (localities), also called *vads* (streets) housed some of the most colorful and vibrant characters. Mumbai (yes, much before Balasaheb Thackeray, they referred to it as Mumbai, not Bombay) was a different planet - its inhabitants might be richer and cleverer, but were not to be envied. Some of these tales may sound fictional but we can swear on our sudreh and affirm that they are true to the smallest detail.

Desai Vad, the *moholla* in which our ancestors were born and died, was quite a stuffy place. Revenue officials and rent collectors for the Gaikwads of Baroda (who also ruled Navsari), they relinquished their original surname - Seervai - for the governmental position they enjoyed. Until 50 years ago, the order of protocol in Navsari gave a pride of place, at weddings and other formal socioreligious functions, to the Vada Dasturji from the venerable Meherjirana family; and thereafter to the Vada Desaiji (not a hereditary position, but appointed by consensus) from the first of the three Desai family branches - pompously called "*Sarkaar*" - its most illustrious member, Khurshedji Desai, having built the Navsari *Atash behram*. So the Desais had more than a bee in their bonnet (something like: "I am Lord Nathaniel Curzon; a very superior person"). In this conservative ghetto of Desai Vad there resided a bachelor popularly called Muncherji *Derki* (meaning a small female frog). Derki must have been well provided for, since he did not work a single day of his long life. Every morning, immaculately dressed in starched dagli and *pugree* (Parsi coat and cap), he would saunter to the Navsari railway station and board the train to Surat, an hour's journey, in the second class (in those days, trains had three clas*ses*). Alighting at the Surat station, he would walk in measured steps to a tiny shop and have his shoes polished. The man would lavishly spread the Cherry Blossom black boot polish from a small round tin having a picture of a grinning monkey. Shoes shining, *Derki* boarded the next available train to Navsari. He followed this routine religiously for over three decades. However, *Derki* does not find pride of place in this column for this eccentricity. As soon as he would enter his spacious Navsari house, where he stayed alone, he would discard all his clothes. Even during the freezing Navsari winters, Derki never wore a garment inside his house and was not too fussy about using curtains or closing the many windows through which generations of children returning from school would peep at this first authentic Parsi nudist. The despairing Desai elders could not do much about *Derki* who was otherwise an exemplary neighbor and a thorough gentleman. Our father told us the reason why he had been christened *Derki*, but that cannot be shared.

In those days - and on a much lesser scale even today - ladies supplemented their income by weaving kustis. Many a kitchen fire was fuelled on the strength of making kustis and selling them to

Zoroastrians all over the world. Rusi, a bachelor residing in Baria Vad, hit upon the brilliant idea of getting non-Parsi ladies serving as domestics in Parsi households to weave kustis. Like a mini cottage industry, half a dozen of these chattering ladies produced kustis faster than their Parsi counterparts, without much regard to the religious *tarikats* (observances) to be followed. Rusi sold these kustis at a massive discount, disrupting the market. A delegation of enraged Parsi ladies (which included one of our grandmothers) knocked on Rusi's door to admonish him. After much shouting, Rusi held the door slightly ajar and told the shocked ladies that there was nothing illegal or irreligious in non-Parsi ladies weaving the kusti. (Had he done this today, like the Russian *navar* aspirant in Sanjan, he would have been given a severe drubbing.) Thereupon, one of the ladies demanded that Rusi permit them to enter his house and discuss the matter. Rusi simply replied: "I am a devout Zoroastrian and always wear my sudreh and kusti; but that is all I am wearing now." The delegation dispersed in disgust. This episode occurred before World War I, which makes Rusi a man ahead of his times.

Another outstanding character was a gentleman named Vakil, a sort of mofussil lawyer; suave, sweet and a bit of a smoothie. His principal client was a rich Parsi widow many years his senior, and the Navsari grapevine had it that their relationship was not only that of lawyer and client. Vakil soon lost interest in his ageing client, who consequently accused him of stealing a Chinese lamp. The charge was found to be baseless and Vakil counter-sued for defamation. The great Sir Pherozeshah Mehta would come down from Bombay, along with a large pot containing drinking water (a sensible precaution) and stay in a bungalow called "*Dhadaka no bungalow*" at Lunsikui. Mehta appeared pro bono for Vakil and, of course, won the case. Within weeks of the judgment Vakil had reconciled with his old client, but the "Lamp Case," as it came to be known, provided much salacious gossip in the dusty by-lanes of Navsari.

Prudish looking towns have their little secrets too. This is borne out by the story of a lady (long deceased) whom we shall call Dina, a

very young widow and then a very young grandmother at 46. She resided with her mother in a two-storeyed house, typical in Navsari *moholla*s. One of our cousins, her neighbor, then a child of eight, was very fond of Dina Aunty who would always treat him to some delicacy or the other prepared by her mother. During summer vacations, Dina would require the child to "guard" the house, as she would retire

A Parsi vad in Navsari

to the second floor to take tabla lessons from a youngish Gujarati 'master,' as he was called. Dina and the tabla master would descend from the second floor, ostensibly enthralled by their musical sojourn, and reward their little guard with a *paavli* (a 25 paise coin, enough to buy snacks plus a Kolah ice-cream). One day, our little cousin asked Dina Aunty why he could hear the tabla being played for only the first 15 minutes. Without losing her composure, the witty Dina replied that Masterji first physically demonstrated a tabla lesson and the rest of the time was spent by lecturing her on the nuances of the *raga, laya* and *taal*. When Osho (then known as Bhagwan Shree Rajneesh) first came on the scene, Dina became one of his disciples in Navsari.

And the final tale, is quite touching. A certain Ms P, then young and attractive and known for her Bohemian lifestyle, befriended a much older gentleman of great wealth - Mr K, who was married. The pair met at K's sprawling residence in the unbearably hot Navsari afternoons. One such afternoon, K suffered a massive heart attack - a classic case of too much passion. Ms P had every reason to dress up quickly and slink away from the back door (every Navsari home has one, called *paachhlubaar*). She did not. Instead, she ran out screaming for someone to save her beloved K's life, as shocked neighbors gawked at her clothes-

Kusti-weaving, a source of income

less form. Alas, K perished. However, for years after that, most men silently admired the integrity of this daring lady, whilst dunking large *batasa* biscuits in glasses containing milky mint tea.

Bawas don't seem to die

Is longevity a curse on the community?

*B*awa, *aay ummaré bhi golat marvanu nai chuké* (even at this age, father gladly has a roll in the haystack)," says a 48-year-old son for his 72-year-old father's libido, with unabashed admiration. There is much merriment in an old age home in Navsari at the wedding of a toothless octogenarian to his well-preserved co-resident in her late 60s; with the newly weds making a valiant effort not to let their alliance remain purely platonic. A 90-year-old matriarch who has lost her only son never mis*ses* her two Parsi pegs of whiskey before dinner. A group of 70 somethings plan an excursion to oxygen starved Leh. Grandfathers share a bawdy joke with their grandsons without the slightest inhibition. A 68-year-old lady with oodles of bad cholesterol polishes off a dozen oysters at a fancy Parsi wedding party at a five star (Hilla *masi é étla* oyster *afaari kaarya ké,* hotel *ma thi siddha* hospital *ma gaya*). Bristling joie de vivre, irascible sense of humor, an unending zest for life and a 'who bothers about wrinkles' existence.

Languishing in the chronic ward of a charity hospital with painful bed sores, as water mattres*ses* are too expensive. Elderly suffering from a disproportionately large number of Parkinson's and Alzheimer's. Old spinsters glumly staring outside the window at dusk in an increasingly alien environment. Childless couples barely managing their infirmities and humiliation. Depleting savings and unwise investments compelling the old to survive with only one meal and often without critical medicine, being too self respecting to seek charity help. Gnawing loneliness, arthritic aches and pains, enduring adult diapers and other geriatric indignities in silence; the rising sun brings no joy but frustration, at having failed once again to pass away in sleep. The body and mind seek deliverance from physical and emotional pain.

Which of the above two scenarios best describes the state of our elderly, one of the few ethnic groups in the world to have 30% of its members above the age of 60. Amongst fellow communities in India, the highest longevity rate. Bawajis don't seem to die, goes the wonderment. Is longevity a curse on the community?

Relative economic prosperity coupled with Western mores results in children living independently from their parents even if the house is large enough to accommodate. Joint families simply don't exist. Large numbers migrate leaving their parents behind. Severe winters don't go well with congenital disea*ses*, better to endure loneliness in a warmer clime. Decades of marrying first cousins have resulted in disproportionately high incidence of neuroticism, rheumatic disorders and cancer. Loneliness is a slow poison. Dementia makes fools of those who once strode proudly on the national stage. There is no fool like an old fool.

Old age homes have not been popular. Most Parsis value privacy more than camaraderie and prefer to stay alone in large dark hou*ses* with unswept bedrooms; grandfather clocks chiming every quarter hour, often out of synchrocity due to bad maintenance. You can smell sadness in these hou*ses*. Frequently cheated by dishonest relatives and caretakers, they become paranoid and suspicious of all.

Fear of a fall and a fracture deters them from venturing outside. Old ladies praying in the evening from the *Khordeh Avesta*, repeating the same para a dozen times due to forgetfulness; old gentlemen downing half a glass of cough syrup as they can no longer afford their evening drink; waking up with anxiety attacks in the middle of the night with none to soothe them back to sleep; staring blankly at their visiting children whom they no longer recognize. Blessed are those few old who enjoy the warmth and company of their loved ones. Little great-granddaughters fascinated by the wrinkled fingers of their great-grandpa and nonagenarians striding proudly with a walking stick in the park are fast diminishing images.

We do seem to focus on our youth but we appear to be indifferent to our elders. Diseased minds and bodies do make them irritable, unreasonable and crotchety. But nevertheless they have to be cared for and loved. Only supporting them monetarily is not enough. How many times do we make them laugh or celebrate their birthdays, however unwelcome to them, and how many times do we discuss newspaper headlines with them or feast together on nostalgia by taking them through pleasant memories of the yesteryears or pamper them by putting a chocolate or a date in their toothless mouths? A very popular Gujarati song titled *Bhoolo bhalé biju badhu, ma baap né bhoolso nahin,*(you may ignore all else, but never your parents) contains a memorable couplet: *lakho kamaata ho bhalé, ma baap jéthi na tharya, é lakh nahin pun raakh chhé, é manvoo bhoolso nahin* (you may be earning lakhs but if you cannot keep your parents happy, those lakhs are worthless ash). A dying community with great financial resources must invest in its youth and ensconce its old.

Parsi Ward at JJ Hospital

Domestics help

Dissecting the symbiotic relationship between the maid and her Parsi master

Parsi men make benign masters of the household. Most maids will concur. The lady of the house may sound a trifle shrill and crochety and demanding and irritating; but the gentleman has a twinkle in his eye and a helpless look which seems to suggest that he is constantly transposing the roles of his wife and the maid. Not that the lady is unaware of her husband's intentions but she would rather turn a blind eye, so long as the line is not unduly transgressed.

Decades ago, we had visited the K. N. Bahadurji Parsi Sanatorium in Deolali (where in the early part of the last century, terminally ill tuberculosis patients convalesced, awaiting certain death after having their ribs cut by the surgeon). Though well kept, its environs appeared gloomy, at dusk; its old English style cottages retaining the smell of many deaths. The heaviness was dissipated by a small girl, barely seven, skipping outside the servants' quarters. Extremely fair complexioned with fine features, she was a picture in contrast to her dusky mother, working in the Sanatorium as a maid. Her father was a Parsi, the mother volunteered. "My daughter has inherited her color from him." This little girl's enchanting smile is still embedded in our consciousness.

Parsi farmers in the villages of Gujarat routinely forged alliances with their domestic help who bore their children. Today, they would perhaps be regarded as common law wives. There was nothing clandestine about these relationships. Gandhian social worker, Burjorji Bharucha with renegade priest, Dastur Framroze Bode performed mass navjotes of these children ('the Vansda Navjotes'), which, as one would expect, created an uproar. In the decades that followed, stigma soon attached to such relationships. As a result they went underground. One such employer had his appointment as the Vada Desaiji (who sat next to the Vada Dasturji till 1980s) of Navsari nixed, due to his being spotted exiting from the hut of his longtime help. He was not too bitter about missing the cold adornment at funerals and weddings and continued to enjoy the warmth of the pulsating hut.

At times, the domestics are an oasis of affection for henpecked Parsi husbands. Anecdotally speaking, it is wrong to presume that this so-called affection is induced by monetary consideration alone. Quite often, the attraction is mutual. Harassed by a chauvinist husband, the maid finds succor in her kind and compassionate Parsi employer.

At the risk of being baked in an oven, we must make bold to state that quite a few Parsi men find their Parsi wives rather aggressive and nitpicking. In contrast, the hardworking and docile maid appears to be more optimal spouse material from every perspective. On the other hand, as the Fiddler on the Roof would put it, Parsi ladies are simply unable to fathom as to how their husbands could condescend to be interested in the working class, which unlike them, are not talcum powdered or Eau de Cologned. Will you take your maid to a Zubin Mehta concert or treat her to a romantic dinner at Wasabi? Lust must be the sole motivating factor, these matrons conclude. More often than not, they are wrong. In most compassionate Parsi men, genuine affection ari*ses* for the lady who silently serves them, without any weekly break, come rain or sunshine. Silently, being the key word.

We do know of some Parsi men who had the courage of their conviction and married their onetime domestic help. Almost without exception, such marriages have been successful. Society initially frowns, and in due course, forgets and accepts. Such wives are often wary of themselves engaging any domestic help.

One of our acquaintances, who passed away recently, widowed early and was thereafter for a period of 30 years, cared for by his domestic help, also a young childless widow. The bonding between them was touching. He left his entire estate, under his will, to her, much to the chagrin of his enraged nephews and nieces. In his last years, he sought our counsel whether he should marry her. He did not follow our advice.

While tales of this symbiotic relationship between master and maid abound, it would be appropriate to mention a young seafaring lad who fell in love with his comely cleaning lady. In a moment of indiscretion, the master and maid forgot to lock the bathroom door; and they were rudely interrupted by his stentorian grandmother who said that she was surprised. (If the lad had heard of the similar predicament of the famous lexicographer, Dr Webster, he would have replied, "No, *Mamaiji*, you are astonished. It is we who were surprised.")

Finally, there was a legend in the by-lanes of Mahim (whom we shall simply call 'M') who, clad in sudreh and lungi, would whistle early in the morning from his terrace to maids proceeding to work. M was a handsome rascal, whom AIDS claimed young after ensnaring many a maid, for love and not money.

Lust may trigger a dalliance, but it often turns into genuine affection, if not exactly love, effortlessly transcending the barriers of caste, race, class and religion. The ugly exploitative element is mostly absent; with the domestic relishing the attention showered upon her by that sweetheart of a bawaji.

The maid is often depicted in nataks as easy prey

Worshipping mummy

Most Parsi mothers seem to have mamma's boys

They come in all shapes and sizes. Mamma's boys. Effeminate or macho, heterosexual or gay, married or bachelor, youthful or grey haired, wealthy or poor, orthodox or liberal, learned or lumpen. The number of Parsi men who are excessively attached to their mothers is startlingly large. According to Sigmund Freud, the Oedipus complex denotes a son's latent desire to have sexual relations with the maternal parent. However, a child who subsequently identifies with the same sex parent successfully resolves this complex. If this identification fails, the boy remains a lifelong mamma's boy. Unlike the BBC teleserial, "Some Mothers Do 'Ave 'Em," most Parsi mothers seem to have them.

Here is a do-it-yourself test for determining if you are one. You are 60 but still call your mother 'Mummy' (with an unusual emphasis on the double 'm's). Your mother decides when you should have a haircut. You have rejected an extremely attractive matrimonial proposal because your mother will not approve of your wife-to-be.

Though you reside in California, you connect with your mother on FaceTime twice every day (and your mother wears a wrist watch in India showing West Coast time). If it was not for Dr Rusi Soonawalla's professional fees, your mother would have readily believed that your birth was a case of immaculate conception. You sheepishly smile when your mother criticizes the excessively long length of your *sudreh* and the excessively short length of your *lengha*, although only the two of you reside in the house. Even though you are an agnostic, you visit the *agiary* every month on your mother's *roz*, 10 years after her passing into the Great Beyond. If you are terribly affronted by this quiz. Two or more affirmative answers make you a Mamma's boy.

We must, of course, confess to our own idiosyncrasies. A few years ago, we had this morbid fear as to who would cut fruits (particularly, mangoes), at breakfast, as neatly and daintily as our mother, then approaching 90. Our fears were dissipated due to the skills in fruit cutting fortunately imbibed by our little maid, functioning under the old lady's eagle eye. Again, we gladly sacrifice a crucial board meeting in order to have lunch with Mummy on our *roz* birthday.

Then there is this bachelor friend of ours who celebrated his 40th birthday in an exotic location abroad with a select band of friends, and his beloved Mumma. One evening, the merry group amused themselves by blindfolding and one had to guess the identity of the individual touching you. Mumma touched our blindfolded friend lightly on his lips. He instantly said, "Of course, this has to be you, Mumma!"

We must exclude from the list of mamma's boys those Parsis who are deferential to their mothers only in order to grab some property or inheritance. Every time mamma visits the family solicitor to discuss her fifth codicil to her ninth will, these Parsis have sleepless nights. They are imposters. A true mamma's boy is one who worships his mother with unadulterated love and devotion. We have seen the most dispassionate and calm Parsi gentlemen go ballistic if anyone even slightly berates their mother's record in public or social life. Machiavelli, a 16th century political pragmatist, had observed that men are more willing to forgive the murder of their father than the confiscation of their patrimony (inherited property from father). If Machiavelli had been a Parsi, he would have perhaps said that Parsi men are more willing to forgive any insult or injury, however severe but will not tolerate the slightest slur on the Mummy Goddess.

Decades ago, there was a Parsi conman who was called PM, who, apart from carrying out minor capers like credit card frauds, was a serial fantasizer. He amused his circle of friends which included many Parsi senior judges and senior lawyers of today. He published a compendium of articles titled "Zoroaster was the first cosmonaut in space"; "Pipe smoking cures lung cancer" etc, and claimed to have received honorary doctorates from Harvard, Oxford and Yale. Despite the many troubles he got into, his mother thought he was god and a wasted genius. He, of course, worshipped mummy. He would narrate his fantasy tales (including some unprintable ones about his alleged encounters with Marilyn Monroe and Donna Summers) to his fan club and, upon seeing disbelief on their faces, would call out to his mother and shout, "Isn't this true, mumma? *Mè tamuné kaheloon nê.*" (Hadn't I told you)?" His mother, with a deadpan expression, would regally sail past and say, "Of course, *mara jaan, tè mané kaheloon!*" (Yes, my love, you indeed had told me) Post that maternal validation, PM cared a damn if the world disbelieved him.

Such devotion can reach great heights. We know of a busy counsel of the Bombay High Court who, after a hectic day in Court, slept every night in The B. D. Petit Parsee General Hospital for two and a half years, despite his ailing mother having a private nurse.

Mercifully, Parsi girls (who, according to Freud, have the Electra complex) do not display any such ob*s*essive devotion towards their fathers. The women of our tribe are obviously more formidable than men.

One of the primary reasons for the horrific demographic

decline of our community is this mummy worship. This can best be illustrated in the words of Rusi, a handsome Cambridge postgraduate who, when repeatedly asked as to why he would not marry, simply stated: "Why on earth do I need to marry, when my mumma is there?".

Poster from the movie Percy that sensitively dealt with the relationship between a mother and a son

Even in murder, class matters

A tale of two Parsi murderers about half a century ago

One was dashing and handsome; the other a shifty eyed psychopath. One killed for honour and passion; the other for greed. One confessed but was hero worshipped; the other denied guilt but was despised. One was pardoned, lived a free man and died in a comfortable bed, the other, hung from the neck until he died. Both were convicted and both were Parsis.

Commander Kawas Nanavati, a highly decorated officer of the Indian Navy, having served as an attaché to defence minister V. K. Krishna Menon in Jawaharlal Nehru's cabinet, was well liked even by Nehru and Indira Gandhi. Tall and good looking, Nanavati looked like the hero who had stepped out of a Mills and Boon novel. He married an English beauty, Sylvia, and had three children. This picture perfect tableau was soon to be shattered.

Pheroze Daruwala was also tall, not bad looking and bespectacled. A divorcee, he remarried Marie, a comely Roman Catholic telephone operator, whose adoptive parents had a small cottage in Bandra. They had a tiny daughter whom Daruwala adored. After passing Senior Cambridge, the future murderer was a conman who lived by his wits. A hardcore gambler, he frequented 'social clubs' to play rummy and poker, and at night, he eagerly awaited the *Matka* number (a digit released daily by a then don called Ratan Khatri, literally from an earthen pot or *matka*). He had strong and wiry hands, which he would later use to snuff out many lives.

During Nanavati's frequent trips abroad, a bored Sylvia was seduced by a family friend, a Sindhi playboy called Prem Ahuja, who promised to marry her. When Prem reneged on his promise, an enraged Sylvia confided in her husband. Nanavati froze in silence at this double betrayal. He dropped Sylvia and the kids to Metro cinema to watch a cartoon film; went to Naval Headquarters, got a revolver, and went to Ahuja's house. A smiling Ahuja stepped out of

Phiroze Daruwala (l) and Commander Kawas Nanavati

his bath, draped only in a towel, to meet his friend from the Navy. "I don't marry every woman I sleep with," were Ahuja's last famous words; as Nanavati shot him through his heart twice, point blank. The assignment completed with the clinical precision of a disciplined serviceman, Nanavati surrendered at the Colaba Police station.

Daruwala pretended to see a ghost in his in-laws' cottage and started to sleep in his old father-in-law's room. A few days later, the old man never woke up. Daruwala told his wife and mother-in-law (whom he also later unsuccessfully tried to poison) that burial was bad for the soul and got the gentleman cremated to leave no evidence of suffocation by a pillow. Within days, he sold the cottage for Rs 68,000 and shifted his family to a shady hotel at Marine Lines. Marie told the police later that her husband had also hatched an audacious plan to abduct the *Matka* don and make him declare the desired digit at night, to make a fortune. He also tried to kill a Gujarati money lender with a heavy stone but the latter somehow survived. Desperate to repay his mounting gambling debts, Daruwala dabbled in the bullion trade and lost heavily in a single day. His desperation was reaching its peak.

When Nanavati's trial by jury began in the Bombay *Sessions* Court, the courtroom was packed with swooning ladies, enraged Parsis who insisted Nanavati could not be tried for this 'honor killing,' and angry Sindhis, amongst whom Ahuja was a likeable fellow. Grave provocation, not premeditated, argued the defence led by Karl Khandalawala. But Ahuja's famous towel was intact on his bloodied body and therefore Nanavati's version of a scuffle with Ahuja and the shots being fired accidently should be disbelieved, said Ram Jethmalani for the prosecution. The jury returned a verdict, by 8:1, of guilty. Ahuja was guilty, Nanavati was "innocent" and not guilty. The veteran *Sessions* Judge Ratilal Bhaichand Mehta termed the jury's decision "perverse" and referred the matter to the High Court, which convicted Nanavati of premeditated murder and sentenced him to life imprisonment. The Supreme Court upheld his conviction.

Nusserwanji, also a small time conman in his youth, resided in Jehangir Mansion, a dilapidated and dark building with a gloomy staircase, at Dhobitalao, inhabited mostly by Parsis. Nusserwanji's wife, Gaimai, then in her seventies, was once upon a time, a ravishing beauty of Dhobitalao. Nusserwanji and Gaimai were maintained by the latter's lover, a bachelor called Dorabsha, who stayed with them and who worked as a court clerk in Crawford Bayley & Company, a law firm of antiquity (this writer recalls, during his stint with this law firm, oldtimers taking about Dorabsha's salacious conversations with Gaimai over the phone). The three old Parsis were served by their faithful domestic, Bawla, who spoke fluent Parsi Gujarati.

The Nanavati affair took a distinct communal turn. The Bombay Parsi Punchayet (BPP) supported Nanavati. The governor of Maharashtra issued an unprecedented decree placing Nanavati into naval custody, pending his appeal to the Supreme Court. This enraged the Sindhi community. The Parsis held a public meeting at Cowasji Jehangir Hall to support the governor. Around 3,500 Parsis packed the hall and nearly 5,000 stood outside the hall. *Blitz*, a tabloid owned and edited by Rusi Karanjia, was Nanavati's greatest supporter. Those days, a copy of *Blitz*, priced at 25 paise, sold like hot cakes, for two rupees.

Nanavati spent a little more than three years in prison before he was pardoned by Vijayalaxmi Pandit, Nehru's sister and governor of Maharashtra, along with a Sindhi convict called Bhai Pratap, to allay the growing tension between the two communities. Jury trial was abolished in India following Nanavati's fiasco (and survives as a remnant only in the Parsi Matrimonial Court). Nanavati's pardon raised a huge outcry but, in the early 60s, there was no aggressive social media or television, and the Nehrus could do no wrong. In any event, the popular view was overwhelmingly in favor of Nanavati who had already undergone the ignominy of three years in jail with other murderers, thieves, pimps and conmen. After his release, stripped of his naval honors, Nanavati migrated to Canada, Sylvia et al, and kept a very low profile, till his death in 2003 in a Toronto suburb. A moment of great anger had destroyed a fairy tale existence. The only consolation was that, in the eyes of the public, he was a hero avenging his honor.

On February 2, 1971 afternoon, Daruwala placed a *gupti* (a small sword-like knife) on Gaimai's throat and demanded money. The old lady foolishly offered Rs 60, which enraged Daruwala to slit her throat, and then he continued to stab her, even though she was long dead. Her husband suffered the same fate, and so did poor Bawla, who rolled in sheer agony under the sofa. Enter Dorabsha, during his lunch break from Crawford Bayley. Slumping in an easy chair, his Parsi white *dugla* turned crimson red from Daruwala's stabs. Totally, the assailant stabbed 147 times. Daruwala left no fingerprints and no clues. Dorabsha's gold pocket watch and money were untouched, deliberately to confuse the police. The murderer then filed his candidature for Bombay North Lok Sabha seat, to ward off suspicion, and in the belief, that the police would not touch a parliamentary candidate from a minority community.

Nanavati's crime of passion was celebrated in a Bollywood film (*Yeh raaste hai, pyaar ke*), several Gurarati plays and novels. 'Ahuja towels' and 'Nanavati revolvers' were sold by vendors at the Gateway of India. The power to pardon was taken away from State governors and is now exercised only by the President of India. Many rumors circulated that Ahuja was blackmailing Nanavati, as both were part of a smuggling racket and though the adultery did happen, it was used as a defence plea of grave provocation and

Nanavati murder coverage in Blitz

'honor' killing to escape the noose. Nanavati and Sylvia led a happy married life, ever after in Canada.

Daruwala was not so lucky. Despite his clever criminal mind and ability to destroy evidence, he made the unbelievable error of dumping the murder weapon (which he could have easily flung, along with a few stones, in the Arabian Sea) in the compound of Byramjee Jeejibhoy High School. Some intrepid detective work led the police to confront him. His alibis came unstuck one after the other. For all his violent tendencies, Daruwala could not withstand even a few hard slaps, and before some serious police third degree could start, he sang like a canary and confessed (confession in custody is however inadmissible in evidence). All the stolen gold ornaments were traced. The State of Maharashtra's case against Daruwala was open and shut. P. R. Vakil, who had been part of Nanavati's defence team, appeared for the prosecution, and another Parsi criminal lawyer, M. B. Mistry, for the accused. On the last day of the trial, this writer attended court and remembers Daruwala's bespectacled angular face, with those deadly protruding eyes, looking like a cornered hawk. The *Sessions* Judge convicted him and pronounced that Daruwala hang from the neck until he dies. The Bombay High Court and the Supreme Court rejected his appeals, as did the President of India, his clemency plea to commute hanging to life imprisonment. Daruwala donated his kidney to a well known social worker, Hamid Dalwai, to gain sympathy, but to no avail. On a Thursday morning, Daruwala was hanged at the Yerawada jail in Poona, and his corpse handed over to his father.

The multiple stabbings notwithstanding, his mental fitness to undergo a trial was never argued. No tears were shed, no society ladies were upset, no community leaders intervened. Neither BPP nor any newspaper supported him. No political pardon was contemplated. Society shows no mercy to career criminals. Daruwala died, clutching his little daughter's photo, in his hand. Nanavati must have read about Daruwala's hanging over a cup of Earl Grey tea in distant Toronto. When the Lok Sabha election results were declared, Daruwala's election symbol, ironically, 'scales of justice', received 896 votes.

Matchmaking still works

Matrimonial efforts are among the few constructive activities being pursued by the Bombay Parsi Punchayet

In Jane Austen's *Pride and Prejudice*, Ms Bennett spends most of her waking hours in trying to get her five daughters married. No Parsi mother has five daughters, and even if someone did, she may not care less. Marriage is not an aspirational matter for the community. On the contrary, it is almost fashionable to be unmarried. To make a provocative generalization, Parsi men in the matrimonial market are insipid and unexciting, while their female counterparts are overtly aggressive. The more educated and the more affluent tend to marry interfaith. Parsis seldom distinguish between sons and daughters in matters of inheritance. Women are most certainly not unequal. Pre-marital and extra marital sex is not such a taboo any more. Most women work and there is little economic compulsion to marry. Parsis are not children obsessed, like other communities. Bachelors and spinsters are envied; not looked down upon. All this makes for a deadly cocktail of dramatically falling marriage rates. Dolly from Cusrow Baug simply won't marry.

If one were to analyze the statistical trends at first blush, it may appear that more and more Parsis are marrying interfaith. The number of Parsi marriages is declining at a rapid rate, while the number of interfaith marriages is rising. In 1989, 383 Parsi marriages were listed versus 62 interfaith. In 2013, only 156 Parsi marriages were listed while the interfaith increased to 98. We are dealing with those Parsis who will not marry interfaith but also find their own kind uninteresting. Most in this category are more steeped in Parsi religion and culture. They just cannot imagine living, on a day-to-day basis, with non-Parsis. They cannot withstand any intercultural shock. Matchmaking comes into play here. These Parsis may not bother going to a restaurant but don't mind being spoon fed. Matrimonial advertisements and *kaajwallis* (traditional matchmakers, usually women, who operate by word of mouth) are no longer effective. Mutual friends may arrange a meeting or two, but hardened singles will not vigorously follow up. The Bombay Parsi Punchayet (BPP), the Zoroastrian Youth for the Next Generation and a few other Parsi organizations arrange mass dating, picnics and social gatherings to create mating opportunities for singles. Most of the organizers not only take the horse to the water but also make it drink. A majority of the candidates are in their mid thirties to mid forties and expectations are not too high. The strike rate may not be great but it is well worth the exercise. If these combined matchmaking activities can result in 50 more marriages every year and about 50 more children, there is hope yet for the community.

Divorcing under Parsi matrimonial laws is not too easy, and woe betide, if it is a contested divorce. Again, unscientifically speaking, the rate of divorce in such matched marriages is lower than in love marriages. Cultural homogeneity ensures easier adjustment. The differences are usually trivial (you cannot make *bheeda per eedoo* like my Mumma). Most of the matched ones come from the middle class*es* and predominantly from the baugs. Emphasis is more on steady companionship rather than pulsating romance. Familiarity with the B. D. Petit Parsee General Hospital wards scores more brownie points than attending a concert at the National Centre for the Performing Arts. In any event, the matchmakers do not target the "caviar" Parsis but the "*masoor-pau*" ones; admirers of Rafi and Asha Bhosle rather than Zubin Mehta or Freddie Mercury. This class requires external intervention to goad them into matrimony. Once they tie the knot, however, they are most likely to make a decent try at begetting a child or two. The BPP can provide them with priority, out-of-turn housing allotment, which is a huge attraction to would-be wedders. Can this result in marriages of convenience, like marrying a US or British citizen to get right of residence? Unlikely, in the present situation.

For those who spurn these matchmaking efforts, here is some stellar advice from that shrewd observer of men and matrimony, Jane Austen herself: "Happiness in marriage is entirely a matter of chance. If the dispositions of the parties are ever so well known to each other or ever so similar beforehand, it does not advance their felicity in the least. They always continue to grow sufficiently unlike afterwards to have their share of vexation; and it is better to know as little as possible of the defects of the person with whom you are to pass your life." Of course, Jane Austen herself, like Dolly from Cusrow Baug, never married.

A traditional ses and an engagement gift

A matter of taste

The community appears to be rather divided between Zubin Mehta and Shakila Banoo Bhopali

D ear Kaklaat,

    Aapro Viraf Violin invited me and Kavas Kishore Kumar to Zubin Mehta's concert at the NCPA. Khojeste Mistree is absolutely right that *Parsiana's* statistics about our declining population are utterly misleading. There were hardly any non-Parsis, *dikra*. If our number is only 40,000 in Bombay, how can there be 800 *Sirpas* (Parsis) at a single concert? Though, I must confess, I hardly knew any of them. One of them looked like my classmate in Bharda New High School; but he snubbed me and said he was a fourth generation Cathedralite. They were, of course, all suited and booted, while Kavas and I were wearing a tee shirt and bush shirt, respectively. Viraf Violin was looking most uncomfortable in his marriage suit.

When we settled down in our seats, the atmosphere felt like an *uthamna*, bossy. People were talking in hushed tones and all that. Then the *firangi* (foreign) musicians walked in and took their positions next to all vague looking musical instruments. And an unbelievable number of violin wallas (Viraf said they are called First Violins and Second Violins!). Though not a single fellow on the drums or tabla, which was a bit strange. *Aapro* Zubin, looking really handsome at 80, walked in, with a little stick in his hand. Throughout the concert he fidgeted with this stick as if he was trying to hypnotize the orchestra. Kavas and I asked Viraf, during the interval, as to why Zubin, like our Goody Seervai and Nelly Battiwala, did not play any instrument. We got some very dirty looks from a lady in a purple gara and large pearls, who was dressed as if she was at a navjote. Kavas was most disappointed that, like our Dadar boy, *aapro behesti* (our late) Freddie Mercury, Zubin did not even sing.

The program said that the first item was a Carnival Overture; but there was nothing carnival about it, boss. The music was so slow that Kavas started snoring and several suitwalas around us took deep breaths. Luckily, Tehmi called him on his mobile with the Kishore Kumar ringtone, and he woke up, with a rude start. Viraf Violin *bichaaro* went white in the face.

The next item was called Concerto in D Major. I asked Viraf as to whether Concerto was Italian for concert. He just put his finger on his lips. I thought this item was dedicated to some army Major, but again, it was too slow and no military music. Suddenly, *Dadaar Hormuzd* knows what happened to Kavas that, at the end of the piece, he loudly clapped. Believe it or not, Kaklaat bossy, none else applauded. Viraf whispered that it was only a movement and the piece was not yet over.

On our way back to Dadar, Viraf explained to us that Zubin was one of the greatest orchestra conductors. But he was the only person on the stage who did not make a sound, argued Kavas humming a Kishore Kumar tune. A conductor interprets a great composer's music, he sets the tempo and unifies the orchestra, explained Viraf Violin. But none of the musicians were even looking at Zubin, I argued. Viraf took a deep sigh and explained that top quality orchestral players can watch the score and at the same time watch the conductor who is also listening to the other sections of the orchestra. What has cricket score got to do with all this? queried Kavas. If Zubin has memorized all the scores, he would make a great scorer at our IPL cricket matches, he added. Score means printed music, exclaimed a harassed Viraf Violin.

The next day, Viraf attended another concert of Zubin at the Brabourne Stadium (of course, he did not take Kavas or me), where Zubin conducted a male singer, who is visually impaired, called a tenor; and a nice Mexican lady called a soprano (you remember that Sunnu soprano, who taught us Algebra in school, and whose voice could be heard three lanes away near the *agiary*?). So I asked Viraf Violin as to how the tenor, due to his handicap, can follow our Zubin. Viraf sighed and said that it is the conductor who looks at the soloist and then imparts to the orchestra. All very confusing, *dikra*!

Qawwali singer Shakila Banoo Bhopali

I mean, Kaklaat *dikra*, Zubin is the most famous Parsi and all that; but I did not really enjoy myself. As compared to this concert, you will recollect the programs of Shakila Banoo Bhopali, the queen of qawwali that we used to attend on Saturday nights. Although she was a bit plump, what mesmerizing eyes she had! Our Pallon Petrol Pump used to rush to the stage and shower her with five rupee notes and she would so warmly reciprocate by taking out from her hair the *mogra no gajro* (floral hair arrangement) and fling it at Pallon who would be orgasmic with joy. We would take a swig from the quarter bottle in the pocket of our jeans. The audience applauded after every couplet and shouted 'once more' a thousand times. Such a *boi*sterous crowd it was. Shakila Banoo's singing would reach a crescendo and then she would smash a glass on the stage; and the audience would be on fire. From industrialists to stockbrokers to taxi drivers, all were enthralled. That is what you called a performance, bossy. Your each vein would be throbbing with excitement. I know you will laugh at me, comparing Zubin Mehta with Shakila Banoo Bhopali; but for me, brother, she was like hot and spicy *kolmi-na curry chawal*, and this concert was an insipid bowl of asparagus mousse, to be eaten in funereal silence.

Yours affectionately
Cyrus Critic'

Zubin Mehta conducting the Israeli Philharmonic Orchestra in Bombay

From qawwalis to concertos

The range of the community's taste in music is extensive.

A few know whether to applaud or not after the first movement of a Tchaikovsky concerto; many swing to hot rock; a micro-minority is transformed by Amjad Ali Khan's sarod; only a handful have heard of Bhimsen Joshi; lots are fans though of Kishore Kumar and Geeta Dutt. The community's taste in music is eclectic. One can know the socioeconomic background of a Parsi from the music she enjoys or abhors.

The distinction, evolved by us between NCPA (National Centre for the Performing Arts) Parsis and *masoor pav* Parsis is relevant in this context. If you are standing in the foyer of the NCPA, at the end of a music concert (Western classical, of course), you will certainly agree with Khojeste Mistree that all talk of a steep demographic decline is hogwash. The NCPA Parsis are not necessarily rich or aristocratic; but mostly Anglophiles (those who read yesterday's *London Times*, rather than today's *Times of India*). One will also spot the NCPA Parsis searching for symphony albums at Rhythm House, across the road from the Jehangir Art Gallery. In the good old days, they would have requested Western music numbers on Radio Ceylon. Their children would be receiving piano and violin tuitions, from Catholic ladies in Bandra.

Zubin Mehta, perhaps the world's best known Parsi, conducted the Los Angeles Philharmonic and the Israeli Philharmonic orchestras. The world's second best known Parsi was Freddie Mercury, born Farrokh Bulsara, lead vocalist of the rock band, Queen. You may be surprised, however, to learn that a famous vocalist of the Kirana Gharana was Pandit Firoz Dastur. Dastur was a disciple of the legendary Sawai Gandharva whose pupils included Bhimsen Joshi and Gangubai Hangal. Perhaps, more know about Padma Shri Penaz Masani who has more than 20 ghazal albums to her credit.

Qawwali exponent Mahajabeen, the stage name adopted by Dhun Baria

The first few waves of migrants from Gujarat became rich and prosperous and constantly endeavored to endear themselves to their British masters. These were the opium and silk traders, shippers and builders and the first families of Bombay — Wadias, Jejeebhoys, Petits and Tatas. German governes*ses* gave piano and violin lessons to their children who found the strains of Indian musical instruments jarring. Till today, several of their descendants cannot bring themselves to listen to Bismillah Khan's magic on the shehnai. Those who have a piece of grilled chicken breast for dinner have naturally not heard of Geeta Dutt, the playback singer who enthralled India and died heartbroken of cirrhosis at 42. Generations of Parsis, of course, who enjoy *bhinda pur eedu* were also brought up on a staple diet of Lata Mangeshkar and Mohammad Rafi, Asha Bhosle and Rahul Dev Burman, the versatile Kishore Kumar as also the haunting melodies of

Hemant Kumar and Manna Dey. If you walk through Navroz Baug on a lazy Sunday afternoon you can still hear popular Bollywood numbers of yesteryears. In the days when there was no television, Parsis were glued to Radio Ceylon, and then Vividh Bharati, to hear the inimitable Amin Sayani compere Binaca Geetmala. When the fledgling Doordarshan appeared, Parsis enjoyed Chhaya Geet on Thursday evenings.

Bollywood got its second ever female music composer, Saraswati Devi, from the community. Born Khorshed Minocherhomji, she composed the score for *Achhut Kanya* which had several hit songs. Orthodox Parsis tried their best to have Bombay Talkies dismiss her and her sister, Manek, an actress, but did not succeed. The sisters adopted Hindu names. A young and comely qawwali artiste called Mahajabeen enthralled Bombay audiences with her rendering of authentic Urdu qawwalis, in the league of the then legendary Shakila Banu Bhopali, a famous qawwal. Mahajabeen was none other than the feisty crusader for "*cremate ni bungli*" at *Doongerwadi*, Dhun Baria.

Aban Mistry, India's first female solo tabla player

In the sixties, the Vada Dastur of Navsari, Kekobad Meherjirana, was noticed at many Hindustani classical music concerts, humming a *thumri*. Needless to add, this was considered unbecoming of a high priest, by the fundamentalists of Navsari. He was a bon vivant, a happy soul, who loved to interact with sufi fakirs and ash covered sadhus who often dropped in at his Dastur Vad residence for a cup of tea. He truly loved his similarly inclined wife who, after his rather early death, made eyebrows rise in the mohallas of Navsari by her continuing acquaintance with her late husband's *juddin* friends. He was succeeded by his nephew who was neither interested in *thumris* nor sadhus.

Aban Mistry, under the watchful eye of her guru, Keki Jijina, mastered the tabla and was the first solo female tabla player in India. Jijina, a priest, faced many hardships, social and financial, in his life long sadhana of Hindustani classical music. Few Parsis know of Jijina and Mistry, both deceased, but almost all knew the familiar portly figure of Goody Seervai playing the accordion at Parsi weddings and navjotes of the well heeled. Later, Seervai was a regular fixture at Adi Marzban's Parsi New Year comedy revues, providing music to the talented crooner Uma Pocha, wife of the legendary comedian Jimmy Pocha who horsed around in *Parsi Harishchandra* as Taramati, the hapless queen. Competition to Seervai came in the form of the talented Nelly Battiwala and her band from Dadar Parsi Colony. The middle clas*ses*, of course, had to do with Dara and his Darling Orchestra belting old English hits as you gorged on *saas ni machhi* and *kid gosh* with the ubiquitous raspberry flavored aerated water from Rogers. Dara Mehta's son, Marzban was a popular Parsi singer whose services were enlisted during the AFP (Adult Franchise for Progress) election campaign in 2008 to subtly suggest that AFP too were traditional Parsis. Unfortunately, the music was only heard by the community seven years later.

Wholesome, peaceful and pure

Only half a century ago, Navsari was so Parsi

At dawn, lying in bed, you heard the sound of water, drawn from the house well, being splashed to settle the dust outside the entrance. Followed by the sound of the box containing limestone powder being smacked on the ground to produce designs (chalk *purya*). The huge brass *boi*ler gurgled ominously in the *paachloon bar* (back entrance) heated by chopped wood and charcoal. You cleaned your teeth with crushed twigs from the neem tree. Maybe, some monkey brand tooth powder from a tin on which a happy monkey grinned, displaying his sparkling white teeth.

The fire in the kitchen was fuelled just like the brass *boi*ler. The large aluminum kettle took some time to *boi*l. A spoonful of tea leaves, lemon grass and mint leaves in a no nonsense white teapot awaited the hot water from the kettle. Milk was delivered at your doorstep, just like fish and mutton and veggies. The brood of hens, fluttering all over the *paachloon bar*, would provide fresh eggs and, of course, chicken. The rooster, angel of dawn, enjoyed immunity from execution. He was your pre-dawn alarm clock anyway. You dunked your rough, largish, drum shaped *batasa* biscuit from Surat into your tea. Quarter of the cup would be absorbed by the *batasa*, to be rescued just in time, from turning soggy. The mint and lemon grass cleared your sin*uses* and yet another day had begun in one of the many Parsi *mohallas* of Navsari.

Your biceps were exercised by pulling water from the well, one of the holiest spots in the house, often shared with your immediate neighbor, having access through a window in his wall, just above the well. Every couple of years, a tortoise would be lowered in the well, both as a destroyer of worms and an auspicious symbol. Believe it or not, but even 50 years ago, there was no flush in Navsari. Just behind the Indian style toilet embedded in the floor, there was a passage which could be accessed from behind the house. Twice a day, a service

Parsi homestead in Navsari

person entered the passage and emptied the straw bucket containing the night soil.

A brass bucket with scalding hot water was sufficient to wash the *chana no aato* (gram flour) and rose petalled milk on your birthday, though some sparingly used the transparent Pears soap. Pick up a thin sandalwood stick from a niche in the wall and make your way to the serene precincts of the *atash behram*, avoiding the benign cows and gambolling goats. Esconced in His protection, your aura cleansed, you gorged on a fairly heavy breakfast: A dollop of pure ghee on thick parathas, fresh cream from milk, frozen overnight in the severe winter, sprinkled with sugar, mean looking liver curry in an aubergine base, fried fish, sweet and sour mutton kheema, brain lovingly delivered by an ageless Muslim lady with countless wrinkles called Boo, transformed by mixing it with sautéed spinach (*bhaji ma bhéju*). Even the genial doctor uncle, who knew more compassion than medicine, had not heard of cholesterol or clogged arteries or even calories.

Disciplined beggars appeared only on their designated days. A mother-in-law with her daughter-in-law would only accept food but not money on Monday afternoons and was christened *jamva ni dosi*. People had plenty of time to converse with these regular beggars before retiring for a quick siesta. Middle aged ladies spent their evening playing a card game called bisque or bezique, fiddling with little cardboard mounted dials; or enjoyed the serialized Parsi novel in the daily *Jamé*, which was flung into the portico before noon; the Gujarat Express having brought the dak edition from Bombay. There was an old men's club at Lunsikui, a bit on the outskirts where juddins resided; only qualification was that you had to be a Parsi, economic or educational status did not matter. Even idiots waxed eloquent on Nehru and the Indo-Chinese war and exotic cures for common cold by inhaling the fumes of asafoetida underneath a camel's posterior. Almost everyone abused the toddy and booze-banning Morarji Desai (derisively called Moryo), the Parsi hater.

This routine was energized by a six-day wedding celebration in the *mohalla* or the cathartic camaraderie after a death, even of someone whom you did not particularly like. Both the ends of the *mohalla* were sealed off to prevent entry of non-Parsis, who were strangely not affronted. Life was celebrated and death was mourned together, and at such times, there were no enemies. It was near impossible to keep secrets.

By twilight everyone returned to dimly lit hou*se*s, amidst the cacophony of dark, fat sparrows called *dev chaklis*, and a surprisingly spartan supper. Some placed a black carbon record on an old gramophone, which had to be wound up and its needle changed regularly. At night, if stray dogs created a ruckus, stones were pelted at them, from a straw basket strategically placed near the balcony. If the rhythmic clip-clop of the *ghora gari* (horse carriage) on the cobbled street woke up the *mohalla*, at four in the morning, everyone knew that Cawas was going to Bombay by the early morning train. Few were disturbed anyway, as it was almost time to splash water to settle down the dust at the entrance.

Community members in a Parsi mohalla in Navsari

Ancient secrets of the Faith

Our religion is a veritable storehouse of occult knowledge

Circuits of protection, vibratory intonations, purification rituals, aura healing and white magic to cure illness. Some pagan religion in Polynesia? Some heathen practices in South America? No sir, the Zoroastrians of India. When agiaries, *atash behrams* and *dakhmas* are built, elaborate circuits of protection are created, according to liturgical directions, to protect their sanctity; our prayers unleash powerful vibrations when intoned correctly; *mobeds* and behdins undergo periods of seclusion called *nahan;* nirangs cleanse the aura and Avestan magical spells can cure scores of illnes*ses*, both physical and mental. No Polynesian paganism this.

Good words, thoughts and deeds; and nothing more, assert the liberals. Priests are babblers for money, rituals have been invented to impress the gullible and magical charms are mumbo jumbo. Unlike religions which prescribe fasting (Jainism), or proscribe alcohol

(Islam), or ban beef (Hinduism), or mandatorily require church attendance on Sundays (Roman Catholics), or forbid work on the Sabbath (Hebrew), Zoroastrianism hardly has any dos and don'ts. Even if you never visit an *agiary* or never open the *Khordeh Avesta* or do not wear the sudreh-kusti, you are not a lesser Zoroastrian, say the rationalists. Maybe, but you are missing out on the rich, possibly the richest, occult heritage, counter the traditionalists.

It is rather unfortunate that most knowledgeable Zoroastrian occultists are also rabid sounding fundamentalists. They use jargon which only a few beyond their ilk can understand. They are violently opposed to interfaith marriages and alternative methods for disposal of the dead. Intolerant of dissent, they oppose equal rights for interfaith married women and blood and organ donation, while emphasizing racial purity. As a result, they don't appeal to the youth and are dismissed as comical figures on the fringe. Their low credibility is compounded by poor communication skills. Some deliver dreadfully boring diatribes on abstruse topics in *agiary* halls before half-a-dozen geriatric listeners; most of the latter are more interested in consuming the *chasni* (temple offerings) served after the lecture.

Late Adi Doctor (left) and Dastur K. N. Meherjirana

Quite a few of these speakers are Ilm-e-Khshnoomists (literally, science of ecstasy, followers of late Behramshah Shroff who claimed induction into esoteric aspects of the faith by some divine beings near the Caspian Sea) and some are Pundolites (followers of one Minocher Pundole who purportedly performed many miracles including conjuring cutlets out of empty Udvada hotel fridges). At the risk of generalizing, the former are usually knowledgeable and the latter, a bit gullible. The talks cover topics like Magav Sahebs of Demavand Koh; celestial customs of Mazdayasni din and the advantages of reciting the *Moti Haptan Yasht*. Parsi theosophists, followers of Madame

Blavatsky, Annie Besant and C. W. Leadbeater, speak occasionally on astral travel and vegetarianism. Shroff's followers, Pheroze Masani and Jehangir Chiniwala, published newsletters on occult teachings, titled *Parsi Avaz*, *Dini Avaz* and *Parsi Pukar*, some now defunct. Masani founded the Parsi Vegetarian and Temperance Society (interestingly, Pundole forbade his disciples from partaking meat but himself did so, on the basis that the atoms of his mortal coils were so finely tuned that they were immune to the polluting effects which flesh has on lesser mortals). Dastur Kaikhushru N. Dastur Meherjirana of Navsari is among the last of the knowledgeable Khshnoomists, as was the late Adi Doctor.

While some of their rabid assertions about genetic purity may repulse, it is unfair to dismiss all Zoroastrian occultists as loonies. Some of the most revered scholars believe that Zoroastrianism is a storehouse of esoteric or occult knowledge. While many may find it meaningless to recite prayers in a dead language which hardly anyone understands or find even its translation not so impressive, several will vouch for the efficacy of the vibratory intonations of some potent capsule prayers (at the end of the *geh sarna*, when the priests thrice utter the earthly memory severing words, *Nemascha ya Armaitish izhacha*; or the magical *Ahunem vairim tanum paiti*; or even a sonorously recited *Yatha Ahu Vairyo*, it does give goose pimples to the attuned). You may chortle at the awful smelling albino bull in the *agiary* compound or revere it as the holy varasyaji whose urine is the purifying nirang of many a sacred ritual. You may term the Vendidad prayer ceremony as an invention of post Zarathushtra clergy or find it an uplifting experience at dawn when the priest completes his all-night vigil. You may regard guardian spirits of fire temples as a hallucination of tired *mobed*s or trust in the collective experience of countless boywalla *mobed*s who have witnessed first-hand these mystical beings shrouded in all white sweeping through *atash behram* corridors in the early hours of the morning. You may mock those who daily invoke the protection of the Dog Star, Sirius, known as *Tir Yazad* in the *Avesta* or relish the stupendous cleansing energy it unleashes. Reputed occultists regard Zarathushtra as a great initiate and the first of the white magicians.

After the Prophet, the magician king Shah Faridoon was the greatest ever Zoroastrian occultist. He paralysed the demonic Zohak and composed miracle rendering nirangs in Pazand and Avesta which can cure many a debilitating illness of body and mind. Recited even today by the faithful, *fe naame yazad, ba farmaane yazad baname nik Faridoon gaav daye*, is the magical formula. King Vistaspa's astrologer was the great Jamaasp who predicted, Nostradamus like, about the eons to come in his magnum opus, the *Jamaaspi*. In recent times, the much revered Dastur Jamshed Kookadaru of Kappawala *Agiary* performed many a miracle including turning a brick into gold to finance the stalled construction of the Anjuman *Atash behram* despite knowing that he would pay a terrible price for this selfless act of alchemy in the form of losing his young son. His mantra, "*Ya Noor e dastagir, ya dastagir e Noor, karam kar karimaar, raham kar parvardigar, madad kar ya nabi, Zarthosht Teri Paadshahi,*" is recited daily by the faithful to ward off evil and survive through difficult times.

Of course, rituals are commercialized and praying has become a business. Most *mobeds* are ignorant of the glorious heritage of this ancient faith. And xenophobic scholars do not help the cause. Nevertheless, the fact remains that Zoroastrianism is not an elementary faith merely espousing good and simple living but an ancient knowledge system of great power whose many divine secrets will be revealed to those whose time has come to know.

Can you hear me, Tehmi?

Parsi spiritualists provide solace to many

Sholapurwala lovingly looked at the tiny *planchette* (a heart shaped wooden arrow mounted on tinier casters) sitting motionless on his glass table top in the Nariman Point office of India's premier vaccine maker. A large chart, containing letters of the alphabet and numerals from one to nine (an Ouija board in medium parlance), is spread eagled. Sholapurwala, a genial man in his seventies, is a scientist by training. He lightly touches the *planchette*, which literally comes alive before our bewildered eyes, and starts furiously zigzagging over the chart. "Who are you?" asks the old Parsi. "R-U-S-I," goes the planchette. "Oh! you again," exclaims Sholapurwala, "What do you want?" "I-WANT-TO-F_ _ _," replies this disembodied entity called

Ouija board and planchette

211

Rusi. Disgusting, grunts the old gentleman, he has lots of desire but no body to fulfill it. Burning in the hell of desires, we sheepishly state. Sholapurwala nods enthusiastically.

Sholapurwala is well versed with occultists and their works: Helena Blavatsky, author of *The Secret Doctrine* claimed to have been dictated by the Masters of the Great White Brotherhood; the Theosophists, Annie Besant and Charles Leadbeater; the German occultist, Rudolph Steiner's *Karma*; Alice Bailey's *Agni Yoga*; Sri Aurobindo's *Life Divine* - the list was endless. Though a practising Zoroastrian, Sholapurwala firmly believed in the twin principles of karma and reincarnation. At death, you merely discard the bodily robe - the journey continues through eons, in multiple bodies.

Sholapurwala was not alone; Parsi spiritualists abound. They are neither charlatans nor in it for any gain, at least their motive is pure - providing solace to those who have lost someone beloved as also to seek guidance from the other world. Whether they are truly psychic or merely hallucinating is a different matter.

Years ago, we recollect our clients, two Parsi spinsters of blue blood, telling us that they had evidence that their brother was murdered. Before we could take them to the police, they fortunately (for us) revealed their source of information – the deceased brother himself, who spoke to them during a séance.

The most famous of the Parsi spiritualists were Khorshed and Rumi Bhavnagri of Rustom Baug who lost both their young sons in a car accident. During our stint with *The Bombay Samachar*, we had visited them. You lit a lamp, recited *Yatha Ahu Vairyo* thrice, grabbed a ball point pen which would initially scribble gibberish on a note book, and gradually full sentences would form. Was it your subconscious or an incarnation awaiting denizen of the other world, you had to decide.

Khorshed authored a book called *The Laws of the Spirit World* which became quite popular even though believers found its contents to be quite puerile including a chapter on an exclusive heaven for dogs, cats and parrots. They had a large following amongst non-Parsis too. The distraught mother of the air hostess who had perished in the Air India crash on New Year's eve became ob*sess*ed by 'automatic writing,' an alternate method of communicating with the dead. "Darling, I found my missing earrings in the second drawer of the bedroom cabinet, exactly as you had told me," the mother would tell her daughter, who would reply by stating that she enjoyed the most pretty purple sky in the nether heavens, yesterday.

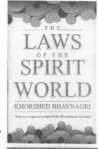

A Parsi lady of aristocratic lineage learned to communicate with her son, a lad of 12, who had succumbed to a rare heart disorder. Behram, as we shall call this boy, turned into a powerful 'guide' for his mother. We were privy to an episode involving

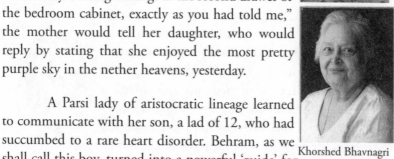

Khorshed Bhavnagri

Behram. Noted counsel of the Bombay High Court, Firdaus Taleyarkhan, an avid mountaineer who explored the Himalayas every court summer vacation, fell into a crevice, and all attempts to rescue him by the Indian Army and other agencies were proving unsuccessful. On behalf of his father, the well-known Parsi politician, Homi Taleyarkhan, a relative requested Behram's mother to conduct a séance. The rescue team was stunned by the precise instructions given by Behram as to the exact position of Firdaus in the crevice and the suggestions to extricate him. He must be pulled out in the next two hours, warned Behram. Unfortunately, it proved impossible to reach Firdaus. Just before dawn, Behram told his mother that Firdaus was happy and now with them and the rescue operations may be called off. At that very moment, the rescue team had reached an identical conclusion. Some years later, Firdaus's well-preserved body was discovered by another Himalayan expedition team.

Karl Umrigar was India's best upcoming jockey who had saddled many winners at a very young age. Umrigar was thrown off his mount and his lungs punctured by the hoofs of the horse which followed. After a brief battle, he succumbed. Like the Bhavnagris, his mother, Dhun (Nanny) Umrigar emerged as a powerful medium over the years, claiming an ability to communicate with her son and other departed ones including Meher Baba, a popular Parsi Irani godman, who kept a vow of silence when alive. Seasoned occultists claim, however, that the souls dwelling in the subtler mental and higher realms seldom communicate with mediums who are lulled by the lesser disembodied entities masquerading as some celebrity. Bona fide mediums too often fail to distinguish between the impressions emanating

Nanny Umrigar

from their subconscious and messages coming from the other world. A rather thin line exists between sanity and hallucination.

The internationally famed dancer and choreographer Shiamak Davar is a committed spiritualist and so is noted stage actor Sorab Ardeshir who, along with his octogenarian mother Silla, holds séances once a week at their Bandra home. They have acquired quite a fan following among Parsis and non Parsis. There are plenty other Parsi spiritualists of various hues and colors from Pasta Lane to Thana. Of course, many who think they are mediums are plain barmy. We know of a retired lady manager of a public sector bank who is convinced that Zarthosht Saheb is in constant communication with her.

The great playwright and theater personality Adi Marzban dabbled in the occult too and wrote a memorable skit for All India Radio called *Maro Raincoat*, where the raincoat of a deceased best friend forewarns Marzban of many a disaster by falling off the peg on its own. In fact, Marzban wrote a superb parody in which comedian Dinshaw Daji wailed for his recently departed wife, Tehmi, who admonished him even from the distant heavens. Hearing the cackling voice of the old thespian, like a tenor gone terribly wrong, "Tehmina, *tu paachhi aav, èm mané na sataav* (please return and stop torturing me thus)," had the audience rolling in the aisles.

Our no nonsense grandmother often warned us never ever to participate in any séance or other mode of contacting the dead. She vividly narrated as to how cups and saucers flew on their own in the house of her Navsari neighbor who was an exponent of this practice. This prevented us from a foray, as we did not want a saucer containing hot English breakfast tea hurtling at top speed towards us.

The orthodox, including the Ilm-e-Khshnoomists, frown upon these unZoroastrian practices and warn exponents of dire consequences (antithetical to the Kyani *tokham* (genetic make-up) and the pure *berjisi jiram* (soul fibre). Asho farohars of the departed are not to be thus disturbed in their celestial realms, say our priests.

And finally, this rather touching tale, narrated to us by the managing partner of a law firm. After a hearty repast at the Colaba *Agiary*, a well-known spiritualist and his mother took a car lift. The spiritualist burped loudly, whereupon his mother said, "Oh I forgot to tell you, dikra (son), daddy did warn that the paatru (food) will not be nice!" The spiritualist replied, "Please ask him now whether I should take Baralgan or will Digene suffice".

Keeping our promise to be loyal

The patriotism of Parsis is in keeping with their character

During Indira Gandhi's Emergency (1975-77), the income tax authorities raided two Parsi spinsters, bred in the purple, brought up by a German governess and a doting father. The raiding team froze in awe as they walked into the palatial bungalow bristling with a thousand antiquities and artefacts. As they patiently awaited the arrival of the ladies in the (ballroom sized) dining room, they were struck by the life size portraits of Queen Victoria, George V, George VI, the perennial favorite lover boy, abdicating Edward VIII and, of course, Queen Elizabeth II.

A British guinea

"Madam," stuttered one of the raiding officers, "why are there so many British kings and queens here?" The reply was curt and swift. "Because," said the noble lady, "we do not recognize your government." At which stage their tax consultant felt dizzy.

For gifting at the birth of a child and for navjotes, engagements and other auspicious occasions, Parsi ladies seem to have a limitless supply of English guineas, even though they ceased to be a valid currency unit in the UK as early as 1814. The tiny Queen Victoria quarters in little red pouches elicit much gratitude from non-Parsi receivers. When Queen Elizabeth made her only state visit (as head of the Commonwealth, not as Queen of England) to India in early 1961, her entourage passed close to the Khareghat Colony, whose outer buildings were jam packed with Parsis desperate to catch a glimpse of the beatific vision. We recollect one very ancient lady in her late 90s being roused from her semi-comatose condition to behold the monarch of her dreams. Ambafui, as she was fondly called, was made to sit on a chair placed on the large verandah of her ground floor flat. She sat morose and speechless, slumped in her seat, oblivious to the great commotion around her. However, just as the royal personage passed, slightly waving her little gloved hand (that is, the Queen, not Ambafui), Ambafui shook off her decades long stupor and joyously shouted, "*aapri rani, aapri rani* (Our queen, our queen)!"

When the last Shah of Iran, Mohammad Reza Pahlavi visited Bombay, the Bombay Parsi Punchayet led the community in organizing a Persian carpet welcome for "the other King," who was a closet Zoroastrian. Many Parsis believe that had he not been deposed, we would have perhaps realized the dream of having our fatherland back.

Let not the above lead anyone to believe that Parsis are not patriotic. The first field marshal of India (Sam Manekshaw), many admirals, air chief marshals and generals as well as numerous awardees of the highest national gallantry awards (like Paramvir Chakra, mostly posthumous), were Parsis. The list of freedom fighters for India's independence is too long and too well known to enumerate. Madame (Bhikaiji) Cama designed the first "Indian Independence flag" in 1907. As a minuscule community, our contribution to every branch of the state - legislature, executive and judiciary — has been abnormally disproportionate, as compared to any ethnic group of a similar size anywhere in the world.

Bhikaiji Cama with the first Indian flag of independence

More significantly, we have been an exemplary minority. We have never displayed any dysfunctional behavior or insecurity. Our compliance with the laws of the land is immaculate. The apocryphal promise, to dissolve like sugar in milk, given to the refuge granting Indian ruler by the first wave of Zoroastrian migrants, has never been breached. In an era of affirmative action, and although justified, we have never asked for reservations in education or jobs or seats in the legislature.

Some cynics may say that this is more out of compulsion than choice. An ant is bound to politely smile and give way to the elephant. Inwardly, quite a few Parsis continue to believe that the British were perhaps better and more benevolent rulers than their Gandhi-capped replacements. Some even secretly yearn for returning to Iran one day. Is our patriotism ambivalent and do the cynics have a point? In all migration waves from India to the UK (1960s), USA ('70s), Canada, Australia and New Zealand ('80s), Parsis have been pioneers. Parsi migrants are seldom misty-eyed about India, unlike their counterparts in other communities. Parsis feel more at home in a Western environment, which they find more to their liking - cleaner, more disciplined and honest, quieter, politer, more civilized. Those in India too envy their relatives and friends who have acquired foreign citizenship. Many are ill at ease with the sounds and smells of the multitudes.

The ancestral promise to remain loyal to the country which so readily granted them refuge is to be observed at any cost. Is it then a case of patriotism out of promise rather than emotional fervor for the nation? Hypothetically, if the Brits were to grant citizenship to all Parsis, would not most make a beeline for *"Velaat* (England)?" After 1,200 years, do we still feel like refugees in a foreign land? In our collective subconscious, do we harbor a desire to go back to Iran? Delicate questions, indeed. The head has always done what is right even though the heart may have sometimes felt otherwise.

Our anthem, *Chhaiyé Hamé Zarthosti* (the rendering of which makes most misty-eyed), seems to suggest so, when it recites: *"Jeni vafaadari par, padya nathi koi daag; Aa Rajnee yaari par, ladshè misalè vaag; Nimakhalalee jaalvi; te par bani dilsoj* (Whose loyalty to this country is spotless; who has fought like a tiger for this kingdom; who have been always grateful to this land)." The late poet Firoz Batliwala must be complimented for this very subtle couplet.

There are two types of migrants. Those who zealously root for their adopted country, even more than its natives; and those who are grateful and law abiding but not having that emotional connect with the ethos of the nation. If, even after 1,200 years, touring Iran gives you goose pimples and the rani remains *'aapri,'* you may be a loyal citizen all right, but not a passionate nationalist.

Ardent admirer of British royalty Boman Kohinoor meeting the Duke and Duchess of Cambridge in Bombay

Foul mouthed parrots and a privileged hen

Apart from dogs and horses, Parsis love exotic pets too

Amongst all Indian communities, Parsis are the loneliest. Bachelors, spinsters, widows and widowers and the childless are to be found in a staggering number of households. Considering their yearning for companionship and severe emotional deprivation, it is surprising that so few Parsis keep pets. While the community boasts of many dog and horse lovers, some of its members are also fond of the odd and the exotic.

Our earliest memory of this incarnation is being rocked on the protruding belly of a genial bearded dasturji lying on a four poster bed with laced mosquito nets. He was our grand uncle in Navsari who had returned from Aden after officiating as a priest in the local *agiary* and had brought along with him a handsome grey and white African parrot of the cockatoo family (*kakatavvo*, in Parsi dialect). This particular bird had an amazing ability to mimic the human voice, coupled with a terrible sense of timing. He learnt the choicest Parsi abuse from the lads roaming around the *moholla* (locality) and would daily shower the same on a prudish neighbor returning from the *atash behram* across the street, defiling his pious state of mind. Later, when our widowed grand-aunt was the lone survivor in a three-storey house where once a family of 100 members resided, Kaskoo, as the parrot was called, would be heard, in the middle of the night, advising her to go to bed.

Many Parsi homes in Gujarat had as pets the less exotic cousin of the *kaskoo*, the green parrot with the curved red bill, in a circular cage hanging in the patio, whose vocabulary was limited to a couple of words like "*popat mithu* (sweet parrot)," but who had the privilege of being the first in the household to be served a vegetarian meal. Our maternal grandfather, a noted caterer who conjured up a mean liver curry, kept a succession of these green parrots and was proud to be known as Behramji Popat. Bombay Parsis, in the yesteryears, were fond of keeping love birds, natives of Madagascar, small and affectionate, who made more noise than love. Our uncle, a professional magician maintained a flock of white pigeons; they smelled awful, would voluntarily return home every evening to captivity and did not seem to mind being squeezed into various parts of the anatomy of our uncle's buxom assistants, only to triumphantly appear on stage with an excited flutter.

In the sultry summer of 1832, the English decided to cull stray dogs, notwithstanding the entreaties of enraged Parsis including a delegation led by none other than Sir Jamsetjee Jejeebhoy. On June 6, the Parsis rioted in the streets of Bombay to express their *boi*ling anger at the treatment meted out to their canine friends. These are chronicled as the Mad Dog Riots. In the years following, Parsis rioted against Muslims too, over some religious issues, with far graver consequences. The *Vendidad* classifies the dog as a divine animal gifted with special sight to detect any sign of suspended animation; hence the dog being brought to eye a corpse at funerals to prevent any Parsi being consigned before his time. The dog is also supposed to destroy the impurities emanating from dead matter or *naso*, surrounding a corpse.

We knew of a Parsi family taking affront if their dog's name was not mentioned in the *lagan ni chithhi* (wedding invite) and would refuse to attend the function. On the other hand, the Bombay Parsi Punchayet (BPP) forbids its tenants from keeping dogs in the premises, under their leave and license agreement; though we have not yet heard of an eviction suit being filed on this ground by the otherwise trigger happy trustees. We also know of a senior counsel in the High Court, much sought after for his scintillating brilliance and court craft, who summarily terminated a critical meeting with a corporate bigwig and returned a lucrative brief, as his nervous client accidentally kicked the counsel's Pomeranian who was sniffing at his ankles.

Parsis, usually, though not always, of aristocratic lineage, were pioneers in founding and managing animal hospitals, stray dog shelters, the Society for the Prevention of Cruelty to Animals and dog shows. Muncherji Cama, the chairman and managing director of *The Bombay Samachar* would brave ill health and fly to Tashkent and far flung countries near the Caspian Sea to judge dog shows. After appreciating disciplined dogs for decades, he resigned in disgust from the BPP trusteeship. The reverence and love which Jains and devout Hindus bestow on cows is showered by Parsis on dogs.

Few Parsis like purring felines though. Years ago, in search of paying guest accommodation, we came across an old Parsi spinster staying alone in a seven-room house at Dhobi Talao, reeking of eucalyptus oil, and to complete the bizarre tableau, more than a dozen cats perched on window sills and the furniture, eyeing the nervous jugular of the visitors, who, of course, beat a hasty retreat.

While tortoise and fish are fairly common, some display more exotic taste. A couple called Nagrani Nargis and Yogiraj Jimmy, leaders of a cult which once upon a time had a sizeable following amongst Parsis and still has amongst non-Parsis, reportedly kept colorful snakes at home, including a defanged cobra. On *naag panchami* day, the snake couple were said to visit the *dakhmas* with their Parsi followers to perform some strange rites, until some enraged orthodox Parsis reportedly manhandled the rather frail Yogiraj who beat a hasty retreat.

During the days of the Raj, in Bareily Cantonment, a Parsi who ran a popular shop selling liquor, ham and cheese to the British soldiers, kept with him at the till a fully clothed chimpanzee who greeted the customers with an eerie smile and followed his master home where he dutifully untied the owner's shoelaces and carefully placed his shoes in the closet.

In Gujarat towns and villages, Parsis reared poultry for eggs and meat. However, each home had a pet hen or two, who would live to a ripe old age instead of suffering the usual fate of their less fortunate kind, that of ending up on a plate alongside potato chunks. The pet hen was easily identifiable by a colorful chain round its neck and would strut around pompously, having instinctively realised its special status. The rooster, on the other hand, regarded by Parsis as the angel of dawn, was sacrosanct and never consumed. He dominated his harem with gusto and kept the eggs and chicks coming. On Dassera, a red *kanku* (vermilion) *tilo* would be applied to its forehead and he was garlanded with marigolds.

Of course, the ultimate exotic pets were the ones aspired to by the then trustees of the BPP, who made extensive plans to breed vultures in captivity and wanted well-off Parsis to sponsor a vulture baby. One paid for its feed and upkeep, including medicines. The BPP said it would forward a quarterly progress report with a photograph of one's adopted pet ('Silla's baby is cuter and more cherubic than Pilloo's, isn't it?'). Unfortunately, there were no takers.

On noses, twitches, gaits and traits

You can spot a Bawaji (and a Maiji) from a mile

Considering how handsome our Iranian ancestors were, and how exquisitely featured the Indian women who they surely intermarried in large numbers, the resulting product is rather disappointing. The Persian features were vulgarized perhaps by the practice of marrying our first cousins, mostly paternal. You can yet spot a Parsi from a mile.

Although the pink glow of Iranian cheeks is rare, the complexion survives almost unscathed despite the harsh Indian sun. Its shades are becoming darker however. From the near Caucasian (some aristocratic Parsis may be very fair due to marrying Anglo-Saxon and European ladies!) to the somewhat derisively referred to as the *doodh paoo* variety (white bread soaked in milk); to the Oriental yellow pale anemic look; to the Mediterranean dusky; and the rare, dark Parsi.

Physiognomy, the study of correlating physical features with psychological characteristics, may be assailed as a pseudoscience; however, there is something to be said about the link between Parsi no*ses* and Parsi peculiarities. Most of us have a longer one than other Indians, which sharpens our olfactory sen*ses*. Many of those who inhabit the fringe believe that a Parsi, provided he is born of both Parsi parents, has no body odor; and the long nose ensures that you are repulsed from having any bodily interaction with non Parsis.

The typical Parsi nose is often hooked like a beak and classified in physiognomy as a Roman nose. Anecdotally speaking, the blue-blooded families often have long proboscis, and the clan is proud of it. One gentleman from one of these 'proud of nose' families, in his seventies, fell hopelessly in love with a lady a quarter century younger who was upset by the thick clutch of grey hair peeping out of her prospective beau's nose and gifted him a conical shaped battery operated nasal hair remover (strangely available only in Singapore chemist shops). The elated man thrust the object in his nostril and pressed the switch. Designed for gently nipping a protruding hair or two, the device got terribly entangled in the thicket with excruciatingly painful consequences. He ran screaming with the device still whirring inside his nose, until his clever cook deftly removed the battery and ended the torture. He took it as a cosmic sign to remain a bachelor.

The Parsi ear is a close rival to the Parsi nose in its distinctiveness. Few Parsis have small ears. Thick and large ears is the norm, which indicates vitality and courage, according to Chinese face readers. Rarely, you get different sized or shaped ears; such a person experiences many crisis in early years and much success in the later part of life. Parsis often have protruding or sticking out ears, called *bakkra na kaan* (goat ears). Elderly Parsi gentleman are averse to trimming the crop sprouting from their ears as they are considered a mark of prosperity. We remember, as a lad of 11, being castigated by a rather severe looking Parsi tailor called Jassawalla, who had his shop on the top floor of the old Bombay Stock Exchange building, for not standing still during measurements, as we bent forward curiously to examine the rich clutch of hair emanating from his ears, long enough for a tiny plait to be weaved. He was an authentic Parsi eccentric. After a cardiac episode, he used to climb the staircase backwards, in this building without an elevator, and in the process, fractured his femur.

An overwhelming number of Parsis constantly twitch and tick. A leading cardiologist, kind and affable, boarded a domestic flight in the USA to attend a medical conference. His fellow passengers summoned Homeland Security to forcibly evict him as he was behaving suspiciously. All that the good doctor did was to constantly touch his forehead in sudden jerky movements, a twitch from childhood, which terribly unnerves his new patients. Like neuroticism and breast cancer, the community has a grossly disproportionate number of twitching and ticking Parsis. We had a paternal grand-aunt, who must have been extremely pretty in her hey day, suddenly contort her face as if she had just swallowed half a glass  of unrefined castor oil. In those days of formal matchmaking, this must have upset dozens of prospective suitors, forcing her to marry our uncle, who looked like a cross between Dr Spock and R2-D2, apart from being rather dark complexioned, and which resulted in some wags uncharitably saying that *kaagro dahitroon lai gayo* (a crow snatched a delectable piece of baked yoghurt sweet).

To generalize unscientifically, most Parsi men have a rather kind and benign look of helplessness about them (save and except when they are debating some utterly irrelevant point at a meeting of the Federation of the Parsi Zoroastrian Anjumans of India, when their facial expressions resemble the early onset of dementia); while the ladies appear imposing and those who cannot be trifled with. Parsi ladies approaching the 40s have a general look of disapproval about them. You often find them snorting or gently placing their index finger on a nostril and inhaling lightly; as if they were doing *pranayama* (breath control). Some of the aggressive ones flail their arms in an exaggerated fashion, as they stompingly march with a penetrating Medusa-like gaze. There are, of course, angelic ones who neither twitch nor tick. Just a few days ago, we had a business meeting in the foyer cafe of a hotel. Three gents with us, all non Parsis, observed that there must be a big Parsi function somewhere in the hotel, as dozens of Parsis were relentlessly passing by. Pray, we asked them, how do you know that all these people passing by were Parsis. Come on, one of them guffawed, how on earth would anyone not recognize a Parsi. They are from a different planet.

No pride in prejudice

The line between mild bias and being communal is rather thin

Gujri jafaaon bhaari, to pun na chhodiyo dharam (endured many tribulations but did not forsake the faith), goes a couplet from the Parsi anthem *Chhaiyé Hamé Zarthoshti* which continues to make most misty eyed. It conjures up many a thought in our collective consciousness — survivors against all odds; honest and loyal refugees who created wealth only by hard work and daring; pioneers in every walk of life; excelling disproportionately to minuscule numbers; different from the natives; racially and ethnically superior; cannot forget the marauding tribes who robbed us of our fatherland; my beloved community first, merit be damned. Legitimate pride soon gets converted into distrust, if not a morbid dislike of strangers.

The pressure to be politically correct often conceals this smouldering prejudice within. Of course, there is a micro minority which is ethically and intellectually pure enough not to be affected by any such embedded prejudice. For the rest, this affects rational decision making and often compromi*ses* the conscience.

If all other things are more or less equal, would you prefer to hire a Parsi employee or engage the services of a Parsi doctor, lawyer, chartered accountant or other service provider? Would you rather have a Parsi tenant even if it means a slightly lower rent? Would you appoint your trusted non-Parsi friends as executors of your last will and testament? As an air steward, are you thrilled to serve a Parsi passenger? On a long haul flight, do you feel more secure on learning that the captain is a Parsi or make a special effort to be friendly with a Parsi co-passenger? If you are a judge, would you give greater latitude to a Parsi counsel arguing before you? A handful will answer, "Of course not." A few will squirm in discomfort and shrug their shoulders. Many will proudly say, "Why not? We must look after our own first."

The last mentioned group gets vociferous — "cut off this sanctimonious claptrap; we will perish if we don't support our own; look at the Jews and the Kurds and other great surviving refugee groups who always stand united against the enemy without; each one of us is duty bound to prefer our brethren." At least, this lot is honest. Most of us harbor these prejudices on the sly. This is often a gut reaction even in the otherwise secular minded.

Many a justification can be advanced. We are like a drop of water in the ocean, in great danger of dissipation. We must look out for each other, otherwise we simply cannot survive. We are so different from the others — our culture, our ethos, our way of life — naturally, we feel comfortable and happy with our own. We understand and appreciate each other the best — our idiosyncrasies, our eccentricities, our unique sense of humor. The world over, ethnic groups are becoming more close knit and parochial. Look at Brexit, Donald Trump, the rise of extreme right populist leaders in Western democracies, ISIS and the migrant crisis. All are closing ranks. Political correctness is being dumped in the dustbin, along with once cherished liberal values.

There is no room for woolly headed intellectuals. If we have to choose between survival and communal bias, the answer is self-evident.

The road from mild bias to gross prejudice to xenophobia is rapid. We have never been a prickly minority. We have not demanded special status or reservations or protection from the State or society. We are perceived as honest, fair, soft-spoken, gentle and harmless. Is all this about to change?

Parsi properties should only be in Parsi hands, contend the hardliners. Even secular charities controlled by Parsis must give preference to Parsi beneficiaries. Buildings, such as some in Dadar Parsi Colony (DPC), though not bound by the Parsis only covenant, must retain their Parsis only character. The Bombay Parsi Punchayet must only appoint Parsi staff. Paranoia is infectious. The hard line is becoming popular. Even those who have married outside the faith or those who advocate the throwing open of funeral ceremonies to non-Parsis are beginning to believe that having a communal bias is permissible.

Often the dividing line is thin and grey. Recently, our long time bank relationship manager, not a Parsi, changed jobs and wanted us to switch our investment portfolio to his new institution. As his performance was good, we readily agreed and directed a transfer. We were soon confronted by a teary eyed young Parsi lady from the old bank who begged us to retain at least a part of the portfolio. A bright young lass from DPC, brought up by a widowed mother overcoming great odds, then softly said, "Sir, all things apart, we are both Parsis." We agreed to retain half the portfolio with her. We questioned ourselves whether our decision was based on compassion or subconscious communal bias; and if we, accused of being anti-Parsi a million times, can think thus, what about the rest?

Decades ago, a viciously litigating Parsi client of ours was advised as a litigation strategy to write to the government authorities about his bitter and equally vicious opponent. The otherwise ruthless gentleman exclaimed, "He is my enemy all right, but a Parsi. I will lose the case but never set the *juddin* government against him." This will warm the cockles of the hearts of the vocal brigade who proudly prefer to wear communalism on their sleeves. In an unspoken manner, expectations are growing within the community that we will, in all situations, first look after our own. Many don't even have to make a conscious decision, it happens automatically from within. As this attitude spreads like slow poison, our community's image as being a cut above the rest in fairness is bound to suffer. "Don't worry about the image, *dikra*. If we don't fend for each other, we just won't survive," says the openly communal brigade. No prizes for guessing who is winning the debate.

Traditionalists disrupting the Federation of the Parsi Zoroastrian Anjumans of India meeting in Ahmedabad in 2004

Respecting Priests

*From sublime heights, our priests have descended to becoming an
underprivileged class*

The diktats of imams and maulvis are faithfully followed. Hindu priests rule the roost in most parts of India. Not only archbishops and cardinals, even the parish priest is held in affectionate regard. Buddhist monks are considered evolved souls. Bohris regard their head priest as a direct descendant from the Prophet. Jains revere their maharaj sahebs and mahasatijis. Sants rule Sikh hearts and Rabbis rock. Parsi priests, an underprivileged class, are given only cursory respect.

Zoroastrian prayers reverentially refer to the great dasturs of yore who sacrificed all to protect the holy fire and the faith from the marauding Arabs. It was a dastur(Nairyosang Dhaval) who secured us refuge in India by convincing a sceptical king in power about our bona fides. Dastur Meherjirana attended Emperor Akbar's court and significantly contributed to Din e Ilahi, a new secular faith conceived by the Emperor. For believers, even today, Meherjirana's image which has mystically surfaced on the marble wall opposite the sanctum sanctorum in the Navsari *Atash behram* is proof of his high spiritual status. In more recent times, the many miracles of Dastur Jamshed Kookadaru, including alchemically transforming a brick into gold to finance a fire temple, are the stuff of legend. Our priests were giants of men, both spiritual healers and leaders in thought.

From these sublime heights, the priests descended into unseemly factional strife, asserting territorial rights to perform ceremonies and indulging in parish grabbing, and even violence. Since one had to be born into a priestly family to become a priest, it became a calling by compulsion and not choice. Even if a non-priestly behdin had eminent qualities to be a good priest, he was barred by the accident of birth. A non-merit based hereditary calling often degenerates. Young lads dropped out of school to practise as priests to feed families. Lack of education led to penury, poverty and poor thinking. The priests began to be perceived by the behdin laity as babblers for money. There was reluctance on the part of behdins to marry daughters of priestly families [*Andhyaru ni dikri andharoo lavé* (a priest's daughter brings bad luck)] which resulted in intermarriage amongst priestly families further aggravating the problem.

While the priests were in decline, the behdins prospered. A Brahmin elite elicits respect from other economically superior classes provided the former possesses a sharp intellect. Our uneducated priests could not provide leadership in thought. Nor did their lifestyle inspire reverence. Unlike Roman Catholics, Jains, Buddhists and some Hindu sects, our priests took no vows of celibacy. Unlike the maulvis, they were not teetotalers. Personal sacrifice and a spartan life dedicated to the faith inspire awe and respect. Our priests are indistinguishable from the laity. Many overindulged in worldly pleasures. There was no demonstration of a spiritual life. Neither was there any centralized hierarchy whose commands were sacrosanct. Instead of being able to galvanize the flock, the priests often became objects of ridicule. Priests dozing during recitation of prayers or taking short cuts by omitting stanzas are the butt of jokes. Of course, there were a few who were highly educated, cultured, erudite, learned and pious. But not enough to compensate for the rest of the mediocre army.

Behdins pay paltry fees for religious ceremonies. Poor income makes full-time practice of priesthood difficult, compelling many to take day jobs and become part-time priests, a contradiction in terms. Crass commercialization displaces devotional fervor. Priests have to appeal to charity for housing and hospitalization. A vicious cycle is continually fed. Various *mobed* amelioration schemes are inadequately funded. A rich and prosperous community with huge charity funds has priests who live in penury.

High priests, appointed by heredity and not merit in most ca*s*es, have refused to adapt with the times. Some are unduly orthodox and a few positively repugnant to the youth. The irony is that most po*ss*ess stellar intellect and an ability to impress. However, by toeing an excessively conservative line, they are alienating the youth. We need to lift the priests from this rut and turn them into an army of enthused preachers of the faith. A flock which does not look up to its shepherd is doomed to dissipate.

Jashan at H. B. Wadiaji Atash Behram Hall in December 2013 Photo: Jasmine D. Driver

Permitting behdins and women to become priests, allocating liberal resources to educate and equip young initiates, providing free and highest priority in community housing, medical aid and free life insurance to full-time priests, investing in sprucing up our athornan madressas and making the community conscious of the critical importance of priests, may yet stem the rot. Non-resident Indian Parsis with large hearts are ready to help. Our miserable punchayets are too busy squabbling to take the lead. The high priests themselves have to uplift the priests. Sometimes, ridicule can rapidly turn into reverence.

Not fair, but lovely

The bias in favor of the pale skinned still exists

Rustom (name changed) migrated from Rustom Baug to San Francisco and became a successful businessman. His widowed mother made impassioned pleas to her son to marry — even a *'mudum'* (foreign lady) would do. In his early 40s, Rustom wrote to his mother that he had married a nice American lady and would soon return home with her. His mother and assorted aunts, equipped with *aacchhoo michhoo* thalis (German silver trays containing flowers, coconut, eggs; to be passed over the heads of the newly weds, to wish them an auspicious beginning) anxiously awaited Rustom and his bride. When finally the doorbell rang, Rustom and his lovely bride with beaming smiles, greeted them. His mother took one look at the bride, an attractive African American, and fell unconscious to the floor, the contents of the aachhoo michhoo scattered. She never spoke to her only son, for the cardinal sin he had committed. Unbelievable, but true.

A Parsi official of the Turf Club wooed a smashingly good looking hostess with Air India. When she was introduced to the person's grandmother, she squinted her beady eyes and remarked, "Quite beautiful, I must say, but rather dark, isn't she?" Our paternal grandmother, a pragmatic sort of person, observed about our father's close friend, a certain Vishnubhai (all deceased), that "Vishnu is an excellent human being, if only he was not so black."

Matrimonial advertisements do not care for being politically correct, when promoting "a fair, slim bride." One comes across the occasional advertisement which even talks about the complexion of the bridegroom. Traditional *kaajwalis* (matchmakers) and matrimonial bureau services of Parsi organizations testify to the demand for the fair skinned. You may just manage if you are horizontally or vertically challenged but not if you don't "look like a Parsi."

Burjorji Bharucha, the noted Gandhian social worker, organized mass navjotes of children of Parsi fathers and mothers hailing mostly from the scheduled caste. The 'Vansda Navjotes,' as they came to be known, generated heated controversy in the Parsi Press (Kaiser-e-Hind espousing the liberal perspective). Several, who were not so aghast at the purported sacrilege committed by Bharucha, wondered as to how these "unfortunate children" would be assimilated in the community due to their dark complexion and 'unParsi' looks. We have observed how the composure of portly ladies praying in agiaries, talcum powder embedded in their double chins, is disturbed on spotting a new *chasniwala* (fire temple worker) who suspiciously looks like a non-Parsi.

Complexion though does not seem to be an issue when it comes to the trustees of the Bombay Parsi Punchayet, now elected by universal adult franchise. One, elected thrice in succession as a trustee with a huge majority, bewitches the electorate with his twinkling eyes and beaming smile, even though he, in his own words, looks "more like John than Jehan."

As the most forward looking and Westernized of all Indian communities, the Parsis nevertheless retain their bias for the *doodhpak* (a sweetened rice and milk dessert) complexion, with the ultra thin purple colored 'Kayani' veins visible on pink cheeks and whose sheer presence lights up the room during a power outage. For many Parsis, black is still not beautiful.

All Parsis are not Zoroastrians

Parsi Hindus, Parsi Muslims, Parsi Christians and,
of course, non-Parsi Zoroastrians all exist

Many believe erroneously that all Parsis are Zoroastrians, and vice versa. The nearly three lakh practising Zoroastrians in countries around the Caspian Sea are not Parsis. And quite a few Parsis are not Zoroastrians, like late Rajiv and Sanjay Gandhi. Though born of a Parsi father, neither was navjoted nor believed in Ahura Mazda and his prophet, Zarathushtra. After his assassination, when Rajiv Gandhi was accorded national honor, his Parsi relatives did place a sudreh-kusti on the funeral cortège.

Although there is no legal or ecclesiastical authority for the proposition, without a navjote, a Parsi is not regarded as a Zoroastrian. In the absence of any records or system of certification, a simple assertion by a Parsi that he has been navjoted will suffice. Though some do not like to take chances. Neville Wadia in his eighties and

Nusli Wadia in his fifties were navjoted, a little belatedly, through the orthodox Dastur (Dr) Firoze Kotwal who had termed Parsis marrying interfaith as being guilty of adultery. Of course, for the learned priest, goose and gander don't require the same sauce.

It is possible that you may be navjoted and yet not be regarded as Zoroastrian. This can happen in two situations. If you are navjoted but your father is not a Parsi (there are priests now who will gladly navjote you, even if both your parents are not Parsis) and, secondly, if you convert to another faith, openly or otherwise. We know of two unrelated Parsi ladies, both born of blue-blooded Parsi parents and married to a Parsi, and though not baptised, were practising Christians (one of them regularly played the piano during Sunday Mass). When they were widowed, they had to sit outside the *Doongerwadi bungli*, like any other non-Parsi.

Rajiv (left) and Sanjay Gandhi: Parsis but not Zoroastrians

For our younger readers, it is best perhaps to reiterate the legal position. Parsi is a race, Zoroastrianism is a religion. To enter most fire temples and Towers of Silence and to be regarded as beneficiaries of almost all Parsi charities, you have to be both — a Parsi and a Zoroastrian. There are some rare trust deeds where the beneficiary need only be a Zoroastrian (mostly out of inadvertence, not design). To be regarded as a Parsi, at least your father must be a Parsi.

A micro-minority, though born Parsis, never get to be Zoroastrians. The parents may be atheist, agnostic or believe that no religion should be thrust upon a child, and hence no navjote. Then, of course, there are those who begin life as Parsi Zoroastrians but convert at the time of marriage to the faith of their husband (the law requires exacting evidence to establish such conversion — a name change is not enough but another faith marriage ceremony, usually, is). Again some migrate to another faith out of a conscious choice. We knew of a Parsi solicitor (now deceased) who did *namaz* in his office, five times a day, while his irate clients fretted in his Pickwickian office. Or like the born again Christian Parsis mentioned above. Confuse not though those who believe in other faiths but also continue to be practising Zoroastrians. The orthodox would like to disbelieve but a huge number of Parsi Zoroastrians in India fall into this category — perhaps even as much as one-third.

When Sanjay Gandhi suddenly perished in an air crash, his widow, Maneka, did consult lawyers to ascertain which law of intestate succession (those dying without a will) would apply — the Hindu Succession Act or the Indian Succession Act provisions applicable to Parsi intestates. We do not know the outcome but the correct law would have been the Parsi law; even if Sanjay was not a Zoroastrian, he was certainly a Parsi, being born of a Parsi father. You can give up your religion but not your race.

If you think the above is semantics or mere technicalities, you are wrong. It is intrinsically connected to the future of our faith. The day we decide that race is immaterial, and only bona fide belief in the faith is, a revolution will take place. Non-Parsi Zoroastrians will be officially admitted to the faith (perhaps, the aspiring Russian *mobed* Mikhail Chistyakov who was roughed up by orthodox hooligans at Sanjan, will return, to be initiated as a priest). This will provide an unprecedented impetus to millions of nascent Zoroastrians to join the faith and numbers will swell for this modern sounding religion with its emphasis on ethics, environment and equality. A micro-minority of the followers of the Zoroastrian faith will then be Parsis, mingling with their non-Parsi brethren in a vibrant melting pot.

Praying matters

Parsis ought to, but are not praying enough

The Prophet termed priests as babblers for money. Perhaps he was urging every Zoroastrian to pray himself and not contract out for a fee. If so, the Prophet's commandment appears largely ignored by his followers today.

Few believing Parsis pray at all, and even those, not regularly. Apart from the perfunctory tying of the kusti, perhaps. A candidate for *navar* or maratab or a *mobed* readying himself to conduct a *Vendidad* or other ritual prayer, is required to cleanse himself by undergoing a naha n or seclusion period for nine days (during which he cannot use water to gargle or brush his teeth or for cleaning any part of his body). During this nahan period he is required to do *farajiyaat* (mandatory) prayers in different *gahs*. The purist will rise at dawn to recite *Hoshbaam* (which is one of our most beautiful prayers). In each of the five *gahs*, he will do his kusti prayers, followed by *Srosh Baj*, the relevant *gah*, *Khorshed* and *Meher Neyayesh* in the sunrise to sunset *gah*s, being invocations to the sun, the *Vispa Humata* (declaration of the faith), *Doa Nam Setayeshne* along with the homage to the four directions.

Apart from this capsule of prayers five times a day, the devout are expected to retie the kusti after every visit to the toilet (presumably, not after dialysis). At night, you should pray to the moon, particularly on new moon, full moon and no moon day (*chaandraat, poonam* and *amas*). It is mandatory to recite the most beneficial *Atash Neyayesh* to the holy fire at least once a day. Add to this, the *yasht* dedicated to the presiding angel of the day (like Khordad or Behram or Ardibehesht).

On the Avan *Parav* (*roz* Avan, *mah* Avan), many attend the traditional function at Radio Club only after spending a goodly 60 minutes intoning one of the longest prayers, the most boon granting *Avan Yasht*. If you manage, year after year, without a break, to recite this *Yasht* on the *Parav*, whether you are in the hospital or in Havana, it is said to give the most amazing results.

On the last day of the Parsi New Year, you wipe your balance sheet clean by begging forgiveness for your sins through the prayer *Patet Pashemani*. The *Patet* has a laundry list of the various *gunah* (sins) which you could have wittingly or unwittingly committed. A day before the five Gathas, one recites the preparatory prayer contained in the *Framarot no Ha*, and then of course, the recitation of the poetic *Gathas*, composed by the prophet himself.

The behdins visit agiaries to either doze or gossip when the retained *mobed* is zipping through the *afringaan, farokhshi* and *baaj* prayers like the Dehradun Express, often missing a few stations, deliberately or otherwise. The sensible prefer to themselves pray the *Stum no Kardo* for their deceased. During the muktad days, in bustling agiaries, part-time priests have to almost continuously pray for nearly five hours for the departed clients of the panthaky, in quick succession, and could be pardoned for a few short cuts (cutely termed, "Dasturji *gaapchu maarech*"). Some behdins bitterly complain to the panthaky about the voice of the *mobed* not being sonorous enough ("My late Tehmaas loved to hear prayers loudly recited"), as others irately protest at the out-of-turn allotment of the prayer slot to some favored client ("my cousins and I entered the *agiary* much before that stout lady!"). The chaasni (partaking of the prayed upon food) not being edible or the apples being rather small, are other frequent grouses. Tempers are frayed inter se the attending behdins, if the 'name list' (given to the *mobed*) of the deceased family members omits a particular name or about its placement in the order of priority ("Look at her temerity! My father was the eldest brother but his name was listed third! Now, I too will cancel her grandmother's name from our name list"). All this and more happens with amazing frequency much to the consternation of the harassed panthaky. The prayer charges are most reasonable yet a few behdins negotiate a discount ("Now don't you charge separately for the baaj").

A free flowing Gujarati or English translation from Avesta or Pazend may appear simplistic and uninspiring. However, the vibratory effects of our manthric prayers, when recited with devotion and concentration, are claimed to be highly effective. Decades ago, Dame Meher Master-Moos, in her Mazdayasnie Monasterie and its affiliated University, claimed to break window panes by intoning the *Yatha Ahu Vairyo* to a particular high pitch. When Zoroastrian teacher/preacher Khojeste Mistree first descended upon Bombay in the late 1970s with his lectures on religion, he would often round off by reciting the *Ahunavar* in a highly accented but sonorous baritone, endearing himself to many middle aged ladies.

Apart from Moos and Mistree's vocal experiments, the *Yatha Ahu Vairyo* is the cornerstone capsule prayer [*Ahuném vairim tanum pāti* (Ahu*navar* saves body and soul) is a powerful manthra by itself]. So are the words, *Nemascha yā armaitish izha-chā*, recited thrice at the end of the geh sarna prayers, obliterating the worldly memories of the deceased and severing his mortal ties. The lost word, believed by many to be a powerhouse — *Māāthrém* — is also from the *Avesta*. If you cannot spare time for the longer prayers, at least recite these manthras for temporal and spiritual protection, say our scholars.

A micro minority prays daily with great fervor, while observing ritualistic purity. We knew of a very fine gentleman, who would visit every fire temple on its founding day, and in addition pray at home for nearly four hours. If his foot accidentally touched the wire of his old gramophone upon which his *ganga* (maidservant) happened to simultaneously lean while cleaning the floor, he would redo the kusti and start praying afresh, to purge the *juddin* contact and the possible impurity. By this standard, most of his neighbours would have to pray constantly.

Prayers, our wise ones say, are like the umbrella. They won't prevent the rain from falling but at least you will get less wet.

Devotees praying at Bhikha Behram well in Bombay
Photo: Kainaz Amaria

Non-Parsi believers are on the rise

A surprising number of non-Parsis have faith in Zoroastrian prayers

There is this anecdote about a solitary fisherman's tiny boat being tossed around in stormy waters with the shore nowhere in sight. A few years earlier this fisherman had witnessed, in a similar situation, his Parsi master reciting the *Yatha Ahu Vairyo* after which the sea suddenly turned benign, thus saving precious lives. However, the only word the fisherman could remember was "Thavario." With great devotion and faith, he started chanting, "*Parsi taro Thavario* (Parsi, your Thavario)." The miracle is said to have occurred again: the stormy skies cleared and the wind dropped.

In those towns of Gujarat which have an *agiary* it is commonplace for non-Parsis to hand over sandalwood sticks to Parsis entering the fire temple and requesting them to light a divo. Barring some occasional oddball, Parsis gracefully accede to this touching request.

Bhikha Behram Well at Churchgate

Even in Udvada non-Parsis buy sandalwood and leave it at the Iranshah gate. In the 1940s when the revered Sardar Dastur Noshirwan Dastur, designated Head Priest of the Deccan, was in charge of Poona's Sardar Sorabji Patel *Agiary* in Nana Peth (*Gaam ni Agiary*), it was widely known that non-Parsis would leave sandalwood outside the fire temple as offerings to the atash padshah. The benign priest, noted for his spiritual aura, would also reportedly receive written requests (which were tied to the branches of a pomegranate tree in the compound) asking him to make special intercessions on their behalf to solve the problems they were facing. This now occurs in Bombay as well. On *Meher mah, Meher roz,* as the queue winds its way through the narrow lane leading to the famed Aslaji *Agiary*, non-Parsis can be seen handing money to Parsi devotees to offer sandalwood to the holy fire on their behalf. At Bombay's Bhikha Behram Well, located at the southern end of Cross Maidan, several non-Parsis stand outside the venerated premises to offer their devotion.

Our progressive priests (and their number is gradually increasing) who perform funeral rites for those opting for cremation and navjotes of children of intermarried Parsi mothers, are now being requisitioned to conduct *jashans* at non-Parsi homes. The fervor with which these *jashans* are attended by non-Parsis is to be seen to be believed, report the priests. The potency of *manthric* prayers is appreciated. Non-Parsis suffering from chronic illness*es* or inexplicable malevolence request their Parsi friends to recite the *Ardibehesht Yasht* or the nirang of Afsoon-e-Shah-e-Faridoon, the divine healer. A Maharashtrian lady on dialysis recently surprised this writer by reciting the central *manthra* of that nirang, with impeccable pronunciation.

Does this mean that if the faith was to open its doors to non-Parsis there would be an implosion? We think not. Just as Parsis, substantial numbers of whom routinely worship at the temples of other faiths but remain Zoroastrians, non-Parsis who offer devotion at Zoroastrian places of worship would stay with their religion. Many such non-Parsi believers often express a wish to worship in our fire temples and some of them have even done so. This will undoubtedly enrage the orthodox. However, what seems sacrilege today may, over the next two or three decades, may become accepted practice. Closed door practices generally crumble under the pressure of external factors.

Parsis should be legitimately proud of the power of their faith being appreciated by others. Every religion is universal and man-made rules of exclusion are bound to fall by the wayside when the time is ripe.

Does chhaiyé hamé zarthoshti make you misty-eyed?

The Parsi anthem still evokes strong passion

Chhaiyé Hamé Zarthosti [(CHZ) We are proud to be Zoroastrians], the unofficial anthem of our community, continues to evoke strong passion. A nation is what a nation feels. If you are not misty eyed every time CHZ is played; something is amiss with your Parsipanu (a uniquely untranslatable phrase – effectively meaning a sense of belonging to the community). CHZ, composed by Kavi (poet) Firoz Batliwalla who died in 1912, speaks of the heroic few who battled all odds to save their faith from marauding Arabs (*Gujri jafaao bhaari, to pun na chhodyo dharam* meaning endured severe hardships but did not forsake the religion). The poet adds that the secret of Parsi prosperity is this undying devotion to the faith. Batliwalla extols the great charity instinct (*Baholi sakhawat hathé,*

jé chhè jag jaher meaning extensive charitable instincts are known worldwide) and the community's outstanding ability in all fields (*sauv vaat ma maaher*).

Composed over a century ago and sung to the tune of Farewell My Bluebell, composed in 1904, the poet is ahead of his times in emphasizing the role of Parsi women and asserting that female education is the key to a happy family. Women are our legitimate pride, the poet asserts. (*Té kom ni banu thaee, chhaiyé hamé magroor*). However, some liberals have criticized the anthem for its repeated reference to racial stock and genetic superiority (*O tokhum kyani, O jagmashoor*). Almost like the ultra orthodox credo "*tokhum ni jalaavni né boond ni paasbani.*" CHZ, while, propagating a friendly approach to other communities (*kul jehaan saathé dosti*), does emphasize the exclusivity of the Parsis and even a slightly understated sense of superiority over non-Parsis.

The unstinted loyalty of the Parsis to the rulers who provided them refuge is lauded (*Jéni vafaadari par padya nathi koi daag* meaning our loyalty is unstinted). Even our Prime Minister (Narendra Modi) has never lost an opportunity to uphold the Parsis as the 'loyal' minority and a beacon light to others who are more vocal in asking for special rights.

At the 16th North American Zoroastrian Congress, New York, in August 2012, the ZAGNY (Zoroastrian Association of Greater New York) philharmonic orchestra rendered CHZ, with the audience mouthing the lyrics, as teary eyed American Parsis clicked this very emotional moment on their cell phones. The migrants' nostalgia for the motherland is always touching.

Parsi associations like the Rahnumae Mazdayasni Sabha, the Rathestar Mandal, the Bombay Parsee Association, the Navsari Parsi Association, Youths Own Union and the like invariably ended their functions, cutely called a '*mélavdo*,' with a rendering of the CHZ, though the audience did not spring to attention (most of them would not have been able to, even if they had wanted to).

In the collective consciousness of the community, the most powerful thought is our forefathers making the arduous journey from Iran to protect the faith; a people hounded out of their motherland and deprived of their kingdom by barbaric hordes. This thought, being the central theme of CHZ, strikes an emotional chord in most. If you don't feel sentimental when the chorus of CHZ plays, you are either disconnected from the community or do not understand Batliwalla's lyrics couched in *shuddh* Gujarati (not the Parsi dialect).

Apart from CHZ, there are other recorded songs which make us feel devotional. Most are eulogies to Zarathushtra (*O Dadgar dadar Nabiji vandan ho shut var, amara bhav bhav na aadhar, Koi poochhé mané kya chhè tara Zarthosht paygamber, dil chiri né batavoon, mara jigar ni andar*). The Dadar Parsi Association, music director Vistasp Balsara from Calcutta and Mani Rao from USA have, at different times, produced discs containing Parsi devotional songs, some of which are available on YouTube.

Decades ago, Parsis like the Chiniwalla brothers and Pervez Katrak used to sonorously recite or sing monajats (hymns) and passages from Firdausi's Shahnameh – the chronicles of the ancient kings, warriors and pehelvans (a kind of samurai). The most popular of these being the tragic saga of the legendary father-son duo of Rustom and Sohrab; the former vanquishing the latter in a brave battle, not knowing that he was killing his own son. This did not stop Adi Marzban and thespian Jimmy Poncha from spoofing the saga on stage, Shahnameh style – "*Rustom é aapyo Sohrab né jolab; Né Sohrab é kidho léngho kharaab* (Rustom gave an overdose of laxative to Sohrab, who soiled his pyjamas)."

Flippancy apart, Parsi devotional music, with CHZ leading the list, is as much a part of Parsi culture as gahambars, lagan nu paatru, *garo* and dhansak. Even after hearing a diatribe on the demographic decline and a grim future, sung with gusto CHZ invariably lifts spirits and offers hope, reminding us of a thousand years ago when the odds against our survival were stacked even higher than they are now.

Chhaiyé Hamé Zarthoshti being sung at the Federation meeting in Bombay in 2012

No sex please, we are Parsis

Not procreating, but recreating

In 1973, a London West End hit called *No sex please, we are British* played to full hou*ses*. The Brits were pilloried as a nation of flat beer, soggy chips and insipid fish. Our dramatically declining numbers may lead many to believe that, like the Brits, we too have lost it. A disproportionately large number of spinsters and bachelors give an impression that Parsis are no longer like the birds and the bees. Nearly 31% of the community is 65 plus, as compared to the national average of seven percent. Retirees go to bed, and go to sleep, early. May be wealthy and wise, though not always healthy. Has our libido hit a nadir or are we still fit and proper?

The national census does not collate data on sex habits. Although Parsi demographic studies abound, no one has produced a thesis on sexual behavior. The Bombay Parsi Punchayet will allot priority housing to those who furnish evidence that they are engaged to get married [we do know of some fake *lagan ni chithis* (wedding invites)] but not to those who are in a live-in relationship. Perhaps, the trustees believe that our hallowed baugs ought not to be defiled by premarital sex. In the absence of any authentic Parsi sexuality studies, only anecdotal material can be considered.

Those who believe that the genial bawaji is hardly interested in the subject, are mistaken. A few generations ago, Parsis in rural and semi urban areas had large families. Our maternal grandmother delivered her last born (ninth) child, exactly nine months after her first born daughter had already delivered her child. (Spending time on watching television detracts from time in bed.) They married while in their teens and wasted no time in procreating. In the mores of those times, premarital sex was rare, not due to lack of opportunity and space (large houses offered plentiful privacy); but the fear of losing virginity (older women of the household carefully examined the bridal night bedsheet for telltale signs, the morning after). With hardly any access to contraception [barring raw papayas from the backyard tree or for those who had no easy access to trees, boiled concentrate of *ajmo*l or *ajwain* (bishop's weed/carom seeds) in hot water], fear of pregnancy would deter even the most robust. Unlike Hindus, since cousins were the most likely marriage partners, some did begin physical relationships early. Resulting accidents were quickly converted into rushed matrimony, with curious ladies slyly eyeing the bride's belly to estimate the month of conception. Popular Parsi folklore had it that a pregnant bride made a great wife.

In the villages of Gujarat, it was commonplace for Parsi men to maintain non-Parsi mistress*es*. The controversial Vansda navjotes, of children born of such alliances, rocked the community's orthodox bastions. Conducted by the then liberal priest, Dastur Framroze Bode, and encouraged by a Gandhian social worker, Burjorji Bharucha, these navjotes were a bold attempt to assimilate children of Parsi fathers, and Hindu mothers from economically weaker sections, into the mainstream.

Until the 1980s, when some *mohollas* (localities) in Navsari,

Valsad and Surat still retained their Parsi character, the occasional dalliance with non-Parsi women, mostly domestic help, continued. In a particular town of Gujarat, a particular traditional family, whose leader occupied a pride of place at ceremonial occasions decided to fill up their deceased leader's vacancy by somewhat surprisingly appointing a soft spoken, docile, nondescript bank manager. Days before his coronation, the leader elect was spotted exiting his domestic help's hut in the late afternoon and the shocked elders nixed his appointment. Parsis have coined an original term for an afternoon foray — '*baporyoon* (afternoon sex).'

In the bygone era, infidelity, so long as not in the face, was silently admired as a sign of manliness. In the early 1960s, when business travel abroad was in its infancy, a foreign 'returned' Parsi businessman would be asked by his envious friends — "*Kèm, Minocher, Germany ma tipu mooki né aaya ké* (Did you leave any potential heirs in Germany)?" Those who continued to be sexually active until their 70s were admired even by their children: "*Bawa, ajun bhi golat marvanu nai chuké* (Even at his age, father can still perform)!" At the uthamna ceremony of a serial philanderer, the mourners would non-judgementally remark that "*marhoom, manas saara, pan naara na dhilla utta* (The deceased, though a good man, had loose pyjama strings)."

More than three decades ago, in our early days of legal practice, one of our first clients was a Parsi gentleman of leisure with an aristocratic lineage. During a visit to Poona, he made us wait in his Fiat, as he went to visit his tailor. He returned after a good 50 minutes, so we asked with a trace of irritation, as to why it took so long to give measurements. The tailor died four years ago, he replied nonchalantly. Enjoying our perplexed look, he volunteered that the tailor's daughter was his good friend. He sincerely believed that Parsi men possessed unparalleled prowess in matters sexual.

Two fundamentalist priestly brothers from London echoed this gentleman's views, when they told a stunned management committee of AIMZ (Association of Inter-Married Zoroastrians) that Parsi ladies married to non-Parsi men did not know what they were missing. The immodesty of such macho claims apart, quite a few Parsi men find Parsi women a trifle too dominating and aggressive, which acts as a 'put off' factor; resulting in non-Parsi women appearing attractive as partners. On the other hand, as the fiddler on the roof would say, Parsi women find Parsi men to be sissy, insipid and mumma's boys. Decades of genetic inbreeding has perhaps produced a reciprocal revulsion factor — nature's way of restoring a healthy balance — a recipe for the galloping number of interfaith marriages.

Legendary tales abound. There was this famous race horsetrainer of yesteryears, believed to have consumed a live queen ant, which endowed him with enough libido to populate nearly half a village near Poona. A harassed sub-registrar of assurances was bombarded by multiple claims to the immovable properties of the deceased trainer from persons claiming to be his sons and daughters. And then there was this building contractor in his late 60s, popularly known as 'Sam Uncle,' barely five foot tall; but to whose amazing stamina, half of Dhobi Talao swore. Sam Uncle's female counterpart was an air hostess in Dadar; old-timers in the airline would compare her to Catherine the Great of Russia, who was rumored to have died while copulating with a horse.

Someone ought to venture to write a screenplay for a Parsi new year *natak* to be called, *Sex please, we are Parsis*.

Family portrait, circa 1900

Lemon and chilli are not that silly

Many Parsis are superstitious

Until the late 1980s, when there were no mobile phones or email, and crank calls were untraceable, warring Parsis in baugs would arrange to send the *Doongerwadi* hearse first thing in the morning on some *saaro saparmo divas* (auspicious day) to their enemy's home. Just as Behramji was savoring *sev and dahi*, the *khandhias* (pallbearers) rang the doorbell and crudely ask: where is the body? A classic case of *sagan ma vaghan* (bad omen on an auspicious day) would convince Behramji's family that the coming year would be an annus horribilis (not to be confused with a bad attack of piles).

Apart from the path-crossing black cat, walking under a ladder, spilling salt and other international superstitions, Parsis have their own unique collection. Seeing a hearse at crack of dawn on Parsi New Year day, a dog suddenly wailing or moaning without cause, a crow depositing a dead rat on the window sill, and meeting a Parsee punchayet trustee first thing in the morning are the milder superstitions. The hard core ones are a mixture of Iranian and Indian beliefs. That pregnant women must sleep out a lunar eclipse is extensively followed. In the villages of Gujarat, it is widely believed that at such a time, a pregnant woman should not even open her eyes: If she were to spot an owl, the child would be born with owl-like features.

The rooster is much respected as the angel of dawn and almost never knowingly eaten. In the backyard of Gujarat Parsi homes, poultry would be reared for eggs and for *sali ma murghi* but the rooster would be spared and die either of excessive exertions with his fast diminishing harem or being heartbroken at seeing his mate end up on a plate. To complete the bird superstitions, Parsis reacted with horror to a vulture sitting on the roof of a house. It was taken as a sign of an earthly sojourn about to end. Considering that Parsis managed to outlive the vultures, this superstition has proved to be baseless.

Even in Persia, they believed in evil eye. Shah Faridoon, a wise king, was a great white magician who conquered the evil Zohak and whose nirang prayer is even today faithfully recited by community members to ward off black magic. This nirang lists more than a hundred different types of *nazars* or *chashma* (evil eye) to be purged. The healer holds the thumb of the right hand of the victim and recites this nirang with the oft repeated intonation of the mantra, "*Fé naaméyazad, bā farmaané yazad, banamé nik Faridoon é dāāv gayé*," which has very potent vibrations. Some Parsis wear an amulet containing a miniature version of the nirang.

Fixing a horse shoe above the entrance door (more often than not, the shoe was from cattle, and not a horse) to prevent malevolent influences from entering within, tying lemon and chillies and avoiding stepping on those lying on the ground, curing hepatitis (only of the 'A' variety) and sunstroke by performing certain rituals ultimately do have their origin in some superstition or the other. The rational ones quip that superstition brings bad luck, while the believers retort that superstition is nature's way of preparing one for bad news. The glass shade of a *divo* (oil lamp) or a mirror cracking are considered terrible omens (as Tennyson put it: "The mirror crack'd from side to side, 'The curse is come upon me,' cried the Lady of Shalott").

Notwithstanding the Parsi love for food, dhansak is never to be prepared on a birthday; since post the dawn uthamna ceremony for the deceased, the temporarily vegetarian relatives would eat mutton dhansak, cutely called the *charam nu botu* (charam being the fourth day after death and botu meaning a succulent piece of meat). However, one may gladly consume *mora dar chawal* on a happy occasion. Fortunately, there are no superstitions attached to drinking though one may certainly consider it a bad omen if that carefully preserved Merlot turns out to be vinegarish.

Devout Parsis do believe that day and night are divided into sub-periods of 90 minutes each (beneficial, inimical, excellent, auspicious, chaotic, bad, disease) prominently printed for the month in every good Parsi calendar (like those produced by the defunct Karani Brothers or Union Press). Rolled up into a cylinder, the calendars were handy to swat mosquitoes before flattening them under a heavy mattress in time for Parsi New Year. These sub-periods or *chogadiyas* were faithfully consulted and journeys and events planned accordingly. If one was not careful about what one said during a particular chogadiyu, the consequences could be horrendous, if some malevolent entity was listening in then. Similarly, it was taboo to wallow in bed at dusk. Anyone uttering messages of gloom and doom was sarcastically dubbed *"Sagan no ganthiyo"* (virtually impossible to translate) and to be avoided.

The most sinister superstition was that, other than the khandhias, no one must come out alive from the dakhma. Decades ago, when medical standards were poor, an old lady consigned to the Navsari dakhma showed signs of life and was promptly beaten to death in the belief that once the geh sarana ceremony had been performed, one simply cannot come alive again. This is not a figment of our imagination, though obviously we cannot adduce any evidence. Finally, it is not good to die during the five Gatha days preceding the new year, since one will not then have a *masiso*, *bumsie* or *chhumsie* (after death prayear for the first month, two months and six months). Something like being born on February 29. So be extra careful during the Gathas.

Taxing matters

Parsis, with some notable exceptions, are honest taxpayers

About 15 years ago, a Parsi business family was raided by the income tax department. As is the norm, the raid was simultaneously conducted at multiple locations, just after sunrise. A posse of taxmen along with police constables rang the doorbell and gruffly announced their mission to the domestic help who unsuspectingly opened the door. A formidable lady, looking like an enraged Medusa, stormed out of her bedroom and screamed at the hapless income tax officer. "Get out of here," she imperiously commanded the baffled raiding party who was accustomed to seeing fear on the faces of those being raided. "But, Madam, we have a search warrant," whispered the otherwise awe inspiring officer, who instinctively felt that this lady was from a different galaxy. "At this very moment, your husband is fully cooperating with our team at his office," he informed. "I am no longer that bastard's wife," she shouted, "we have been divorced." The officer thought of asking to see her divorce decree but was deterred by the fire and brimstone emitting entity in front of him and sheepishly signalled his team to retreat. Parsi women don't lie, he muttered to his assistant.

It is widely believed, and correctly so, that Parsis are honest taxpayers. A former advocate general of Maharashtra, known for his spotless integrity, had told this writer that when the gold control order was promulgated in the 1960s, he painstakingly explained the salient features of the law to his seven-year-old son so that the child could take an informed decision on whether to exchange the gold buttons bequeathed to him by his maternal grandfather for gold bonds issued by the Government of India.

When Y. B. Chavan was Union finance minister, the highest slab of income tax reached 98%, and along with wealth tax, amounted to 102%. Many wealthy Parsis borrowed money to pay taxes which exceeded their income. They would then attend the iconic Nani Palkhivala's post budget analysis at the Brabourne Stadium and vigorously applaud his denouncing the expropriatory rate of taxation by the banana republic being run by the *dhotiadas* (ruling elite who wore dhotis).

Up to March 16, 1985, there was a draconian death duty levied in India. On an estate of Rs 20 lakhs or more, the estate duty rate was a staggering 85%. What saved great wealth from being wiped out was the Parsi penchant for creating private family trusts which enabled transfer of property to skip a generation or two and thereby avoid estate duty. Little wonder then that the authoritative treatise on estate duty law was written by a Parsi father-and-son lawyer team, Hoshang Nanavati and his late father Dhunjishaw, both partners of the venerable law firm Mulla and Mulla, Craigie, Blunt and Caroe.

A young Parsi girl lost her parents in a short span of time of six months and one day; had she lost them within six months, she would have been entitled to claim an exemption called quick succession relief of only 50% estate duty on the second death. Her tax consultant suggested obtaining a death certificate from the Bombay

Parsi Punchayet (BPP) dated a day or two earlier through some inducements to the *Doongerwadi* staff. The female simply refused and let go of the exemption.

A Parsi liquor baron died 48 hours before the then finance minister V. P. Singh abolished estate duty, which led to much mourning amongst his comely daughters as to how pappa had passed rather prematurely into the great beyond. Estate duty inspired much fear and one blunt son, over lunch at the Ripon Club, suggested to his rich, ageing father suffering from clogged arteries to consider joining the Border Security Force and be felled in enemy action, since there

was total exemption from estate duty for those who had been killed in war!

Parsis are generally averse to greasing itchy palms and quite enjoy litigating against the perverse orders of the tax department before the High Court and Supreme Court. No wonder then that the finest tax counsel that India ever had is a devout and committed Zoroastrian, Soli Dastur, whom we rather foolishly tried to make a trustee of the BPP in the 2008 elections. His chamber has spawned many leading Parsi tax counsel like the much sought after Percy Pardiwalla.

Of course, there have been quite a few innovative Parsi tax consultants (most of the colorful ones are long deceased) who were not averse to playing by the rules of the game. One such consultant, Mr B, who had a largely Parsi clientele, once invited the income tax officer and his twin brats for dinner to his harassed rich client's opulent residence brimming with rare Ming va*ses*. The brats, much to the horror of the host, decided to play cricket in the drawing room. Mr B told their rather sheepish officer father that the brats may break as many va*ses* as they liked, so long as he issued the desired order. Another consultant was a daredevil who would sign off, as auditor, any doctored accounts prepared by his client, provided the client contributed to the consultant's pet charity. Yet a third eccentric consultant brazenly told the income tax officer that his Parsi client must have made a genuine mistake in the accounting, for a Parsi would never indulge in petty manipulation: 'Sir, Parsi *chori bi karé to mottij chori karé* (even if a Parsi cheats, he would do so only on a grand scale)."

Many a Parsi would tell his income tax officer with a straight face that we Parsis never believe in black money, and often get away with blue murder, such being the collective goodwill and reputation of our community. Few know that capital controls or foreign exchange laws did exist even before Independence. Before the much dreaded FERA (Foreign Exchange Regulation Act) of 1973, there was a 1947 version too. Decades ago a retired Parsi businessman proudly narrated to us as to how he sent as little as US $ 500 through hawala every week to build his nest egg in a Swiss bank. Another venerable gentleman of aristocratic lineage visited his bankers in Switzerland to deposit the cash component from the sale of his property and then flung his passport into the Arabian Sea so that his income tax officer would not notice the Swiss immigration stamp. He then proceeded to file a complaint with the police station that he (a forgetful old man) had again lost his passport. Some of the earliest NRIs (non-resident Indians) and naturalized foreign citizens were Parsis.

Most Parsis will fork up taxes to avoid any problems with the tax authorities though they believe that the taxes are being frittered away on wrong cau*ses*. This is in keeping with the Parsi DNA to comply with any law, however odious, unfair or inequitable. Justice Oliver Wendell Holmes of the US Supreme Court memorably said in a dissenting judgment: "Taxes are the price we pay for civilization. I like paying taxes. With taxes, I buy civilization." Most bawajis will vehemently disagree with the learned judge and dub him as "*sadantar ghelsappo* (total idiot)" or its even more unprintable stringent cousin--in-abuse.

No criticism please, we are Parsis

A look at the contemporary community's attitude and approach

Younger readers may not recall an English theater production called *No Sex Please, We Are British.* Our chillingly declining numbers are a testimony to our empathy with the Brits. Though some macho Parsis may contend that we are firing alright, these are mostly blanks. While those on the fringe maintain that the second coming of the Lord shall reverse demographic trends (*Gayomard anda Soshyosh aideryad baad,* our prayers say), their estranged brethren in the mainstream accuse liberals of manipulating statistics (and exposing damned lies).

A decade ago, the above paragraph would have elicited a wry smile. Today it evokes anger and indignation (though not of the righteous kind). The facts are incorrect: (denial mode). Even if they are correct, why publish it: (ostrich approach). You are an enemy of the community: (Taliban attitude). Even if you are only the messenger, we shall shoot you for bringing bad news. Leave us alone in our cocoon of disbelief. Voltaire may have said that I disagree with

you but I shall defend to my death your right to disagree with me. Voltaire be damned, unity of the community is the need of the hour and your dissent is pernicious and we shall not tolerate it. We may have mingled like sugar in milk, as promised to our royal shelter-giver, but now like those suffering from lactose intolerance, we are allergic to criticism.

In fairness to the orthodox, this intolerance is not limited to them alone. It pervades across the spectrum of thought. Is this then the extreme prickliness of those feeling doomed or is it a newfound feeling of bristling aggression? When a person is aware of the weaknes*ses* in his case, he does not want any public expose of such weaknes*ses*. He, therefore, goes the extra mile to stifle any criticism. Respect for another's viewpoint is lost the moment one doubts bona fides. These days, there is too much doubting of bona fides. It is quickly presumed that anyone in community service must be having a personal agenda. True, some do. However, one cannot tar with the same brush the many who don't.

The biggest problem facing the community today is not declining demographics but cold indifference. Most Parsis have a soft corner for the community but nothing more. Only a micro minority is concerned with what happens to the Parsis. Overwhelming numbers believe that the trustees of our charities are a bunch of clowns viciously fighting each other. The beneficiaries greet trustees with a polite smile only so as not to affront them. What the community thinks about our trustees privately is unprintable. The much abused phrase Parsi*panu* is not that annual visit to the *agiary* or watching a putrid Parsi comedy or gorging at the Ripon Club on Wednesday afternoons. Even the intelligent spare little thought for the issues threatening the existence of the community. This has led to the affairs of the community being handled by, believe it or not, a dozen odd Parsis.

This concentration of power amongst the dozen (we shall eschew the adjective), needless to state, is dangerous. The vicious hatred amongst them is very unParsi. Like battle scarred gladiators,

they lick their bruised egos and yearn to see their opponents humiliated. These war games have now spilled over from the media into the courts of law. Many of these worthies are street fighters who love a bloody brawl, merely for the heck of it, as their non-community careers are uniformly boring and pedestrian. They and their followers, of liberal or orthodox hue, sincerely believe that they are the saviors of the community. The indifference of the community feeds their delusions of grandeur. And why blame the tadpole for thinking that he is the master of the cesspool.

As a result, there is no dispassionate expert thinking about how to tackle issues. The cesspool is so turbid that no one wants to step into it. Painstaking sociological research is dismissed as biased. Suggestions to reform charities are seen as motivated. No one wants to be shown a mirror to look into. They do not want confirmation of the ugliness.

A few years ago only those whom we affectionately like to call fruitcakes, reacted angrily to criticism. Now, all do. When few can even bear to be told the truth, disaster is not far away. Our much touted sense of humor was founded on the fundamental premise of having the ability to laugh at ourselves. We have so terribly lost that ability, in the process of protecting our puny egos. The community is already mentally extinct.

Ghaas phoos can be tasty

It's a myth that Parsi vegetarian fare is not delicious

Woe betide the vegetarian diner at a Parsi wedding who spurns the 'Gujarati' thali and opts for what is almost contemptuously called *paréji* (literally, food for a person having multiple dietary restrictions or undergoing penance). The server will dump on his *patru* a medley of lesser vegetables like okra (lady finger), aubergine (brinjal), cauliflower and potatoes from battered aluminum utensils.

These poor veggies look semi-boiled, dull and suddenly 'surprised.' They taste like gooey mash; eminently qualifying as a hospital dietician's recommendation for a patient suffering from multiple organ failure. Some vegan NRI (non-resident Indian) from Los Angeles would then ask the server, "No mushrooms, broccoli, asparagus or water chestnuts?" The server, laden with illicit hooch would give her a smile reserved for idiots. This *paréji* must be singularly responsible for the myth that Parsis cannot conjure up delicious vegetarian fare.

In the olden days, a Parsi vegetarian was an anthropological rarity. You had to be a Theosophist or an Ilm-e-Khshnoomist or a Pundolite (followers of a self styled guru called Minocher Pundole who forbade them from eating flesh, lest it corroded their etheric bodies; though Pundole himself savored mutton dhansak, since he purportedly possessed a superior etheric body) or a member of the almost defunct Parsi Vegetarian and Temperance Society (whose founders were labelled as lunatics, more for their abjuring booze than meat). These days, of course, there are lots of 'out-of-choice' Parsi vegetarians, like this writer. The rest of the *farcha* munching, lobster grabbing Parsis look upon Parsi vegetarians as poor sods who do not know what they are missing. It is like having Marilyn Monroe as your wife and remaining celibate. The reality is, that Parsi vegetarians can have a ball.

You need not enviously watch your brethren enjoy the Sunday dhansak. The same light brown rice, garnished with crimson fried onions, and the same tomato chilly *kachumbar*, and the same thick brown dal, a perfect mixture of aubergines, tomatoes and ground spices. Only those meat balls will be replaced by soya chunks — never to be over*boi*led, marinated in curd overnight or dunked in the dal. Many a gourmet will fail to single out these imposter meat balls. What about the mutton kebabs though, snorts the carnivore. *Sooran* (yam) comes to the rescue of the Parsi abstainers. Soft *boi*led sooran is soaked in pure ghee and mixed with lime and ginger paste in a grinder; then placed in little cups of potato mash, rolled into balls, dipped in whipped egg and rava (semolina) and then fried or grilled. Blindfold the mutton lover and see him fooled by the transformed yam. Similarly, try and distinguish mutton kheema from nutrella nuggets run through a liquidizer, its inadequacies cured by a deft application of the magical *vaghaar* (tadka) comprising of diced onion, tomatoes, green and red chilies, ginger and garlic paste, sauted in desi ghee (according to Ayurveda it actually unclogs blocked arteries).

The lowly *papdi* (Indian flat beans) have their Cinderella moment when mixed with tiny soya kebabs and simmered on slow heat, to preserve their essential juices and flavor. Onion rings soaked in vinegar, mixed rice and jowar flour whitish chappatis and *methiya nu achaar* (mango fenugreek pickle) are its critical accompaniments, for a veritable vegetarian feast.

Most Parsi vegetarians are eggetarians. Thinly sliced potato diamonds, slapped with yellow *haldi* (turmeric) and red *mirchi* powder, packed in a pan. Greatly whipped eggs with a little cream are then gently poured over the potatoes — some of it percolating to the bottom of the pan, which is lightly oiled, to avoid sticking. The resulting *papeta per eedu* is to be eaten with thick, ghee laden, multi layered wheat rotlis and *gor keri nu achaar* (sweet mango pickle). Perhaps, a thin fried papad too (though strangely, we are told by those who do colon wash that undigested papads remain in the dark corners of the intestines for decades, as they are most difficult to digest).

Titori dal (sprouted averakai), harvested during the winter months and soaked overnight in water, made slightly (not overtly) sweet and sour, by tamarind and jaggery paste is an outstanding Parsi vegetarian delicacy. Some prefer its subtle pungent and astringent taste. Never to be mashed up, like other dals, each seed to remain clearly intact, when serving. Lovingly simmered over a very low flame, with a dash of coconut milk, and garnished with fresh coriander. The same accompaniments as the papdi.

Large brinjals sliced into circular rings are marinated in multi spice paste and a little vinegar, and then lightly fried, to retain the softness of the flesh which melts on the palate. Some embellish it with eggs, à la papeta per eedu, converting the oft detested vegetables into the rather lurid sounding *vengna per eedu*, but tasting divine. Many a brinjal hating Parsi can be converted by its spruced up avatar.

Vegetarian Parsis retain their genetic penchant for non-vegetarian fare and secretly yearn for its allegedly superior taste; alleges our carnivorous wife. May be so. Simulated kheema patty, undistinguishable mock frankies and other delicacies conjured by the intelligent use of soya and egg, masked with hot spices will satisfy their taste buds and yet make them feel superior, as not participating in consuming our animal friends, who are evolving into the next humanity and are our brothers in evolution, according to the Theosophists.

Vegetarian meals ready to serve

Time to test the waters

There is a fair chance that interfaith married Parsi women may gain parity with men

An interfaith married Parsi lady apprehends that someday the priest in the *agiary* will prevent the entry of her toddler son. Can he? she queries. Yes, we reply, as the law stands today. Instead of waiting for that humiliating experience, why not move the High Court? Her chances of success are good indeed. *Petit* vs *Jeejeebhoy* and *Bella* vs *Saklat* are no longer good law post the Constitution of India which confers the fundamental right to equality of the sexes (no intelligible differentia exists against putting children of interfaith married Parsi men and women on par). In addition, India is a signatory to many conventions on human rights which further strengthens the chances of these two old judgments being bypassed.

The judgment, of Justices Dhananjay Chandrachud and Anoop Mohta of the Bombay High Court in the banned priests' case makes helpful observations in this regard and indicates the present thinking of our judiciary. Our young lady is still not convinced. What if I fail? she asks. Presently, many interfaith married Parsi mothers blithely take their children to the fire temple and virtually no one objects. If I fail, all this can stop, they reason. So why invite trouble? This is exactly the reasoning of the matronly ladies of AIMZ (Association of Inter-Married Zoroastrians) who have been unable to make this leap of faith.

But look what happened to Goolrookh Gupta's case, they contend. While we believe that Gupta will ultimately succeed, we have always maintained that her individual facts were not ideal to make a test case of [name change to Neha, purported filing of income tax returns as HUF (Hindu Undivided Family) member, etc]. None of the so-called legal infirmities in the Gupta case will, however, apply in this case.

Recently, a non-Parsi journalist lady married to a Parsi recounted the story of her four year old daughter, on her first visit to Iranshah, Udvada, loudly shouting *"Ganpati Bapa Moriya"* in the sanctum sanctorum, to the horror of the not so amused devotees and a stern priest asking her to be taken away. The moral of the story being that culture and way of life is imbibed from the mother, and not so much from the father. All the more reason to end this irrational discrimination. In this article, it is not possible to reveal the precise legal strategy for commencing such a test case. Suffice it to say, that all it requires is a daring Parsi lady. She will receive overwhelming support from the who's who of the community across the country and several eminent senior counsel would be happy to represent her, without charge. For all you know, the mainstream orthodox (like the World Alliance of Parsi Irani Zarthoshtis) may not even resist much. Many in the community believe that this discrimination must end.

Will the AIMZ take a lead, as it logically ought to? We think not. Hence, we require a couple of Parsi ladies, married under the Special Marriage Act (registered marriage), preferably to Hindus, and born of both Parsi Zoroastrian parents. This is only to ensure that some irrelevant objections do not deflect from the main objective.

Some candidates will emerge to bell the cat. It is ludicrous to put a number on the outcome of litigation in India, nevertheless we shall make bold to assert a 80% plus odds of success.

Those who anticipate this will open the floodgates are mistaken. The number of such children (born of Parsi mothers and non-Parsi fathers, the latter willing for the entry of their children into our faith) will not be more than 300. Out of these, hardly 10% are likely to avail of Parsi charities, which anyway are running out of beneficiaries. No sensible liberal is advocating outright conversion, which would be politically disastrous and destroy our unique ethnic identity. However, justice and fair play demand that both sexes must be treated equally. Someone from the fringe elements is bound to quip that if you are so keen to end discrimination, why don't you also exclude children of intermarried Parsi males? If the fringe elements wish to accelerate our already dramatic demographic decline even further, then what is one to say? There may be a dearth of Parsis, but not of idiots.

Sign outside Seth Cowasji Behramji Banaji Atash Behram requesting
"Parsi ladies who are married to non-Parsis... with their children" to refrain from entering

From dadgah to dargah

Extra-religious worship is endemic in the community

Ervad Homi, a *navar* maratab from Navsari, devotedly serves a Bombay fire temple as its managing trustee. Homi offers prayers twice a day at his *agiary*. He is a diehard conservative who disapproves of interfaith marriages and crematoria. Homi believes our faith and its prayers to be potent and powerful, capable of bringing about miracles. Yet, every year, Homi makes a pilgrimage to Tirupati and is ecstatic with the 20-second darshan of Lord Balaji. He also visits Shirdi and prostrates himself in abject surrender to Sai Baba. Homi wears around his neck an amulet of protection given by a Sufi saint, Hazrat Tajluddin Baba to his grandfather which, he asserts, has guarded him against many a disaster. The Brahma temple at Pushkar, the famous Shani temple at Shignapur, and the most revered Ajmer Sharif shrine, are all on his annual list. A carnivore who loves his daily tipple, he turns vegetarian and teetotaler during Navratri and the Ganesh festival.

Homi's example is the rule, not the exception. Parsis like Homi do not feel guilty for a moment about extra-religious worship.

Even mainstream orthodox bodies like the World Alliance of Parsi Irani Zarthoshtis (WAPIZ) seldom raise this issue, knowing fully well that many of their ardent supporters would be offended at any diatribe against extra-religious worship. Of course, the readers of The Parsee Voice and Traditional Zoroastrians online, regard such worship as betrayal of our faith.

At first blush, extra-religious worship alongside an abiding belief in our faith may be puzzling. It is not so. Even Hindus, while being ardent Krishna devotees, do worship Muslim pirs, particularly in villages and small towns. This is true secularism. Being irreligious, atheist or agnostic is not necessarily secular. Treating all faiths as roads leading to the same goal is secularism. Parsis too have adopted the same approach.

The majority of Parsis like Homi are usually from a Gujarati speaking background and are either first generation Bombayites or closely bound by their roots in Gujarat. This accounts for their close connect with fellow communities and their religious practices.

This extra-religious interaction begins at birth. A Hindu astrologer is consulted to draw up the child's horoscope. Often the astrologer may suggest a pooja to remove some malevolent aspect in the life chart. If the child suffers from jaundice, a Muslim healer is contacted to drain the yellowness through water therapy. It is common to worship at the local pir's dargah and come away with an amulet of protection, worn with the same fervor as the kusti around the waist. Numerous rites, customs, superstitions are observed — pregnant women forbidden to venture out during a lunar eclipse, not touching jars of homemade pickles during menstruation. The night of Kalichaudas is feared, the evening of Dhanteras is spent in praying over new books of accounts and Divali is celebrated with gusto.

And this is not a new phenomenon. Parsis began to visit Shirdi from 1930 onwards. Iranis and Parsis constitute a majority of the devotees of Avatar Meher Baba (an Irani Zoroastrian who became a Sufi Master). Prominent Parsis regard late Kamubaba of Goregaon as their guru. On novena Wednesdays at the Mahim church and at

Siddhivinayak Temple on Tuesdays, you will see many Parsi faces. The list is long.

Although most of these Parsis continue to believe in the potent vibratory power of the Avestan prayers, they do not derive solace as it is a dead language. Succor is, therefore, sought in the more intelligible. A preacher expounding the Bhagwad Gita with its twin principles of karma and reincarnation provides greater solace to a Parsi who has lost a loved one, than placing ro*ses* in a silver vase and listening to the drone of overworked *mobed*s in a smoke filled *agiary* during the *muktad*. The increasing number of interfaith marriages adds grist to the extra-religious mill. Displaying the photo of a non Zoroastrian saint or guru alongside Prophet Zarathushtra on the mantlepiece is no longer frowned upon.

The hardcore traditionalist cannot figure out the mindset of his co-religionist who, while being a practising Zoroastrian is, like Homi, seen to be dabbling in alternative avenues. He is willing to ignore the indifferent Parsi but Homi is an eyesore. However, believing in other faiths, while giving primacy to ours, is a part of Homi and his ilk's DNA.

This is also a manifestation of a culture being swamped by larger ones. Parsis do not live in ghettos any longer (ironically, those living in the baugs and colonies indulge more in extra-religious worship). The magic appeal of miracles has disappeared from our faith. There are no longer personages like the revered Dastur Kookadaru who performed many a miracle and healed body and soul. However, such personages do exist in many other religions and thus attract the Parsis.

Homi is misty eyed before Iranshah, Udvada and would gladly sacrifice his life for his *agiary*. He regards himself as a pucca (true) Zarthoshti. However, he is equally lost in the religiously ecstatic quawaals singing outside Ajmer Sharif and equally moved to devotional fervor while attending the aarti at dawn in the Sai Baba temple at Shirdi. Castigating Homi and his ilk will be counterproductive and even drive some of them away from the faith.

Are we xenophobic?

Fear of strangers lurks in our collective consciousness

Xenophobia is a morbid dislike of strangers (Greek, *xenos* = stranger). Worldwide, the mood is xenophobic. From Trump's America to Putin's Russia to Erdogan's assault on the Kurds; the rise of far right populist parties in aristocratic Austria and egalitarian France; Brexit and other potential exits from the European Union; the Shia-Sunni conflicts and many more, the planet is looking inwards. As a community and ethnic group, do we harbor fear of the foreigner and the stranger?

We forbid all those, however close, who are not Parsi Zoroastrians from viewing the face of the dead after the last ablutions. We do not permit children of Parsi mothers married to non-Parsis from entering our fire temples. We keep our hospitals empty but do not permit their secular use. Even for our ancient dhansak clubs, we restrict membership to Parsis. Our charities may have run out of beneficiaries to help, however, the funds will not be utilized for non-Parsis. We largely patronize Parsi service providers including doctors, lawyers, accountants and architects, irrespective of merit. Although the Prophet wanted the faith to be a universal religion, we continue to maintain that a non-Parsi cannot be a Zoroastrian. We will not open the doors to anyone, howsoever genuine and deserving, even if it means certain extinction in the foreseeable future. Clearly, fumes the liberal, we are indeed racist, paranoid and xenophobic.

The traditionalist disagrees. We do not wear religion on our sleeves. We neither entice nor compel others to convert. We are polite, docile, compassionate, easygoing and non-aggressive. We do take interest in the affairs of others. We certainly do not dislike strangers nor are we fearful of them. It follows that we harbor no xenophobia.

Our bonhomie and joie de vivre and graciousness and fabled sense of humor notwithstanding, most of us do harbor a clear notion that we are different from the original natives of the land. We do still fear being swamped and inundated. There is a core area, which is out of bounds for non-Parsis, and where we would like to see only our own. This is effected in a rather subtle and non-offending manner; and others have learned to accept our area of exclusivity.

Our track record in preserving our unique identity intact, in the most dismal circumstances, is remarkable. The proposition that had we been less vigilant in creating entry barriers, the floodgates would have opened and our identity submerged, is indeed correct. Our ability to endear ourselves to the rulers, whether local satraps or the British, bought us protection from external onslaught. Our pioneering entrepreneurship, laced though it was with opium, made us rich and influential. Our small size was a shield which made others believe we posed no danger. Our innate ability to be politically tactful and correct and harbor no ambitions made us non-threatening to the powers that be. A well honed survival instinct ensured that there should not be any attempt to preach, propagate or proselytize our faith. This is not the time or the environment to sell Zoroastrianism.

Undoubtedly, repugnant to the Prophet's message of universality, the early migrants decided wisely and sagaciously that a low profile alone can guarantee survival.

Parsi funerals, with the face of the deceased exposed, meandered through the streets of Bombay until the rise of communal tensions meant that funerals were defiled. Quickly, the funerals and the ceremonies became a closed door affair. Entry to fire temples was restricted to Parsis for the same reason. When you are terribly outnumbered, those who fight are not heroes but fools. The pain of expulsion from the Iranian fatherland was indelibly etched in the collective consciousness of the community. Strangers had caused great harm; strangers were strong; strangers were to be feared; strangers had to be kept at the gates. When your existence is at stake, xenophobia is a legitimate weapon.

A closed door approach, however, always extricates a price. Marrying cousins, the greatest blunder we ever made, resulted in irreversible genetic decline which led to a demographic disaster. At some stage, this blunder became evident, albeit unconsciously. When Parsi men married or 'mistressed' interfaith women (from French madames to the tribals of Gujarat), a much needed boost of gene diversity resulted. On the other hand, Parsi women marrying non-Parsi spouses meant a loss of precious resources. When more equal times came, this gender injustice appeared odious. By then, the gender bias had been sanctioned by law. The orthodox erroneously believe that this is what the religion had decreed. As they controlled community institutions and trusts, a survival tactic was elevated to a tenet of the faith.

When the Constitution of India came into force, had we gradually eliminated this gender bias, our numbers would have looked much better. Children of interfaith marriages are not strangers. Nor are their spouses, who could have been partially assimilated without ruffling too many feathers. Xenophobia can rapidly turn into a weapon of self destruction. Is it then, demographically speaking, too late to reverse the entrenched position? Perhaps, yes. Nevertheless it is the need of the hour. When it is inevitable that closed doors will result in death by suffocation, better open a window.

The apocryphal promise, of dissolving like sugar in milk, was never kept; and rightly so. Loss of unique identity has always been our biggest fear. We have preferred to float like an indissoluble almond in a corner of that milk jar.

Class without brass

The social elite of the yesteryears is caught in a time warp

The senior naval commander's widow was greatly relieved when her monthly pension was substantially increased by the Government of India. She would now be able to afford the salary of a live-in maid-cum-cook. Just the previous month, she had sold with a heavy heart, her antique jewelry including the pigeon blood red Burmese rubies, to pay for some much needed repairs to her tenanted but spacious residence in one of Bombay's richest neighborhoods. For a long time now, she had stopped eating her favorite pomfret, the most expensive flesh in the city, pretending she was allergic. Her mode of transportation is the rickety black and yellow taxi, as even the Uber and the Ola are beyond her reach. All this is a far cry from her world, some three decades ago, when she enjoyed palatial residences all over the country, thanks to the Indian Navy; had a retinue of cooks and servants, and was ferried around in a chauffeur driven car, albeit an Ambassador.

Her story is not unique. The social elite of the yesteryears is steadily being impoverished. Accustomed to being fawned over by deferential servants and service providers, a certain standard of living was taken for granted. Circumstances have conspired to substantially erode this standard of living.

Scions of illustrious families, some of whom built Bombay, brought up by German governesses in the lap of luxury and often products of a Swiss finishing school, are suddenly being told that there was little money in the bank. Gentlemen at large and ladies of leisure are not accustomed to working from nine to five. Neither do they have the acumen of augmenting wealth through sagacious investments. This was never a superrich class, and whatever corpus or fortunes was accumulated in the past got dissipated due to disasters like the Manchester Cotton price crash or some other disruptive event which snatched their only source of income. This was a social and educated elite — Anglophile and Westernized — tutored in convents by nuns and Jesuits, regaled by Western classical music concerts and choir recitals, afternoons spent in playing bridge and mahjong, sipping tea from Wedgewood bone china teapots covered by an intricately embroidered tea cosy. They thought nothing of spending their entire income, or even a part of the capital, on expenses ranging from a luxury cruise or foreign education. They expected, and received, respect from the lesser classes of Parsis.

Rustomji's father migrated from Navsari to Bombay in 1905. Matriculating after two or three botched attempts, Rustomji landed a soporophic job as an assistant secretary at one of Bombay's prestigious clubs and managed to rent a 5,000 sq ft flat in one of the just constructed art deco buildings on Marine Drive for a monthly rent of Rs 12; married his first cousin and remained so for 60 years; his two sons, rather dim-witted, managed to become head clerks in Tata companies. The family enjoyed the services of a *mistaree* (cook; not to be confused with mistry, the carpenter) who conjured up some mean Goan fish curry and delectable kheema pancakes. At 8 p.m., Rustomji would finish his sundowner and with his trembling hands shake a little brass bell to summon the 'boy' (domestic help) to lay a

16-seater dining table for the family, and any unannounced visitors too. A four-course meal was rounded off with a shot of brandy. The family had little savings and investment was an unknown concept. The surviving widow of one of the sons, childless and alone in the 5,000 sq ft house, had to suffer the indignity of seeing the *mistaree*, the boy and all others gradually leave. She heated the meal delivered in an aluminum *bhona no dabbo* (food container), and ate, sitting alone, on that 16-seater, surrounded by dozens of grandfather clocks.

Large tenanted residences in the poshest localities (which they will not sell or surrender for money or love) have become decrepit due to an inability to repair or maintain. The occupants are unable to match the market rate of servants in the richest areas of the country. Caught in a time warp between dignity and desolation, they are too self-respecting to seek charity help even for a medical emergency (exacerbated often by a lack of medical insurance). After death though, when their cupboards are opened by distant relatives claiming to be legal heirs, purple and black Chinese garas along with some priceless set of South Sea pearls and other valuable antiques, tumble out.

Often childless or effectively abandoned or ignored by children, this elite of the yesteryears nostalgically recall the fairy-tale existence when little money provided such great comfort. There is no hope any longer for a Cinderella moment. Mistakenly thought to be rich by the outside world. Fervently praying for death so as not to suffer any further indignities. Yesterdays seldom return.

Indian Dining Room — looking South.

Connecting with Zarthost

Parsis need to be more passionate about their Prophet

We are not adoring our Prophet enough. Nor are we capitalizing on his exalted superhero status. Jesus nailed to the cross, Krishna preaching *Gita* from the chariot, or Prophet Muhammad's march on the city of Mecca, evokes strong passion in their followers. A dying community can be rejuvenated by an enlivened faith. For multiple reasons, Zarathushtra can be the focal point for such a revival. Historically, intellectually and spiritually, Parsis need to connect more with their Prophet.

Occult literature of the East and West accord the status of a Great Initiate to Zoroaster. He is spoken of in the same breath as Rama, Krishna, Hermes, Moses, Orpheus and Jesus (*The Great Initiates: A Study of the Secret History of Religions* by Édouard Schuré). Helena Blavatsky, in her seminal work, *The Secret Doctrine* extols the great antiquity of Zoroastrian scriptures, as laid down by Zarathushtra. She considers Zoroastrian cosmology to be ahead of the Book of Genesis, and the Prophet himself to be the "earliest lawgiver and ruler." Most scholarly Greek and Christian literature regards Zoroaster as the inventor of both magic and astrology. His followers have been referred to as the Magi, from which 'magic' emanated. It is widely believed that the "three wise men" who bore gifts at the time of Jesus' birth were Zoroastrian Magis. The famous philosopher, Freidrich Nietzsche, made Zoroaster the anti-hero of his work, *Also Sprach Zarathustra* (Thus spoke Zarathustra, 1885) and Strauss composed an opera by the same name. W. B. Yeats, the Irish poet and his wife dubiously claimed to have contacted Zoroaster through "automatic writing."

Most Parsis know Good Friday to be the day on which Jesus was crucified; few will instantly connect *Zarthost no diso* to be the day on which the Prophet was martyred. According to legend the Prophet lived upto the age of 77, he had two older and two younger brothers, his first two wives bore him three sons and three daughters, while his third wife, Havovi, was childless (Mary Boyce; West). Few realize that he influenced Islam and that he is venerated as Prophet by the Baha'is and the Ahmadiyya Muslims, amongst others. Paul Kriwaczek, a BBC journalist, has observed in his book, *In Search of Zarasthustra*: "Every country I had ever visited in the area was overwhelmingly Muslim. Yet nobody could have helped noticing an undercurrent of something else — the spirit of Zarathustra, still powerful after 1,300 years of Islam."

Unlike Buddha or Mahavir, the Prophet did not advocate abstinence or fasting or penance or forsaking the worldly life. His is a religion of joy and freedom of choice and spreading universal happiness. It is a fallacy, however, to presume that Zoroastrianism is a simple faith. It is a treasure house of esoteric knowledge. The *Gathas* and other prayers which Zoroaster composed, when recited properly, unleash the most powerful vibratory effects on all of existence. Numerous magical formulae are embedded in these prayers, which dispassionately speaking, are the most potent ever known to mankind.

Parsis hardly display any devotional fervor for their Prophet. Hindus swooning to the chants of "Hare Rama, Hare Krishna",

Muslims ecstatic while hearing qawwalis in praise of Prophet Muhammad, Christians delirious with joy adoring Jesus at evangelical gatherings, Baha'is worshipping Bahaullah; virtually every other faith goes ga ga over its Prophet. The once mandatory picture of Zarthost saheb on the wall of every Parsi living room is missing; only a few reverentially touch his feet in the large photo frame in *atash behram*s and agiaries. Prayer lamps bearing his image on the glass covering are hardly to be seen. Nor are there many artefacts like a marble bust or motifs on wall coverings. Old songs extolling him and recorded by a Parsi music group from Calcutta are seldom played: (*Nabiji, vandan ho shutvaar, amara bhuv bhuv na aadhar* — a million salutations to our Prophet who is our savior over incarnations) or the touching rendition by the chorus of the Bai Avabai Petit Girls Orphanage, at Parsi functions (*Koi poochhé mané, kya chhé tara Zarthost paygambar; dil chiri né bataoon, mara jigar ni andar* —If someone asks where is your Prophet Zoroaster, I will tear my chest to show that He resides in my heart!) or the more recent monajats sung by the melodious Mani Rao (*Khudavand o Khavind, O parvardigaar; namoo tari dargaah né hoon khaksaar* — I reverentially bow before Thee, O Prophet of Prophets! and *O dadgar, O davar, O parvardigar; tu gyaani, tu daani, daya no bhandaar* — 'You are knowledge, you are munificent, you are an ocean of compassion). Our inner spiritual zeal appears to have dulled. No devotional fervor absorbs us.

Ilm-e-Khshnoomists and other occultists believe that it is possible to attune oneself to the all encompassing consciousness of Zarathushtra. Clairvoyants say that his aura is so resplendently bright that it occupies a huge part of the cosmic realms. One very effective and beneficial spiritual exercise is to invoke him as soon as you wake up (preferably at dawn) and fervently pray that his great aura lights up your home and hearth; he protects you against black magic and evil by providing you with the shield of prayers (*mithravaani*); he expounds to you the significance of Ahu*navar* (*Yatha Ahu Vairyo*); and he extends his field of protection over you and your family. Aspirants can hope that their body and mind becomes so pure that it is possible one day for them to momentarily interlock with the great cosmic consciousness of Zarthost. This exercise, done with a clean heart and for non material wishes, is a giver of miraculous boons.

Since he is the only smiling Prophet, better to end on a lighter note. The Prophet's greatness rubbed off on a horse too. Terence Gray, an Irish writer and philosopher, named a thoroughbred horse as Zarathustra (1951-1967), which won the Irish Derby, Irish St Leger, the Goodwood Cup; and finally, was ridden to victory in England by the legendary jockey, Lester Piggott, in a thrilling finish in the Ascot Gold Cup, defeating the favourite, Atlas, owned by the Queen herself. Zarathustra returned to Ireland to stand as a stallion. The Parsis of London led a delegation to the British racing authorities to have the name of this horse changed as it offended their religious sensibilities. However, the delegation's efforts did not succeed.

Unlike the Hindus and Muslims, Parsis seldom name a child after the Prophet. The residents of any Parsi colony, known for their penchant for colorful abuse, must heave a sigh of relief at having thus been spared from cardinal sin.

GLOSSARY

Akuri - Spiced egg bhurji (a Parsi delicacy)

Afarganiyu - Vessel holding Holy Fire

Agiary - Second highest Fire Temple

Ahunavad Gatha - A hymn composed by Prophet Zoroaster

Akabar - Community leader
Aleti Paleti - A dish of offals and goat liver
Andhyaru - Priest

Atash behram - Highest Fire Temple

Avesta - The ancient language of the Zoroastrians

Bafaat - One who makes faux pas, all the time

Bawaji and Maiji - Parsi man and woman

Behdin - Laity, as distinguished from a priestly family

Bhakras - Sweetened dough cake

Bheeda pur eedoo - Okra egg pie

Bichaaro - Poor wretch

Boiwalas - Priests on duty to tend the Holy Fire

Bun pao - A soft bun

Bungli - Prayer hall at Towers of Silence (post death ceremonies)

Chinvat bridge - The Day of Judgement

Cusrow Baug - A charity founded Parsi housing colony in Colaba, Mumbai.

Dadar Hormuzd - Lord Ahuramazda, the Supreme God

Dadgah - Third highest Fire Temple

Dakhmas - Enclosures / wells in the Towers of Silence, where dead bodies are placed.

Dar ni pori - Sugary lentil cake

Demavand Koh - Large cave in Demavand, Iran, where Zoroastrian Spiritual Masters are believed to dwell.

Dhansak - Popular Parsi delicacy of lentils containing mutton / chicken, along with browned rice.

Divo - Oil lamp

Dokhmenashini - Disposing dead by vultures / solar panels

Doongerwadi - Parsi Towers of Silence (disposal of dead)

Farcha - Chicken drumsticks

Gaar - Abuse

Gah - A unit of time during the day (five Gahs)

Gahambar - A communal free feast

Geh Saarna - Funeral prayer before the corpse

Gor Keri nu achar - Pickle of spiced mangoes and jaggery

Garabh nu achaar - Fish roe pickle

Humdin - Co-religionist(Zorastrian)

Jama - A traditional priestly dress

Jamva ni dosi - Old lady beggar who begged only for food, not money

Juddin - A non-Parsi

Karasyo - of brass drinking vessel

Khordeh Avesta - Zoroastrian prayer book

Kolmi-na-curry chawal - Prawn Curry rice

Kusti - Holi thread made of wool worn around the waist

Ilm-e-Kshnoomists - An esoteric, occult,Zoroastrian group

Lagan no dholiyo - Bed for the newly wed

Lagan nu bhonu - Wedding feast

Lokhan ni railing - Iron railing

Madavsaro - A ceremonial day before the wedding day

Mamaiji - Maternal grand mother

Manthric - Zoroastrian science of vibrations to intone prayers

Masoor Paavs - Hoi polloi, the masses

Mobed - A priest

Mora dar chawal - Steamed rice with plain dal (lentils)

Muktad - All souls day (remembering the dead)

Murabba - Sweetened mango condiment

Nassessalar - Corpse bearer

Navar - Priestly initiation ceremony

Paatru -Plantain leaf upon which food is served at Parsi feasts

Panchang - Almanac

Papri - Savoury bread in temple offering

Parsipanu - Parsi way of life

Paidast - Funeral

Pheto - Parsi traditional elongated cap.

Pundolites - Followers of a self-styled Guru, Minocher Pundole

Pugree - Parsi traditional circular cap

Saas ni macchi - Fish in white sauce

Sagan no ganthiyo - Prophet of doom

Sagdi - Minor Fire Temple at the Towers of Silence

Sali ma murghi - Chicken in straw potatoes

Sarosh - Archangel who protects souls

Sethias - Old time, Parsi aristocrats

Sev and Dahi - Sweetened vermicelli with yoghurt

Shuddh - Pristine pure; unadulterated

Sojju - Very good

Stum - Prayer to remember the dead

Su dahra aayach - What days have come to pass! Alas!

Tokham ni jalavni ne boond ni pasbaani - Protecting ethnic / racial purity

Towers of Silence - Parsi cemetery

Uthamna - Post funeral prayers

Vendidad - Ancient Zoroastrian religious text

Yasht - A long form prayer dedicated to an angel

Yatha Ahu Vairyo - Potent capsule prayer of great spiritual significance

Acknowledgements

The author is grateful to:

➢ Darius Khambata, one of India's most sought after Senior Counsel, for penning the Foreword;

➢ Mr. Justice Rohinton Nariman of the Supreme Court of India, for consenting to launch the book;

➢ Jehangir Patel, and his editorial team at PARSIANA, for painstakingly editing every column and giving maximum latitude to the author's idiosyncrasies;

➢ Farzana Cooper, for her brilliant cartoons and illustrations;

➢ Mrudul Pathak and Debojyoti Kundu, for the sizzling cover design;

➢ Ramjee Narasiman and Gayatri R of Zero Degree Publishing, the angelic publishers of this book; and Richard Remedios, vendor of flowers, real estate and occult ideas, for introducing the author to the publishers.

➢ K.P. Ravindran, my friend and colleague, for tirelessly typing and retyping, without complaint.